The Dragon Squisher

the hilarious fantasy novel

by

Scott McCormick

Also by Scott McCormick:

Mr. Pants: It's Go Time!
Mr. Pants: Slacks, Camera, Action!
Mr. Pants: Trick or Feet!
Mr. Pants: Camping Catastrophe!
Rivals! Frenemies Who Changed the World
Rivals 2! More Frenemies Who Changed the World

Printed in the United States of America

First Printing, 2020

ISBN (Print): 978-1-54397-916-9
ISBN (eBook): 978-1-54397-917-6

Storybook Editing Press

Contact Scott at: storybookediting@gmail.com

www.scottmccormickonline.com

"... monsters ..."

My eternal thanks to Andre Calilhanna and Steven Spatz for making this possible, to Joe Clark for being an enthusiastic early supporter, and to my amazing wife Michaela for all her support, encouragement, and feedback.

Dragons smell like farts.

The Age of Magic

BEFORE I CAN begin my tale, you need to know about the king's panties.

So, let me take you back two thousand years to the reign of King Stephanus II, specifically to his ninth annual State of the Kingdom address.

I don't know if you have State of the Kingdom addresses in your country, but they're essentially fancy speeches in which the king drones on for hours about the economy to a room full of dignitaries trying their best not to snore. These events were especially tedious during the reign of Stephanus II, for the man was widely considered the worst public speaker in all of Amerigorn. To give you a taste of how awful his speeches were, Stephanus began his eighth address with a comprehensive overview of his prized dust collection before moving on to a detailed report of "the fifty ghastliest things my cat coughed up last night." Experts disagreed as to how any of this pertained to the economy, mostly because they had slept through the whole thing. But they all admitted that the speech was an improvement over his previous address, which culminated in a two-hour tale of woe about a "friend" who had recently suffered from a nasty strain of foot fungus.

I mention all of this to explain why Stephanus's audience didn't immediately panic when he wrapped up his ninth address by informing everyone how wonderful life was going to be thanks to his new pair of magical panties.

Had he been a more exciting speaker (or at least, someone who stuck to the point), history might have turned out differently. But as I mentioned, the audience was essentially asleep on their feet, and therefore, not paying any attention to what Stephanus was saying. The word *panties*, however, has extraordinary power. It can silence even the noisiest rooms, or, as in this case, wake up the deepest sleepers. And so the sound that filled the great hall was not one of alarm or outrage, but that of four hundred people snorting awake, looking about in wonder and confusion, and mumbling some variation of, "Did he just say what I think he said?"

The crowd turned their attention to the King's Guard, for it was his duty to listen to everything the king said, just in case he were to say something crazy.

You know, like something about magical panties.

Realizing this was his big moment, the Guard stepped forward and bowed low.

"Your majesty, perhaps we misunderstood. Did you say 'magical panties'?"

"Yes!" Stephanus announced. "Silk panties. Pink with tiny blue hearts. And, I have to be honest with you, Bertie, they feel fantastic on my bum."

Women fainted. Panties! Bums! These were not the sorts of things kings were supposed to discuss in public, especially in front of foreign diplomats.

"Magic, my lord?" asked the King's Guard. He had correctly diagnosed this as the most troubling word of the king's announcement. Wearing panties is one thing, but magic? That was crazy talk. "What do these 'magical panties' do?"

"I have not gone mad, sir, I assure you," said Stephanus. "Look, it's quite simple. A mysterious wizard gave me these panties and explained that if I wore them they would bring vast riches to our kingdom. Today is a day for celebration!"

Wizards! People were now openly panicking. Their king had always been eccentric, but now he had clearly gone insane.

The Guard slid out his dagger. He was sad. He loved his king, but Amerigorn had suffered mad kings before, and it was the Guard's solemn duty to protect the people from crazy monarchs.

"And where is all of this magical wealth, sire?" asked the Guard, strolling towards the king as if to have a cozy chat.

"Huh. That's a good point," said Stephanus, looking around. "Oh! I remember. In order for the magic to work, the wizard said I need to be addressed by the words written on the back of the panties."

The Guard was close to the king now. One lunge with the dagger would take care of everything.

"And what words are those, sire?"

"Love Muffin."

"Get him!" yelled a merchant from the back of the room.

The Guard raised his dagger high and whispered, "Rest in peace, Love Muffin."

And then a curious thing happened. A pile of gold, as tall as an olyphant's knee, appeared in front of the king. This awesome sight silenced the crowd and stayed the hand of the Guard.

After staring at the treasure for a long moment, the Guard fell to his knees and cried out: "Long live King Love Muffin!"

Thus began the Age of Magic.

Part One

Chapter One

"GOOD MORNING, MOM," I said as I descended the stairs to the kitchen.

"Good evening, Nigel," she replied.

That's when I knew I was in trouble.

Obviously, it's not a good sign when you can't tell your mornings from your evenings, but Mom had that special tone in her voice. You know that tone. The one where your parent is so angry the only way they can express themselves without exploding is to speak with strained calm? That was the tone of voice my mom used to address me.

I had to think. What could I have done that would make her that mad?

And then it hit me.

I don't know how I could have forgotten, except that when you've slept through an entire day you're not exactly at your best. If I'd had my wits about me, instead of walking into my kitchen I would have climbed out my bedroom window and legged it out of town.

Nevertheless, I tried to remain calm. After all, it was possible she was just mad about me sleeping in and that she knew nothing about last night.

Rule #17: Admit to nothing. (Actually, that's the only rule I have, but it sounds more impressive if people think you have a long list of awesome rules.)

"Is it evening already?" I said with a laugh. "My, how short the days are. I'm reminded of the poet—"

"Never mind the poet," she said. She rose from her kitchen chair and pointed a finger at me. What long fingers she had! Dirty, too! I briefly thought about suggesting she clean her fingernails, but decided that perhaps this wasn't the right moment.

"You," she said, "were supposed to have been up ages ago to help Master Phelps with his fruit stand."

"Ah. Quite right," I said, advancing towards the breadbox and away from that bony finger. "I'll just grab a slice of bread and butter and hop on over there straightaway. Well, maybe not 'straightaway.' Let's say in an hour or so. After all, I don't want to seem too eager."

"You've been fired."

"Have I? Huh. I guess it's a good thing I didn't get up early then, isn't it?" I smiled and winked. I grabbed the breadknife and picked up a loaf of Mom's delicious homemade bread. I even twirled it on my finger, trying to keep things light. Whew! I thought. She's only mad about me getting fired!

"Nigel?" she said, almost as an afterthought. "Did you destroy the farmer's market and extinguish the Phoenix Tree last night?"

The loaf fell. Crumbs scattered across the floor. Mom had totally caught me off guard with her surprise attack. Had she just come right out and asked me about the market and the Eternal Flame, I would have been ready for her. But no!

Clever woman, my mom.

"Market?" I said. "Destroy? Flame?" Clearly, my mastery of the spoken word was failing me. Mom's gambit had worked. "I-I was with you!" I finally managed to say, "At the Phoenix Tree Ceremony! The market was just fine when we left."

So far, so true.

A cough from the corner of the room startled me.

Mom and I were not alone.

A soldier stood at attention over by the front window. And what a specimen he was! He wore all the trimmings: medals, a broadsword, a helmet tucked under his right arm, just so. But what really tied the whole ensemble together was the expression on the man's face, which was one of complete disapproval. I've had expressions of disapproval directed my way countless times before, so I'm a bit of an expert on the subject. This one was notable for its professionalism. Here was a man who disapproved of everyone and everything for a living.

A chill went up my spine. Nevertheless, I tried to play it cool.

"Hallo, old chap," I said, crossing the room, extending a hand in his direction. He was a bald bloke . . . well, sort of. The top of his dome was as bald as a baby's knee, but what hair he did have had formed a sort of blockade around the middle of his head. It began under his nose and ran down his cheek, where it made a feint and charged up to engage his sideburns; from there it performed a flanking maneuver around his ears and then continued the circumvallation all the way around the sides and back of his head. His hair gave him a rugged, dangerous look. Clearly, this was a fellow who was not to be trifled with, which was a pity, since I love trifling with people. "Name's Nigel Pipps-Schrewsberry-Billingsbottom III."

"No it's not," he growled. He sounded like he had just gargled a mug of steaming gravel. "It's Maggot."

"Is it indeed?" I said, not liking the way this conversation was going. "How about that? Sounds like I need to take a gander at the old birth certificate!"

"This is Drill-Sergeant Smythe, Nigel," Mom said. "He's a friend of your father's."

Some friend!

"And that friendship," Smythe said, "is the only thing keeping you out of jail after that stunt you pulled last night."

"Friendship's a wonderful thing, isn't it?" I said, slowly backing away from that seething mound of medals. "By the way, sir, smashing helmet you've got there."

"You can call me Drill-Sergeant."

"Can I? Lovely. Now if you'll excuse me, I'll just be heading off—"

"The only place you're going is straight into the Royal Military Academy," he said. "It looks like your worthless life now rests in my hands. Do you see my hands, Maggot?"

I did. They were tough-looking, bone-crushing, angry hands.

"Military school?" I said in a daze.

Mom began weeping uncontrollably. Drill-Sergeant Smythe walked over to console her. "Look what you've done to your poor mother. Don't worry, Margaret. I'll whip the boy into shape in no time at all."

"Splendid!" I said, clapping my hands and rubbing them together. "I'll just go pack a bag, then, shall I?" I figured all I had to do was get out of sight of this bloke for one minute so I could climb out my window and make my escape. I'd heard stories about military school, and I wanted no part of that.

But Drill-Sergeant Smythe was not fooled. "The only thing you're bringing is your pathetic self! Now MOVE IT!"

Good lord! I thought. *This is actually happening!*

I rushed over to my mom's side.

"Mom?"

"I'm sorry, dear. But you've left me no choice."

"But it was an accident!"

"It wasn't just last night's escapade, Nigel. You've been getting into trouble on a regular basis ever since your father died."

"Crying on your mother's shoulder ain't gonna help you now, Maggot," Smythe said. Then he picked me up and carried me towards the door.

"Would it be all right if I cried on your shoulder?"

I won't repeat what he said as it's not fit for print. But the gist of it was that it would most definitely not be all right if I cried on the Drill-Sergeant's shoulder.

"How long am I going to be in the military?" I asked as we burst through our front door out into the twilight.

"For the rest of your miserable life," said Smythe.

And that's when I proceeded to cover Drill-Sergeant Smythe in vast quantities of vomit.

Chapter Two

DRILL-SERGEANT SMYTHE IS not the kind of man who enjoys being covered in vomit. He is also not the kind of man who thinks highly of people who try to escape from Drill-Sergeants by throwing up on them and running away. I know these facts about Drill-Sergeant Smythe because he expressed them to me in a rather lengthy monologue that was greatly disparaging of my character.

My escape attempt was an abrupt failure. I was immediately nabbed by Smythe's henchman and forced to listen to the aforementioned speech. I won't repeat exactly what Smythe said (I'm endeavoring to keep this a family-friendly tale), but he wrapped up his three-part assessment of me with: "And if you think for one cuss-filled second that you can get away with any more of this cussing cuss-tasticly stupid behavior, I am going to cuss in a watermelon and cram it down your cussing neck. You hear me?"

"What was the part about the watermelon?" I said, suddenly swept away by the Sergeant's vivid imagery.

"Why you little . . ." Smythe lunged for my throat. The guard stepped in between us and held up his hand at the onrushing Drill Sergeant. "Don't, sir," he said. "Maggot here ain't worth it." The guard then tossed me headfirst into the back of a cart, which was basically a jail cell on wheels, and locked the door.

I had a rather long journey ahead of me and this jail cart was not an ideal ride, for not only did it not have plush seating, but its floor was covered in hay. I am allergic to hay, so I spent the entire trip sneezing and trying to blow my nose without the aid of a handkerchief.

Smythe and the guard walked up to the draft horse, and Smythe smacked it on the behind, which set the cart in motion. I watched my house in the fading light of day as it slowly grew smaller. I hoped to see my mother peek out of a window to wave goodbye to me, her only child, but she never did.

We rounded a corner, and it finally hit me that I might never see my house or my mom again. One of those proverbial lumps actually formed in my throat as the cart bounced up and down on the street stones.

We turned another corner and entered the village square. I got up on my knees—the cart was too short for me to stand up—and I tried to get a look through the bars to see what destruction I'd wrought.

It was as bad as I'd feared. A whirlywind couldn't have brought more damage.

Broken stands abounded. And there, in the snow, lay our extinguished Phoenix Tree, with a group of angry people gathered around it consoling each other.

One member of the group noticed me, pointed, and said, "There 'e is, the cussing cusswad," and the whole mob rushed over to my cart and tried to reach through the bars in order to claw my eyes out, all the while hurling insults at me. Neither Smythe nor the guard made any attempt to discourage them.

"Howdy, folks!" I said between sneezes. "Lovely evening, what?" I figured it was best to keep the mood light.

"Throw him to the dire wolves!" said one elderly woman as she jabbed her cane at me.

"Naw," said one mangy-looking geezer who was missing as much hair as he was teeth. "Getting eaten by wolves is too good for 'im." He then proceeded to suggest that they saw my head off and use it for target practice. At least, I think that what he said; he was so angry he was cursing and spitting every other word, so it was hard to understand him.

Who knew adults cursed so much?

Given all of the hate being directed at me, I began to feel relieved that Smythe was taking me away from my village. Imagine if he hadn't come around to whisk me off and I had just walked down the street, minding my own business. The crowd would have literally torn me asunder.

Eventually, the angry citizens gave up, and I was left alone with my thoughts, which is never a good thing, but one thought in particular nagged at me.

"How did you know it was me, sir?" I asked.

"D'ja hear that, boyo?" Smythe said, slapping his guard on the back. "A confession!"

"Your friend ratted you out," said the guard.

Of course. I knew exactly who he was talking about, too. Lance Hightower. Lance was my rival and my arch nemesis. He had been ever since he had first shown up in our village two years ago. As I rode onward, I found myself thinking back to the good old days—before Lance—and how wonderful life had been. Back then, I was the most interesting person in town. Everyone knew my name. Girls paid attention to me—mostly to ask me to leave them alone, but still, it was something. I was someone of importance. Then suddenly—some would say mysteriously—Lance Hightower appeared in our village. No one knew where he came from. He had no parents, no history. No one even knew where he lived. He just showed up one day, introduced himself, the girls all swooned, and that was that. Lance became the Big Man About Town, and I became the Big Zed. And we've been rivals ever since.

So, of course Lance ratted me out, the coward. I found this news to be especially appalling seeing as Lance had been there and had even participated in creating this disaster.

But I wasn't going to rat him out. No. I wouldn't sink to his level.

"There 'ee is," said Smythe. "There's your rat friend."

I turned to look in the direction Smythe was pointing so I could hurl an insult at my betrayer.

But it wasn't Lance who was standing there.

It was Nate.

My best friend.

No way, I thought. Nate would never rat me out. But then, as I rode by him, our eyes locked on each other. He turned and walked away from me, and I could see shame written all over his face. He had actually done it!

I couldn't believe it! Nate and I were besties! We had planned and carried out dozens of mischievous schemes over the years, and we had always had each other's back.

How could he have betrayed me?

I sat there, dazed, bumping and sneezing along in my rolling jail cart, when we came to an abrupt stop, which knocked me over. I crawled to the front of my cart to see what the problem was. And there, standing in what could only be described as a heroic pose, was a figure blocking our path.

"Gentlemen!" said the figure. "I have come to turn myself in."

I knew that voice.

"And who might you be, then?" said Smythe.

"Sir, I am Hightower. Lance Hightower." He bowed low. "I also participated in last night's shenanigans, and I am prepared to meet my punishment."

Oh, brother, I thought. I'm going to have to share this cramped cage—and, apparently, the rest of my life—with this bottom-kisser.

"See that, Maggot?" Smythe said to me. "See how he owned up to his mistakes even though we weren't looking for him? Notice how he didn't try to vomit on me and run away?"

I did notice that. The jerk.

"Now if you will please, sir," said Lance, "I will gladly take my place by the side of my comrade-in-arms."

"Nah," said Smythe. "This cage is only for lowly cowards like your girl-friend here. You may ride on top."

"As you wish."

Lance, with his long, perfect dark-brown hair and his perfect cheek-bones and his perfect jawline and his flawless olive skin, climbed on top of the cage and sat down above me. "Greetings, comrade," he said to me through the bars.

I hated how he called everyone comrade.

"Why the glum look, mate?" he said. "We've got us a free ride to the capital! Chillax and enjoy the ride."

I also hated how he used words like chillax.

Smythe smacked the horse again, and it came lazily to life.

I rode in that cramped, bumpy cage—under my enemy's butt—for the next eight hours. This gave me ample time to reflect on how everything had gone so wrong.

Chapter Three

THE PREVIOUS NIGHT had started off innocently enough. It was New Year's Eve, and I had big plans. Nate and I were going to meet up at Blyburn's after the Phoenix Tree Ceremony and gorge ourselves on the finest treats in the kingdom.

It just occurred to me that you might not know about Phoenix Trees— after all, they only grow in Amerigorn. A Phoenix Tree is a tall, thin evergreen that looks very similar to a cypress. But what makes the Phoenix Tree so special is it has unusually dense wood that burns very slowly. So slowly, in fact, that a single Phoenix Tree can burn for well over a year. And so, thousands of years ago, we started using them to keep track of time. Some brilliant sod figured out that if you cut a Phoenix Tree to be fourteen feet, four-and-a-half inches high, it will burn for exactly one year. And thus began our tradition of the Phoenix Tree Lighting Ceremony.

Every village in the Kingdom of Amerigorn has a New Year's Phoenix Tree Ceremony, but our village's flame was the oldest by far. For one thousand and eleven years, Bletchleysbum had had an Eternal Flame alight in its town square. Even during the Really Big War, our flame had not faltered. All the men in the town had gathered together to protect that flame from the invading gork army. And although many men had perished that day, our flame lived on. The flame had had another brush with extinguishment five years ago during the Farmer's Revolt. My father became a local hero by single-handedly defending the flame from a horde of marauding farmers who were furious with the king's reforms. Many village flames in the kingdom were extinguished during that period of unrest, but not ours.

So, our Phoenix Tree Ceremony was, to put it mildly, a big deal for our town. Every year King Olerood himself traveled all the way from the capital to participate in the event.

Anyway, as interesting as all of that may be, I was only attending the ceremony to shore up my nighttime plans with Nate. After all, if you've seen one Phoenix Tree Lighting Ceremony, you've seen them all. Every year the Mayor gives the same speech, the king mumbles the same mumbles, the crowd sings the same songs, and the Phoenix Queen—the most beautiful sixteen-year-old girl in the village—gets to light the new Phoenix Tree from the dying embers of the last one.

Mom and I walked to the town square together, but as soon as I saw Nate over by the hot cider stand, I ditched Mom and swam my way through the crowd. Unfortunately, when I caught up with him, I realized he wasn't alone. Hender and Petrick were clinging to him like dead leaves on a tree on a windy day.

Nothing against them. They're fine fellows, I'm sure. But they're not the kind of chaps you can count on if you're up to a bit of mischief. Especially Petrick, who has a tendency to panic.

I finally made my way to the boys and exchanged hellos with everyone. Nate raised his eyebrows at me as if to ask if we were on for tonight. I gave him a slight nod. He shrugged as if to ask what time we were to meet. I thought about it for a second. How do you pantomime ten bells? I figured putting up ten fingers was too obvious, but I didn't see any way around it. So I did.

"What are you guys up to?" said Petrick noticing my hands.

"Look, Petrick," I said, "I don't want to tell you. Not because I don't like you, but because you'd ruin it."

"What! I won't ruin anything! Honest! What are you up to?"

He was talking a little too loudly for my liking. I looked at Nate, who shrugged back at me. The only way to get out of this situation with any hope of successfully accomplishing our late night escapade was to tell all and hope for the best.

"I have a key to Blyburn's. Nate and I are going there tonight at ten bells."

Petrick blanched. "But we've got curfew at nine," he said, as though I didn't know this.

"Good," said Nate. "Then it's settled. You stay at home. Nige and I will go to Blyburn's."

"Whatcha gonna do at Blyburn's?" said Hender. "Steal stuff?"

I sighed. "No. No one is stealing anything at Blyburn's." After all, I may be a mischief-maker, but I was no criminal. "We're going to pay for it. But we're going to help ourselves to the King's Select goodies."

"But that's still basically stealing," said Petrick. "After all, only the king—"

"Yes, yes, yes, we all know about the King's Select, Petrick."

"They'll lock you up in the pillory again."

I wonder if they have the pillory in your village. It's a wooden contraption you see in many town squares here in Amerigorn. Someone who has been caught doing something naughty gets their hands and head locked up in this thing, and then they have to stand there all day while everyone in town comes and laughs at you. I have been locked up in the pillory four times: twice for breaking curfew, once for being a public nuisance, and once for hitting the mayor's daughter in the nose with an orange. (That last one was totally not my fault. I had been aiming for Lance, but he selfishly ducked out of the way.)

Most people find being locked up humiliating, but I don't have any shame so that part doesn't bother me. Last time I was locked up for staying out past curfew, people came to scoff at me, and I basically laughed in their faces and said, "Hey, at least I had a good time last night!"

But being locked up at an awkward angle for hours on end is uncomfortable.

Especially if you have to pee.

And believe me, you don't want to pee your trousers while standing in the middle of the town square. You will never live that down. Just ask Pee-Pee McGrew, the melon farmer's kid, whose favorite activity is reminding people that his first name is actually Michael.

Anyway, I understood Petrick's nervousness, but at the same time . . . we were talking about Blyburns! The greatest bakery in the entire kingdom!

"What ho! What have we here?" came a merry voice from behind me.

My skin shivered. I knew exactly who it was; the only question I had was how many adoring girls would be clinging to Lance.

Seven.

As much as I hated to admit it, I was impressed. I mean, seven girls! But then I noticed that Melissa was one of those seven, and my thoughts turned green.

I'd had a huge crush on Melissa as long as I could remember, but part of my continuing infatuation with that beautiful creature was that I had never seen her give Lance so much as a second glance. Here, I had thought, was a girl of taste; a girl who wouldn't be taken in with good looks, talent, and charm.

And yet, here she was, gazing longingly at Lance, totally unaware that there were eight hundred people standing around her.

Totally unaware that I was there.

"And what bit of mischief are you up to tonight?" said Lance with a stupid gleam in his eye.

"We'll never tell you," I said, trying to strike the same heroic pose Lance made look so easy.

"They're breaking into Blyburn's and stealing the King's Select," said Petrick.

I looked at him. "Remember how you said you weren't going to ruin everything?"

"Blyburn's!" said Lance with a nod and a wink. "I commend you on your taste; for I have sampled the King's Select and let me tell you, they are the finest treats in the entire world."

He had a way of enunciating everything and squinting his eyes to enhance certain words so that it made everything he said sound like it was the most important and profound thing anyone had ever said.

I rolled my eyes. "I know. That's why we're going there. But no one is stealing anything. I have money. I am paying for them."

"The King's Select can't be bought, comrade. They are made expressly for the King."

"I know. Nevertheless, I am going to pay for them."

"Then I will join you on your quest," said Lance.

"Oh, Lance, you are such a bad boy!" said Gilda.

"He's a bad boy?" I said. "I'm the one who came up with the plan and stole the key! And no! You can't come!"

There! That put him in his place.

"Can you really get us into Blyburn's?" asked Melissa, placing her hand on my chest. Her giant, green eyes burned right through me. It was, I am rather ashamed to admit, the first time she had ever actually looked me in the eye.

And, well, what can I say? I melted right there on the spot.

To think! I could be showing off my bad-boy self in front of the fair Melissa!

"T-t-t-ten bells," I managed to say. "Meet me in the back of Blyburn's at ten bells."

"Good show!" said Lance, pounding me on the chest right where Melissa's hand had been. "We'll be there!"

"Oh, Lance! You are so daring!" said Bethelda.

"My dear," he said, lifting her chin with his left hand. "I believe one has to breathe if one wants to live." He did that squinting thing when he said the word breathe.

Bethelda sighed. "You're such a poet!"

"A poet?" I said. "He merely stated a biological fact! I believe dragons have scales! I believe babies burp! I believe llamas are larger than frogs!"

But they weren't paying any attention to me. They were too busy following Lance as he strode away.

"Don't let him get to you, mate," said Nate. "Think of the look Melissa will give you when you hand her one of the King's Select."

Good old Nate. He knew how to keep me focused.

The dirty rat.

Chapter Four

As SOON AS I heard the tenth bell, I climbed out of my bedroom window and leapt to the nearest tree. From there, it was an easy drop to the street. I crept from shadow to shadow, keeping an eye out for Nektor, our ancient town watchman. He was a mean old bugger, though he always walked in the same pattern, so he was easy to avoid. I arrived at Blyburn's only a few minutes after leaving my room. I was the first one there, which I had expected since I lived the closest. I peeked in through the back window to make sure Old Man Blyburn and his wife were asleep. I saw no one.

Nate soon joined me and clapped me on the shoulder.

"What say we just go in and eat everything ourselves?" I whispered.

"Let's."

But it was too late. Petrick, Hendle, and Lance, along with Lance's entourage of seven—no, eight!—girls came strolling up the street. My jaw dropped. They weren't leaping from shadow to shadow to hide from the night watch. No! They were striding along like they owned the place.

"Get out of sight!" I said, trying to find that magical balance between yelling and whispering.

"I refuse to skulk, my good man," said Lance. "When I perform mischief, I do it proudly. And if I get caught, so be it."

Says a guy who's never done anything mischievous in his entire life, I thought. But the girls all swooned.

"Do you really have a key?" said Melissa, her gorgeous eyes locking on to mine.

"I do." I kind of hated myself for saying it heroically, the way Lance would have, but that's what I did. I even performed a slow reveal of the key for added drama.

"Let's do this," said Lance, ruining my moment.

I unlocked the door and began nudging it open. But Lance. He had no patience for my stealth. He just shoved it wide and sauntered into the place.

"Idiot's gonna get us caught," said Nate.

Lance cruised over to the King's Select table, and Melissa glided along right behind him. Everything seemed to be happening in a blur. I rushed over to the table, for I wanted to be the one who had the pleasure of offering Melissa her first Select treat, but I couldn't get there in time.

"Here you are," said Lance, proffering her a chocolate-covered gooseberry. "A sweet for the sweet."

She took the treat—casually gliding her hand over his—and bit into it. Her eyes.

They closed deep as she rolled the confection around in her gorgeous mouth. And then she opened them wide, in rapturous delight, clasping her hands around his.

"Oh my word!" she said, gazing into his eyes. "It's heavenly!"

The next few minutes played out like that, with Lance doling out treats to everyone and receiving thanks for being so wonderful.

Then he finally handed one to me.

"And one for you, our hero of the night," he proclaimed. To his credit, he did give me the biggest treat in the shop—a giant slice of triple-chocolate raspberry mousse cake—and everyone said a hearty "hear, hear!" in my direction. But still, it rubbed me wrong the way he had stolen my spotlight.

I was about to bite into my dessert when Gilda spoke up.

"None for you, Lance?" I hated the way she reveled in saying his name.

I looked up at him. He wasn't eating.

"No, no. There aren't any treats left. But that's OK. It gives me greater pleasure to see my friends so happy."

"Awww," said Belinda. And then she looked at me, for I was the only person who still had a treat left.

The implication was clear. I was expected to share my treat with him.

Earlier in the evening—when it was just going to be Nate and me pulling off this caper—I had been expecting to enjoy a half-dozen treats. Now I was not even going to have a single treat all to myself.

But whatever.

I broke the delicate piece of cake in two and offered it to Lance.

"Nonsense, my good man!" he said heroically. "You enjoy that. You earned it!"

I don't know why, but that made me even angrier.

I swallowed my treat. I tried to savor its extraordinary flavor, but my mind was so clouded with anger, I was unable to do so.

"Now, who's up for some more fun?" Lance said, rubbing his hands together.

"I am!" said Melissa, her eyes aglow.

The crowd filed out of the store with Lance, but Petrick stopped.

"Wait! Who's paying for all this?"

"Why, Nibel is!" said Melissa.

Nibel?

She didn't even know my name!

"Good man!" said Lance.

"Thanks, Nibel!" said the girls.

"Yeah, thanks, Nibes!" said Nate with a wink.

I paid and locked up shop, and I followed the crowd as Lance led us out into the woods.

"Where are we going?" I asked.

"To the most beautiful spot in the entire village," he said. "A little clearing, just up ahead."

He helped Gilda to step up over a branch.

"You're such a gentleman!" said Ariadne.

"I believe you have to live by a code," said Lance.

Oh brother. Lance and his code. He was always going on about the stupid thing. Why, just the other day in the square I heard him saying something to his cadre of worshipers as they walked by me.

"I live by a code," he said. "And part of my code is I don't push old ladies in the street."

The girls all sighed. I couldn't believe it. Bethelda cooed, "You're so righteous!"

"Righteous?" I said. "No one is FOR pushing old ladies!"

"Oh," said Gilda, "look who's suddenly against pushing old ladies."

They looked down their beautiful noses at me.

"Suddenly?" I said. "I've never been *for* pushing old ladies!"

"Of course," said Bethany.

And then they all forgot I was there and followed Lance as he sauntered up the street.

Well! I wasn't going to stand by and be outdone by such nonsense. I ran up in front of the crowd.

"I too have a code," I said, striking a bold stance. "I am totally against kicking puppies."

I smiled boldly. I may have even winked. But my statement didn't have the effect I had hoped for.

"Kicking puppies?" said Gilda.

"What kind of sick person are you?" said Ariadne.

"What?" I said, blinking.

"I mean, really. You ought to be ashamed of yourself," huffed Bethany.

"Ashamed?" I said as the crowd followed Lance. "I said I was against kicking puppies. Against it!" But they walked away, shaking their heads with disgust.

I'd learned my lesson. Tonight I wasn't about to trod on Lance and his idiotic code. I merely followed the crowd up the hill.

I had to admit, Lance may be a buffoon, but he knew a beautiful spot when he found one. The view was stunning. Out here, beyond the daily traffic of the town center, snow still coated the ground. As if on cue, the moon emerged from a cloud to illuminate the scene and sparkle the trees. We could see the entire village—which, at that point, had been my whole world. There, between the snow-covered roofs, lay our town square, with the New Year's decorations still hanging on the market stands, and our impressive, brand-new Phoenix Tree, blazing proudly in the middle of it all.

The clopping of hooves behind us broke the spell.

There, only fifty yards away, on the main road into town, was a horse-drawn carriage.

It was unusual to see one on the road at this late hour, for although Amerigorn was a relatively safe kingdom, merchants avoided traveling at night because bandits were a ubiquitous problem. But this driver seemed to be in no hurry as he wound his way around our hill, totally unaware we were standing above him.

I don't know what possessed me, but I grabbed up some snow and packed it into a ball.

"I'll give you a gilder if you hit him," said Nate.

"You're on!" I said. After buying all those treats, I was broke.

I reared back and fired.

I missed.

By a mile.

"No, no, no, comrade," said Lance as he scooped up some snow. "You have to lead the horse a good ten yards in front."

He launched his snowball, and, to my astonishment, he missed as well.

We looked at each other, and the race was on!

We each scooped up some snow, slapped together our missiles, and threw them at the cart.

We both missed. My snowball fell apart in mid-flight due to my haste.

The cart was only a few feet from the town gate, so there was only time for one last throw. In spite of this, I took an extra second to ensure the quality of my snowball.

"You first," I said.

Lance fired . . . and missed!

Here was my chance to prove I was better than him at something.

I aimed far out in front of the horse and threw as hard as I could.

The snowball sailed through the night . . . and smashed into the poor creature's eye.

Startled, the beast whinnied, reared back on his hind legs, and sprinted off into town.

The driver yanked on the reins in a desperate attempt to control his horse, but it was no use; he was spooked and out of control.

The horse galloped haphazardly into the square, where he overturned a fruit stand, sending fresh apples and berries everywhere. This commotion sent him into a panic. He spun around, flinging the driver onto the cobblestone road where he landed with a sickening thud. The horse kept thrashing and kicking, destroying stalls, barrels, and boxes everywhere he went.

And then I watched in horror as he ran into the Phoenix Tree, sending it flying into a snowbank, and extinguishing its flame for the first time in over 1,100 years.

The horse finally broke free of the cart and dashed away from the scene.

Residents rushed out of their houses and into the square. They were shouting and crying and moaning.

My mind raced for a way out. I knew I could sneak back home undetected, but I wasn't sure about everyone else.

I turned to my friends to discuss our options.

They were all gone.

The End of Magic

Sorry to pause the story for another history lesson, but this bit is essential to understanding the rest of my tale. Last interruption, I promise.

You remember our pal Stephanus II, a.k.a., "King Love Muffin?" It turns out he wasn't the only monarch who had received magical panties from a mysterious wizard. All of the kings of Esteria had, even King "Sugar Bums" Selron, who had received a pair of panties that granted all the elves of Riverfell eternal life. (Remember King Selron, he'll play a role in my story.)

The more the kings used their magical panties, the more magic they released into the air. This had a rather nifty side effect: All that magic attracted hordes of magical creatures to our lands, such as dragons, zombies, goblins, giant eagles, moths who could burp the alphabet, and more.

Esteria became the premier destination for knights and adventurers looking to fight giants and slay trolls. Poets wrote epics. Bards told tales of derring-do. It was a golden age of adventure. And it was all thanks to that mysterious wizard who had created those magical panties.

Unfortunately for everyone, that wizard, a bloke by the name of Lord Smoron, wasn't just some nice chap who wanted to make the world a wonderful and exciting place. No, his doling out of magical panties was all part of a devious plot to conquer Esteria.

Frankly, I don't understand how this wasn't blindingly obvious from the start. I mean, how did people not see that making the kings of Esteria wear women's panties and be addressed by ridiculous nicknames was a sign that someone was up to something naughty? But alas, the kings and people of Esteria were too giddy with magic and power to pay heed.

Here was Smoron's plan.

First, he forged a pair of magical cufflinks.

"What's a cufflink," you ask?

It's a fancy button for your sleeve.

"That's ridiculous," you're thinking.

Yes. Yes, it is.

Nevertheless, Smoron made this pair of magical cufflinks, forging them in the fires of Mount Boo-Boo.

"Seriously?" you're thinking. "There's a mountain named Boo-Boo?"

Funny story. Mount Boo-Boo lies deep in the heart of the Gorkish Empire. The Gorks named this massive volcano Graashka, which means "Gash," as in, "this active volcano looks like an open wound upon the earth." It's actually kind of a cool name if you think about it, but if there's one thing humans genuinely excel at, it's finding childish ways to belittle our enemies. So: "Mount Boo-Boo."

Anyway, the panties derived their magic from these cufflinks, which became known as the Cufflinks of Doom. What's more, Smoron was able to use the Cufflinks to secretly control anyone wearing his magical underwear and get them to do his bidding.

And so, with Cufflinks in sleeve, Smoron went to the gorks and said, "Who wants to conquer Esteria and make elves cry?"

There were two wars. In the first one, known as the Big War, Smoron and his gork army launched a surprise attack on the peoples of Esteria and nearly succeeded in conquering the whole continent. But—to make a very complicated story absurdly short—he failed, and his hands were cut off.

"Agh! My hands!" he cried. (Sorry, I know that's a superfluous piece of probably apocryphal detail, but that's how my fourth-grade teacher, Mrs. Kerfuffle, told the story, and I always feel compelled to include that bit. To make the scene come alive the way Mrs. Kerfuffle did, it helps if you imagine Smoron's voice as a high-pitched croak.)

When Smoron's hands were lopped off, that not only separated him from the Cufflinks of Doom, but it also cast him into the eternal void.

Amazingly, it had been boring old King Love Muffin who had delivered the blow and recovered the Cufflinks.

King Selron rushed over to Stephanus. "Quick!" he said. "You must take the Cufflinks to Mount Boo-Boo and toss them into the fire. Only then can we destroy them and forever ruin Lord Smoron's chances of returning to our world."

"Hmmm," said Stephanus.

"Hmmm?" said Selron. "What do you mean 'hmmm'? We must act at once! The fate of the world is in your hands!"

"If I destroy the Cufflinks, won't I also end the Age of Magic?"

"Yes?"

"Magic is cool," said Stephanus.

"Good point," said King Sugar Bums.

"How about this? What if we hide the Cufflinks somewhere no one will ever find them?"

"What could go wrong?"

In hindsight, of course, this seems like an incredibly stupid idea. Although, to their credit, it worked for nearly two thousand years, which is more than one can say about a great many ideas people have.

OK, so flash forward to just twenty-five years ago, when a halfling named Elbo, who had gotten lost in the deepest cave of the What-Ho Mountains, stumbled on to said Cufflinks. Not realizing what he had found, he put them on.

This acted as a magical alarm, waking up Lord Smoron. Even though he was still trapped in the void, Smoron was able to use his magic to charm the gorks and get them to launch another attack. Their goal: recover the Cufflinks and return Smoron to the world so he could finally realize his plan of total domination.

Esteria was plunged into the second war, known as the Really Big War.

Epic battles and thrilling chase scenes ensued, and things looked pretty grim for humanity and their allies, but in the end, Elbo and his friends made an epic quest to Mount Boo-Boo where they tossed the Cufflinks into the fires, destroying them—and Lord Smoron—once and for all.

And that is how the Age of Magic came to an end in Esteria.

Just in time for me to be born.

Figures, right?

Chapter Five

C<small>LANG</small>!

That was the sound of Smythe smashing his sword hilt on the cage, waking me up.

Bang!

That was the sound of my head hitting the top of the very same cage.

"Dang!"

That is a cleaned-up version of what I said after I hit my head.

"Rise and shine, Maggot," said Smythe. "We're here."

I rubbed my head and struggled to climb out of the cart. It was morning. We had traveled straight through the night.

I sneezed a few dozen times. My eyes were so swollen from my hay allergy that I could barely open them.

"You look terrible, comrade," said Lance as he extended a hand toward me.

I hated to accept his charity, but I needed his help.

"Thanks," I mumbled.

I stood up and looked around. What I saw was rather impressive.

The Royal Military Academy is a large castle on the northwestern border of Shropsfordshire. And Shropsfordshire, as you probably know, is the new capital of Amerigorn. (The old capital, Flumpklump, was destroyed in the Really Big War. Amerigorners never rebuilt it, mostly because people hated the name Flumpklump.)

I estimated the walls of the castle to be at least 30 feet high. All along the wall, spread out every hundred paces or so, there was a tower, manned by archers, that was taller still. I saw several large buildings in the castle, including a barracks (where we would sleep), the mess hall (where we would eat), classrooms, stables, the Great Hall, the armory (where the weapons were stored), and more. The castle wasn't just the largest structure I'd ever seen; it was bigger than my entire village.

We were standing in a huge courtyard, or bailey, and everywhere I looked there were cadets in uniforms being screamed at by drill-sergeants: some were being screamed at as they marched, some while they practiced fighting, others while digging ditches, and others while standing at attention. The screaming was very informative. In only a few seconds, I was able to learn that all the cadets in this school were worthless, weak maggots, whose parents had done the world a tremendous disservice by bringing them into it.

I shuddered at the thought that this was going to be my world for the foreseeable forever, but then I felt a tiny bit better once I realized that I would fit right in with these poor sods.

"Let's go, maggots," said Smythe as he marched us into a small building and brought us up to an elderly woman who had clearly never smiled in her entire life. She told us to hand over our clothes. I was a bit shy about undressing in front of this stranger, but Smythe gave me a few hearty words of advice, saying that if I didn't do what I was told without hesitation, I would have my limbs removed from my body and reattached in all the wrong places.

I disrobed and handed my clothes to the unsmiling woman. She handed me a brown and grey uniform whose main purpose, I soon discovered, was to provide maximum itchiness to the wearer.

"Now we're talking!" said Lance. He winked at me. "The girls won't be able to keep their hands off of us."

He had a point. We looked sharp. Well, I didn't have a mirror, so I could only see Lance. But he looked great.

"Girls?" said Smythe. "Madame Luxe here is the closest thing to a girl you're going to see for the next forty years."

I gazed at Madame Luxe. She leered back at me to make it clear that I was not to make any romantic gestures in her direction.

A loud bell rang eight times.

"Looks like you're just in time for your first class, maggots." He then yelled for a cadet to escort us to our classroom.

As we walked down twisting corridor after twisting corridor, I couldn't help but notice my companion's cheery attitude about all of this. I asked him about it.

"I always make the best of every situation, comrade. That's part of my code."

"Please tell me more about this code of yours," I said. Lance looked at me and realized I was speaking ironically.

"Or," he said, "you can wallow in misery for the rest of your military career, which is apparently going to be eternal. Your call."

Ouch.

The cadet led us to a room and told us it was our classroom. It was a room all right, though it was clearly devoid of class. Think of a dungeon. Now add a few benches and about a dozen sour-looking cadets, and you have a better idea of what we were walking into.

"Hallo, my fellow comrades!" said Lance as he entered the room—or, I should say, as he made his entrance, for Lance never merely "entered" rooms. Nor did he ever "walk" anywhere. He strode, he waltzed, he eased, he sauntered. He made going from point A to point B look like it was the easiest and most thrilling thing in the world.

But his specialty was breezing.

When he breezed into a room, it was clear to everyone that the party could now begin.

That was how he made his entrance into this gloomy hole of a classroom.

"Good day, comrade," he said as he slapped a cadet on the back. "Are we yearning to learn?"

By the looks on their faces, I immediately grasped that the only thing these boys were yearning to do was to murder my companion. And while I could completely understand that feeling, I also felt . . . well, I felt like I needed to protect him. It occurred to me that this hale and cheery fellow— whom I absolutely despised, mind you—might be destroyed by this awful place. And somehow that made me sad.

I sat beside him in the back row, dizzy with conflicting emotions.

"What's with all this 'comrade' nonsense?" I asked him.

"I'm a socialist," he said. "We always call our friends comrade."

"A socialist?" I said, having no idea what he was talking about. "Is that an interesting thing to be?"

"Not particularly. But it freaks the heck out of adults."

I looked at him and realized that, as much as I disliked him, I didn't really know him at all.

"Why, Comrade Lance!" I said, "I had no idea we shared a love of freaking out adults."

Just then Drill-Sergeant Smythe stormed into the classroom. "I'd tell you to open up your books but you haven't got any books and we're gonna keep it that way. Why? Because you're all a bunch of worthless vermin, that's why."

"Sound logic," I muttered.

"Now!" Smythe said, clapping and rubbing his hands together, "Today we're going to talk about the Really Big War and how the Gorkish Empire launched a cowardly attack on the Eastern front of our kingdom twenty-five years ago. Does anyone here know why the gorks attacked us?"

The cadets all looked at each other.

"I'll tell you why they attacked us!" he said. "It's because they hate our way of life. They hate our freedom. They hate everything we stand for."

"Sir?" I said before I could stop myself. "Not that I doubt anything you just said, sir, but the gorks said that they only attacked us because Lord Smoron forced them to."

"Are you telling me that you'd take a terrorist's word over mine, Maggot?"

Lance nudged me. "You see what he did there? Turned your own words against you."

"Dashed clever of him."

"That's why he's a sergeant and we're lowly cadets."

"Are you two finished?" said Smythe.

"I was going to compliment you on your fine speaking voice, sir, but it can wait," I said.

"Think you're funny, do you, Maggot?"

"I don't know, sir. Mildly, perhaps—"

"You're not!" he said. "You're a smart aleck! You know what happens to smart alecks?"

I hesitated a moment, not sure if he actually wanted me to answer that question or if it was rhetorical.

"I asked you a question, Maggot!"

"Oh, sorry, sir. I wasn't sure if—"

"They get killed, that's what happens to smart alecks!"

"You kill smart alecks, sir?" I said, genuinely concerned. I mean, I had heard military school was tough, but wow, that seemed a little over the top.

"Are you an idiot?" he asked. And he paused again, just long enough for me to wonder if he was asking yet another rhetorical question.

"I'm sorry, sir, am I supposed to answer that?"

"You don't know if you're an idiot?" he said, practically spitting on me.

"No, sir, I just can't tell when you're asking—"

"You know what happens to smart-aleck idiots?" said Smythe. "They get LD! Now scram! And take your girlfriend with you."

"Girlfriend?" I said, pointing at Lance. "I don't want to rush into any long-term commitments, sir. It's my first day."

"GET OUT OF HERE OR SO HELP ME!" said Smythe. "YOU!" he pointed at a cadet in the first row. "Show them where to go!"

Lance and I left the classroom, and the cadet, who I later learned was named Charles, led us down a long hallway.

"Did he seem cross to you?" I asked Lance.

"Maybe he suffers from irritable bowel syndrome," he said.

"By the way," I asked Charles, "What is LD?"

"Latrine Duty. You're gonna dig latrines for the whole company."

"That doesn't sound too bad. At least we don't have to listen to Smythe anymore."

Charles shot me a look that said, *just you wait and see.* And his look was not incorrect, for LD would turn out to be a loathsome activity—one that Lance and I would get used to over the next few weeks.

"Sorry I got you into trouble," I said.

"Oh, it's all right. Honestly, I don't know that I could have endured Smythe's history lesson."

We exited the building and walked across the bailey, towards the western barbican, which was the main entrance to the castle.

"By the way," I said. "Why did you turn yourself in for that Phoenix Tree fiasco? I was the one who threw the snowball."

"Well, I sort of egged you on."

"Yes, but you were in the clear. I wasn't going to rat on you. Not like some friends I know."

"I needed a change of pace," he said. And then before I could ask him what he meant by that, he pointed and said, "Ah! Look!"

We were leaving the castle, passing through the portcullis and onto the drawbridge, over the moat. From here I could see that the moat was actually connected to the Moor River, which formed the Northern border of the kingdom. I could even see the other side of the river.

"The Great Beyond," said Lance.

I had never seen the world outside of our kingdom. "To think what strange creatures might live on the other side!" I said.

"What, like an antelope?" laughed Lance. "Because that's about as exciting a creature as you're likely to find."

I sighed. "Why did our fathers and grandfather have all the luck? My Uncle Alpert actually fought a dragon once. He even had a scale to prove it."

"We were just born too late," said Lance.

"You never know," said Charles.

"What, dragons?" said Lance. "They're all gone, mate. All the magical creatures are gone."

"They say there's still one magical item left. A relic from the First Age."

"People say lots of things."

"The Cufflinks stayed hidden for two thousand years," said Charles. "Maybe this relic is still hidden."

"Yeah, but the Cufflinks and the magical panties were real. They were the first and only magical items ever. There is no record of any other magical anything."

Charles shrugged.

We left the drawbridge and walked across a large field, just outside of the castle. Charles saluted an old man in uniform who sat on a stool with two shovels at his feet.

"Yes, yes," said the old man as he returned Charles' salute. Charles smirked at us and departed.

I looked at the man and wondered if he just sat there all day waiting for cadets to arrive.

"Looks like Smythe sent me his two finest," he said, standing up. He introduced himself as Staff Sergeant Pip.

"I'm Nigel," I said, "and this is—"

"I can't hear ya, sonny. Lost most of my hearing in the Really Big War. Now," he said as he clapped his hands together, "who's ready to dig some holes?"

He slowly bent down and picked up the shovels. Then he took a deep breath before standing upright again and handing the shovels to Lance and me. "OK now," he said. "See that tree line over yonder? Start digging right in front of that. And don't stop until I tell ya!"

The ground was frozen solid, so the going was slow. We asked Sergeant Pip for some pickaxes to help break up the soil. He laughed for a bit. And then he laughed some more. Lance and I took this as our cue that pickaxes would not be forthcoming, but ol' Pip wasn't done with us. "Pickaxes, he says! Ha! You kids and your newfangled technology! You think we had pickaxes back in the Really Big War?"

"Yes?" I said, fearing that perhaps I was once again answering a rhetorical question.

Pip stopped laughing. "Come to think of it, you're right. We did. Huh. Well, that means nothing because I don't have any pickaxes for you today. Now get back to work before you get into trouble."

"How much more trouble could we be in?" I asked.

"Huh?" he said.

"I mean we're already on LD."

"Huh," he said, pushing his helmet back on his forehead a bit. "That's a good point you make, there, sonny." He looked around and seemed to drop the pretense that he was a man of action. "Look, sonny, could you just do me a favor and go back to digging? Making kids dig is the only job they'll still let me do, and if you don't do that, well, what do I have left?"

I couldn't believe it. Someone *asking* us to do something! Plus, this little exchange gave me an idea.

"It will be our pleasure, sir," I said. "Pickaxes or no pickaxes."

We picked up our shovels and went back to work.

It was awful at first, but once you got used to it, the task wasn't so bad. And it didn't hurt that I had Lance to keep me company.

"Comrade Lance," I said. "I think this institution no longer has anything left to offer us."

"You've been here half a day."

"I'm a quick learner."

"Where're you gonna go?"

"Home."

"Ah," he said. He sniffled a bit, wiped his nose with his sleeve, and then went back to digging. "But there's a flaw in your plan, comrade. If you can manage to break out of here—and that's a big if—home is the first place they'll look for you."

That was true. "But I had a good gig at home. Lots of friends. Good food. A mom who did everything for me. No responsibilities. Girls."

"Girls?" said Lance.

"Well, I mean . . . they were around. Mostly they were following you, but they were there. At least there I had a slight chance of kissing a girl."

"You've never kissed a girl?" he asked. I could tell by the way he said it that the chap probably spent the better part of his day kissing one girl after another. I'm sure to him the notion that one could grow up to the ripe old age of fourteen without ever having kissed a girl was ridiculous.

"I almost kissed one once."

"Almost!"

"I accidentally stood on her foot."

"Sound like love at first trample."

"It was glorious, right up until she said, 'Ow. Get off my foot.' I think about that moment often." Then I leaned in close to Lance and asked, "How about you?"

"Girls?"

"No, don't you want to go home? You were the king of our village!"

"Oh, I don't know. I rather like it here."

"Here? Are you crazy?"

"At home, what was I going to be, a farmer? A merchant? I've always wanted to live the glamorous life of a soldier."

"We're digging a ditch for people to poop in."

"Yes," he said, "but this ditch is for military-grade poop, the most vital poop in the land! Only by allowing our soldiers to poop freely can they defend our realm. If that doesn't make you proud, then I don't know what will." He slapped me on the back and got back to ditch digging.

I laughed. I couldn't believe it: it had never occurred to me that Lance could be funny.

Chapter Six

"**W**AKE UP, MAGGOTS!" Smythe said, banging on our bunks.

We all jumped out of our beds as best we could, which was not very fast, given that it was still dark outside and we were half asleep. We assembled in two lines and stood at attention. I was still sore from yesterday's LD.

"Guess what, ladies?" Smythe said. I seem to remember him gleefully rubbing his hands together as he said this, but perhaps my memory is faulty. At any rate, we all knew we were in for something awful. "Tomorrow is the twenty-fifth anniversary of the end of the Really Big War. To celebrate the occasion, we are going to the reopening of Fell's Palace. All of the military academies are going to be there in a show of support for the kingdom, and I want us to set an example of how a military academy is supposed to look— and behave." He glared at me as he said that last word.

So far I couldn't tell what was so awful about this. After all, I love celebrations and being able to see Fell's Palace in person would be a treat. What was Smythe planning, exactly?

"Now," Smythe continued. He put his arms behind his back and ambled up and down the lines as he delivered the next bit of news. "Fell's Palace is forty miles from here. That's a two-day march—even if taken at a brisk pace."

He stopped his stroll and snapped to attention in front of me. "We're going to hike it in one." He leaned in close to my face: "And guess what, Maggot? It's going to rain. The whole way there." He smiled his evil smile and said, "Now. What do you think of that, Maggot?"

"Sounds lovely, sir," I said, trying to fake a bright smile.

"Oh, it will be, Maggot," Smythe said, cracking his knuckles. "It will be."

It was, as I'm sure you can imagine, not.

Hiking is an unpleasant activity. It is a demented perversion of that elegant and civilized institution known as walking. The phrase "to go for a walk" implies a pleasant stroll on well-paved roads with your friends or family. One might even get to hold hands under the moonlight with a romantic interest. (I never have, but I'm told that it happens.) "Going for a hike," on the other hand, involves hauling a heavy backpack over miles of rugged terrain with zealous nature enthusiasts who feel compelled to point out how beautiful everything is.

But as repulsive as regular, civilian-style hiking is, the military version is absolutely diabolical. Cadets and soldiers are not allowed to walk or even march on a military hike; they are forced to run. They cannot enjoy the luxury of simply carrying a heavy backpack; no, they must lug enough supplies to feed a small village. And instead of being accompanied by rabid nature-lovers, the military places you under the watchful supervision of sadistic drill-sergeants who have devoted their lives to the art of creating insightful and enduring ways to humiliate and emotionally scar their subordinates. Military-style hiking is universally acknowledged as the fourth cruelest activity ever devised by humans (behind stoning, attending State of the Kingdom addresses, and, of course, eating peas).

As Smythe had predicted, it rained the entire way there. My backpack became more oppressive with every drop of ice-cold rain that poured from the sky. (Personally, I would rank military hiking at number two on that list, just behind eating peas.)

It didn't help that I was in terrible physical shape. I collapsed a dozen times from exhaustion. At the 15-mile mark, I thought my lungs were going to burst out of my chest and punch me in the face. But I have to say, Drill-Sergeant Smythe really came through in those critical moments. His screaming of obscenities and promising to rip off my ears and cram all sorts of objects into every orifice of my body was just the sort of inspiration I needed to keep going. Honestly, I found myself respecting Smythe more. After all, I only had to run forty miles. He had to run forty miles while yelling at us, which had to require an amazing amount of stamina.

We ran all through the day, pausing once for a brief meal, and then we ran all night long. The only saving grace was that our journey was on relatively flat ground. Had there been any hills I'm sure half of us would have died.

Just before dawn, we emerged from the Grand Woods to an enormous plain. The sight caused me to despair because I had thought we were getting close, and yet I couldn't see the palace anywhere. The only thing in sight was a small rocky hill. *How many more miles do we have to go*, I wondered. But then we rounded that hill, and there it was: Fell's Palace, glimmering like a ghost in the predawn light.

Somehow we had hiked the 40-mile journey with no casualties.

"Company . . . HALT!" Smythe said. And we all collapsed onto the cold, muddy ground. I fell instantly to sleep and didn't think I would ever be able to stand up again.

At some point, Smythe yelled at us to get up and get changed. We had all packed a fresh uniform in our bags so we could make a good impression for the ceremony. My body fought me as I struggled to stand up. And only when I finally did stand up, did I realize it had stopped raining. It was as cold as a polar bear's poop, but it was turning out to be a beautiful, sunny winter's day.

I gaped at the palace as I got changed. I had never seen it before, and all the while on our hike, I had set myself up to be disappointed, for these things never live up to the hype. But let me tell you: the palace took what little breath I had left away from me.

Fell's Palace was the most famous building in all of Esteria. It was built twenty-five years ago to celebrate our victory in the Really Big War. Fell, the architect the king had hired to design the palace, was just as famous for his brilliant designs as he was for his notoriously eccentric behavior. At this point in his career, he was also an alcoholic, so he was in a drunken stupor during the entire design process. Thankfully his wife Petra had learned a thing or two about architecture, so she was able to interpret his drawings to the builders. (She became so important to the project many people—especially those in the construction trade—refer to it as Petra Palace.) The palace had started out as a pretty-but-rather-dull affair, but Fell kept changing things even after the masons had set the foundation. The first floor of the palace was rectangular, but as the building rose, angles became swooshes and swooshes became curlicues. Engineers feared it would never stand, and they questioned Fell and his wife daily, but the king stood by Fell and demanded the engineers follow his every whim.

Not only did the palace stand, it stood higher than any building in history. It was the grandest, strangest, and most beautiful building human-kind had ever produced. The titanic temples and arenas from the Golden Age, which had inspired poets and artists for millennia, couldn't compare to the magnificence of our palace. People came from all over Esteria to see it. Even the elves and dwarves marveled at the structure, which made our King proud. Finally! A human had created something that caused elves to gawk in wonder!

Fell died the day after his palace opened. The king had been planning on naming it after his son Ethelfred, but the public outcry forced a (much welcome) change of plans. Fell's Palace became an iconic symbol throughout the world of what humanity could achieve.

Last year a small earthquake damaged the building, making it unsafe for occupation. The king closed it down and ordered a complete renovation. Today, on the 25th anniversary of VS Day (Victory over Smoron), the palace was finally set to finally reopen.

After we got dressed and gorged ourselves on breakfast, we lined up with the other schools in Academy Formation—perfectly straight row after perfectly straight row of cadets in gleaming uniforms, all standing at attention. Considering every single cadet had run miles through last night's downpour, this was a rather amazing feat.

We waited, unmoving, for what seemed like hours. Hordes of civilians slowly gathered for the ceremony. By the time the trumpets announced the king's arrival, there were tens of thousands of people in attendance. It was the largest peacetime assembly of humanity in modern history.

The royal family and their attendants slowly advanced up the grand stairs to the main entrance of the palace. The music stopped, and the king turned to face us.

"My dearetht thubjecth," he said. At least, I think that's what he said. It was rather hard to hear him given that he was a couple of hundred yards away, and even though everyone was trying to be quiet to listen to the man's words, the general noise of thousands of people trying to be silent is still pretty deafening. And of course, his lisp didn't help.

Ultimately, it didn't matter that we couldn't hear him, for the king got no further in his speech. Two giant fireballs appeared overhead and, one after the other, smashed into the palace's southern tower.

The first one exploded on the tower's surface, blasting stone and support beams hundreds of feet in all directions, and creating a hole for the second fireball, which set the inside alight.

People screamed and jolted from the shock, but no one fled the scene; mostly because no one was quite sure what was happening. But then there was this sickening moment of silence as we all watched the southern tower slowly lean forward, and then gather momentum and collapse into the northern tower, knocking that one over, setting off a chain reaction that ultimately brought down the entire palace.

Now people scattered, shrieking and yelling, unsure if there was more destruction to come. Within seconds a cloud of smoke and ashes enveloped the crowd, causing more panic.

"Stay in formation!" yelled Smythe. I was too scared to do anything else, other than to duck so as not to be hit by debris, but since I couldn't see, I wasn't about to run anywhere. Lance, who was standing next to me, grabbed my arm to steady me. The cadets in front of us were not so eager to follow Smythe's instruction. They turned to run and smashed into Lance and me, knocking us over.

The smoke cloud finally cleared, allowing us to see the damage. No one could believe it. The pride of humanity was now a pile of smoking rubble.

"This changes everything," said Smythe, more to himself than to anyone else. It was one of the few times I ever saw him be candid.

As it is with these kinds of tragedies, many theories arose to explain what had happened. According to people who were old enough to have ever seen such things, it was dragonfire that had destroyed the palace. Now, no one had seen a dragon in over two decades, so this was a hard statement to confirm, but apparently, dragonfire is very distinct. It is intensely hot, with a deep orange hue. And unlike a regular flame, which has no substance, dragonfire has a forceful impact; it's almost like a physical ball that smashes things to pieces and sets them alight.

That was exactly what we had seen strike the palace.

But there was one problem: no one saw a dragon.

Dragons aren't the kind of creatures you can easily miss. They're rather big, and, from the tales I'd heard, smelly. According to Elbo's book, *Remember That Time When I Saved the World?* dragons positively reek of brimstone, whatever that is. Also, dragons are notoriously obnoxious. They love to brag about how they can fly and breathe fire and you can't. Their favorite expression—and I'm not making this up—is "Nyeah-nyeah-n-nyeah nyeah."

In other words, if a dragon had been present, we would have seen it, smelled it, and been annoyed by it.

Is it possible that a dragon stayed out of sight, shot a couple of fireballs at the palace, and flew away before anyone could see it?

In a word, no.

See, dragonfire can only stay focused for about a hundred yards or so. In order for a dragon to have destroyed the palace, it would've had to have been right in front of it, where everyone would have been able to see it.

Plus, we have Lookout Stations positioned throughout the kingdom, precisely for this kind of thing. Not one of our Lookout Station guards reported seeing a dragon flying over any part of the kingdom that day.

So if a dragon didn't destroy the palace, what did?

One theory was that a powerful wizard had somehow gotten a hold of a magical spell and created those fireballs. But there are several problems with this. First of all, aside from Smoron, there were only four wizards who ever lived: Brondork the Beige, Pépé the Puce, Timbob the Taupe, and Kimrod the Khaki, and they left Esteria with Elbo for the Undying World after the Cufflinks of Doom were destroyed. And speaking of the Cufflinks, as I have already mentioned, when Elbo incinerated them he also killed all of the world's magic, so even if a wizard had stuck around, he wouldn't have been able to do any magic. Lastly, no wizard ever had ever been able to conjure up dragonfire; not even Brondork. (Frankly, aside from creating some nice fireworks displays, no one was really sure what wizards did, besides grow beards and annoy people.)

Another theory—one that seemed to take hold of the public's imagination—was that Lord Smoron himself was back and that he and his gork army were getting ready to destroy humanity once and for all. It didn't matter that Smoron had never gone around smashing things with dragonfire before. People were scared, and Smoron had been such a boogeyman for thousands of years, it made sense to them that he was back and that he had newfound powers.

Our King certainly bought into this idea. The day after the attack he sent a Royal Raven to bring a message to the court of King Skidmark, ruler of the ever-shrinking Gorkish Empire. Skidmark sent a raven back, denying having anything to do with the attack. And soon they began trading insults.

Here is their infamous exchange in its entirety:

Olerood: Destroy my palace, will you? I'll destroy your face!

Skidmark: Say what now?

Olderood: We're declaring war on you.

Skidmark: Oh. OK. Sounds good. What's this about your stupid palace being destroyed?

Olerood: Don't play dumb with me! You and Lord Smoron used a couple of dragonballs to blow up my palace. Don't even try to deny it.

Skidmark: OK . . . You know Smoron's dead, right? I mean, I'm glad your ugly palace is gone, but we didn't do it.

Olerood: Ha!

Skidmark: You are as eloquent as you are stupid. And ugly.

Olerood: You're stupid and ugly!

Skidmark: Good one.

Olerood: Anyway, I just wanted to say that we are officially declaring war.

Skidmark: Bring it on, human scum! We're tired of you gobbling up our lands.

Olerood: Righto. Well, I guess in that case, I'll see you on the battlefield. I'm going to bed now, so don't bother writing back.

Skidmark: Nighty night. Jerk.

Olerood: I can't hear you! I'm asleep! Oh, and your face looks like a butt.

It's because of that last line that the exchange has become known as the "Butt Declaration."

Anyway, we were now officially at war with the gorks. This was a rather terrifying prospect for us cadets, for we had all heard stories about the gorks from veterans of the Really Big War. Gorks were huge, angry beasts who weren't happy unless they were chomping on human flesh. They had the strength of two men and they never got tired—they could march for weeks without stopping. Frankly, if Elbo hadn't destroyed the Cufflinks, it's very likely the gorks would have completely overrun all of humanity.

And now we were at war with them.

Thankfully, Smythe did not force us to run back to the academy. He seemed to be as stunned as we were, trying to figure out what this new reality meant for us.

We marched at a steady pace, all the while, my mind was racing to find a way out of this awful situation. I had already been eager to get out of the Royal Academy, but now that we were at war, I was desperate. I knew that war meant certain death for me.

I needed to escape.

Chapter Seven

AFTER MARCHING FOR what seemed like years, we emerged from the Grand Woods to see the city of Shropsfordshire. It was the first time I had gotten a good look at the city because I'd been asleep when Smythe first brought me here in the cart.

As impressed as I had been with the size of the Royal Academy, Shropsforshire was ten times as big. A thirty-foot wall ran around the entire city, and I could see several heavily armed guards at each gate. Now that we were at war, the guards were thoroughly examining each and every person who tried to enter or leave the city. This complicated my plans, which had been to escape from the school into the city, and then to freedom through one of these gates. But now I could see that even if I did manage to break out of school, one of these guards would arrest me and bring me back to the academy. I didn't know what the penalty was for going AWOL, but I knew it had to be worse than LD.

I briefly considered trying to hide in a cart of some sort, but I saw a guard dig through the contents of a laundry cart, so I gave up on that idea.

So that left me with one option: escaping from the main academy gate.

Not to go too deep into a geography lesson, but the Royal Academy is surrounded by a branch of the Moor River. There are two ways to get into the school, and both require traveling over a drawbridge. One gate goes from the school into the city. The other, which was the one we were marching towards, connected the school to the outside world. Unfortunately, this gate was just as heavily guarded as the city's gates. Frankly, the academy was starting to look more like a high-security prison than an institution of higher learning.

As we marched over the drawbridge and through the barbican, a sense of real panic started to settle in. There was no way for me to escape. I was going to be sent off to war.

But then, as we entered our barracks, I remembered something.

"Comrade Lance," I whispered as I unpacked my things. My clothes were still damp from our first hike, and they smelled moldy. "I've figured out how I'm going to get out of here."

"And how's that?"

"I'm going to get thrown out."

He laughed. "Good luck with that, old sport. We're at war now. They're gonna want every warm body they can squeeze into a uniform—no matter how scrawny."

"Just you wait and see. I'm good at getting thrown out of places. It's my specialty. All I have to do is annoy the poop out of poor Smythe, and he'll have no choice but to throw his hands up in the air and give up."

"I look forward to seeing the master at work," he said with a bow in my direction.

He didn't have to wait long. An hour later, we were assembled out onto the bailey to begin some drills.

We all stood at attention while Smythe walked down the line, inspecting the troops.

"Awright!" he snarled. It was then that I realized he didn't waste much time pronouncing the letter L when it was in the middle or end of a word. I was pondering this and not giving the drill-sergeant my complete attention.

He noticed.

"Oy! You there!" he pointed his sword at me. "What did I just tell you to do?"

"I have no idea, sir. I wasn't listening." I figured the truth was the best course of action.

"You wot?" he said. There was more puzzlement than anger in his response. I wondered if anyone had ever said that to him before. Then I stopped wondering things as that is what had gotten me into trouble in the first place.

My fellow soldiers-to-be started snickering.

"Quiet, you rotters!" Smythe said as he advanced towards me.

"Hallo there, Drill-Sergeant!" I said as he approached, his sword coming ever so close to my Adam's apple. "Lovely, day, what?" (Once again, I thought it was best to keep things light.) I glanced over at Lance. He just shook his head slowly.

"Don't be looking at your girlfriend," Smythe said. He pushed his sword right up to my throat.

"May I just say you have done a rather lovely job of sharpening your sword, sir?"

"You know what it would take for me to run this through your throat?" He paused. Once again, I wasn't sure if I was supposed to answer that question.

Smythe waited some more, so I spoke up. "Was that a rhetorical question, sir?"

"Do I look like someone who knows what the word 'rhetorical' means?"

My eyebrows shot up, which was dashed arrogant of them. Another tough question! This would call for some diplomacy.

"You look like the smartest person I've ever had stick a sword in my throat, sir."

"Are you being funny, Maggot?" He said this as he pushed the tip of his sword just a teensy tiny bit into my throat. I could feel a few drops of blood slowly snake their way down my neck. *This would be the absolute worst time in the world to sneeze*, I thought to myself. I was starting to reconsider my decision to annoy Smythe. I guess I wasn't expecting him to react with violence.

"No one doesn't listen to me, Maggot."

I wanted to correct his use of the double negative, but one dim part of my brain sensed that perhaps this wasn't the best time.

"Are you about to correct my use of the double negative?"

He must have seen the look on my face because he got even angrier, which I didn't think was possible.

"Do you think you are smarter than me, Maggot?"

"No, sir!" That was an easy one.

"Well then," he said, withdrawing the blade. "If you're so smart, let's see how much you know about sword fighting." My mind was racing to grasp all of the things wrong with that sentence, but then I told my brain to shut up because I needed to focus on fighting this maniac.

He grabbed me by the shoulder and pulled me out from the line. We walked a few paces, and he turned me sharply around, so I now faced my colleagues. I gave them a wink and a little wave, which they promptly ignored.

"Here is your sword, Maggot," Smythe said, handing me what looked like a large toothpick.

"I thought you said we were going to use real—"

I never got to finish that sentence. Smythe howled and swung his enormous, two-handed blade from hell. At my head, no less.

I ducked and squealed like a little girl—although, not necessarily in that order. This caused my colleagues to laugh.

"Nice moves, Prindella!" sneered one of the cadets.

I know he meant it as an insult, but I knew a Prindella back in Bletchleysbum. She was so agile I once saw her catch a blistergoose in mid-flight. The bird was so stunned it didn't even squawk. It simply turned its head and gaped at her, almost as if to say, "brava!" She would have made quick work of Drill-Sergeant Smythe.

Speaking of Smythe, he came charging at me again, swinging his sword so close to me, I could feel my hair move from the swiftness of his attack.

"Blimey!" I said. "Are you trying to kill me?"

"Of course I am," said Smythe. "The enemy will be trying to kill you, too. So you'd better be ready for it."

"Ah," I said, dodging a thrust.

"Fight back, damn you! I didn't give you that sword for nothing."

"This is a sword?"

Smythe slammed his weapon down as if to slice me in two. I jumped out of the way.

"Fight back, or you'll be digging ditches for the next three days."

He sliced through the air at my midsection, and I only just managed to step back to safety. He had swung so hard, he was a little off balance, so I surged forward and poked him in the belly.

"Ow!" he said.

That only made him madder. He was so mad, in fact, that he kicked me. Hard. In the stomach. The force of it knocked me down, and I banged my head on the ground.

Smythe rushed up to me and brought his sword up high.

I couldn't breathe; he had knocked the wind out of me.

I could tell by the look in his eye that he was going to kill me.

"Sergeant Smythe!" came a voice from behind him.

Smythe lowered his sword and turned to face his inquisitor.

"Captain Phoughton, sir." Smythe snapped to attention. (The name Phoughton, true to the ridiculous nature of the Amerigornish language, was pronounced "Fuffton.")

"Did you just kick this poor cadet, Sergeant?" Captain Phoughton reached down to me and hoisted me up.

"Easy, son," he said. "Take a second to catch your breath."

He was a nice-looking, middle-aged man. Had a scar down the right side of his face, but a kindness in his eye. That surprised me, as I didn't expect there to be any kind people in the army; only screamers like Smythe.

"I did kick him, sir. Have to train these mag—I mean, cadets properly. After all, the gorks aren't going to play nice with them."

I was impressed at how subservient Smythe was to this distinguished gentleman. Captain Phoughton instantly became my hero.

"Be that as it may, Sergeant, this is still a school. And you are not to harm the cadets in any fashion."

"Sir, yes, sir."

"Are you all right, cadet?" Phoughton asked me.

I finally caught my breath. "I am, sir."

"Good. You may get back in line." He turned to Smythe. "I have my eye on you, Sergeant. As you were." Captain Phoughton marched away.

Smythe saluted the Captain and then turned his angry eyes on me.

"Just because I can't hurt you doesn't mean I can't send you to LD for being a smart-aleck, back-talking, lowlife scum. Get out of my sight, you little cussing cuss."

"So, comrade, how would you assess your progress so far?" Lance asked me when I got back from LD that evening, four hours later.

I collapsed on my bunk.

"Give me time," I said.

"I think you may want to reconsider this insane tactic of yours. Smythe is liable to kill you."

"Ha," I said. "I've already won."

And I promptly fell asleep.

Chapter Eight

OVER THE NEXT few days, I set about trying to annoy Smythe every chance I had. Needless to say, I dug a lot of latrines. I think I have glossed over what backbreaking work latrine duty is. It isn't just digging a hole in the ground. A proper military latrine for the Royal Academy has to be at least two feet deep. And, during peacetime, we had over 500 people in the castle, which meant that we needed enough space for 500 people to go potty. So, there wasn't just one two-foot-deep hole. I had to dig a trench, two feet deep and forty feet long. And when that trench got filled halfway up with poop and urine, whoever was digging the next latrine (me) had to fill in the old latrine first.

With the kingdom gearing up for war, the army needed to train more and more soldiers. So all the military academies were adding soldiers faster than they could train them, which meant each school was filled way past capacity. I heard our school at one point housed over 800 people, so soon my latrines needed to be fifty feet, and before long, seventy feet in length. And of course it was still winter, so the ground was frozen, which made the detail even more challenging.

In other words, this was grueling, back-slaying work that gave my hands blisters and made my muscles ache. And my awful, military-issue boots were utterly useless, providing me no support or comfort. So I got blisters on my feet, too.

Usually, I dug latrines by myself, but sometimes Lance got roped into it, too, like if he got caught laughing at my comments. So, I soon found myself trying to make Lance laugh in my attempts to annoy Smythe, not just because I preferred having his company, but also because he was a tough chap to make laugh. So if I said something funny enough to make him giggle, I counted that as a minor victory.

On the second day of my attempt to get kicked out, we were all lined up for battle practice, and Smythe whipped out that giant, two-handed sword he had used to nearly kill me the day before.

"Listen up, girls. Does anyone know what we call this?"

I stepped forward. "Compensating, sir!"

Lance burst into laughter, which is what I think made Smythe understand that I was having a go at him. The other cadets started to snigger, too, but they stopped when Smythe screamed a half-dozen obscenities at them. He stormed up to my face. I thought for a second that he was going to punch me, but he managed to reign in his anger, and he sent Lance and me off to LD.

"I thought you were going to get kicked out right then and there," said Lance.

"I'll get him next time."

But it soon became apparent that I had underestimated Drill-Sergeant Smythe. I tried to back-talk him every chance I could, and he would send me off to LD, but he didn't get nearly as angry as I wanted him to. I needed him flustered, but I wasn't getting that.

For instance, that very afternoon he told us to line up in marching formation, and he stood at the front of the line and shouted, "Do you know what we're going to do today, ladies?"

"Give peace a chance?" I offered.

"LD, Maggot!"

"Sir, yes, sir!"

The next day, at a sword-fighting drill, Smythe asked, "Who can tell me the best way to slice through a rampaging gork?"

I raised my hand, "With a song in your heart and a skip in your step, sir?"

That was, apparently, not correct.

"Out!" Smythe said.

Later, Smythe drilled us on how to effectively use a pike, which is a long spear you use to thrust into your enemy. He asked if there were any questions. I raised my hand, "Have you ever considered trying to find less violent ways to solve your differences, sir?"

He simply snapped his fingers and pointed towards the LD field.

Other comments that landed me in LD:

"Did you do something different with your hair, sir?"

"Those medals are very slimming, sir."

"That's a very manly pose you're striking, sir."

"I love the way you swish your sword, sir."

That last one got a laugh out of Lance, so we were both sent off to LD together. At this point, however, I was really starting to have second thoughts about this stupid plan of mine. Not only didn't Smythe seem to be any closer to snapping, but I was also feeling bad for Lance.

"I'm sorry I got you into trouble. Again," I said.

"No you're not," he said with a wink.

"You're right. You see right through me, Comrade Lance."

We waved to Staff Sergeant Pip and grabbed our shovels and started digging.

"You know, Nibel," said Lance. (He had taken to calling me that.) "I have to confess; back home, I didn't think you liked me."

"I didn't."

"Why?"

"I guess I was just jealous."

"Jealous?"

"Yeah, jealous! You had everything! Respect! Girls! Good looks! Girls! And more girls!"

We dug for a few moments in silence. Then Lance sniffed. Then he sniffed some more as though he was trying to hold back laughter.

"What's so funny?"

He stopped digging.

"I have another confession to make. I've never told anyone this, but I trust you. And it's weird to trust you because before we came here, you were the last person I felt like I could trust."

"OK, weirdo," I said. "What is it, already?"

"I don't even like girls."

"Ah, right," I said, immediately grasping his point. "You like women." I think I even winked at him.

He looked at me like I had seven and a half heads.

"No," he said slowly. "I like boys."

I sat there, trying to understand where he was going with this. "Is that some sort of slang expression for a gorgeous woman? Because if it is, it's a rather confusing one."

"No. I'm gay. I have romantic feelings for males and not females."

I stared at him. Anger slowly rose up inside of me until I couldn't contain it.

"Are you serious!" I slammed my shovel on to the ground and started flapping my arms up and down as I spoke. "You could have any girl in the kingdom! And you don't even like girls?"

"Calm down, old sport."

"Calm down? This is an outrage! I love girls, and not a single girl wants anything to do with me."

"Well, you are kind of a mess."

I sat down and tried to slow my breathing. Staff Sergeant Pip started to wander over to make sure everything was all right. I waved him off, and we started digging again.

"So," Lance said cautiously, "you're not mad that I like boys, you're just mad that I don't like girls?"

"Like all the boys you like," I said. "I'm just mad at the injustice of it all. Seems like a waste."

"Well, that leaves more girls for you," he said with a charming wink.

"That's right! You don't like girls!"

"Didn't we just go over that?" he said.

"Ah, who am I kidding? Girls won't even give me a second look as long as you're around. You and all your 'I believe snow is cold,' nonsense."

"Ha. People love that stuff! You've just gotta sell it." He stood close to me, "I believe one needs water to quench one's thirst."

"Wow. You're good."

"You try it. Say it as though it's the most profound thought in the world. Then, no matter how stupid it is, people will think there's a deeper meaning, and they'll pretend to get it, so they don't look dumb."

I grabbed him by his vest and pulled him close, which surprised him. "I believe latrine duty stinks."

He laughed and pushed me away. "We'll work on it, mate. And your breath."

"Maybe you could wear a sign or something? Just, you know, to make it clear to all the women out there?"

He smiled a sad smile. "Others aren't quite as enlightened as you."

"Oh. Right." It was true: guys like him were not exactly welcome in our kingdom—and certainly not in our military. I won't say exactly what they do to people like Lance, but it's not pretty. I cringed at the thought, and once again felt that need to protect him.

"So this whole time I've known you, you've been pretending to be a ladies' man?"

"Best way to throw people off the scent."

"Then why are you so keen on staying in the military?" I asked him. "You know what they'll do to you if you're found out."

"Right now, it's the safest place for me. I left my home because people found out I was gay, and the situation was threatening to turn ugly. So I ran away to Ansley." He was referring to a town near our southern border. "But a bounty hunter found me."

"What?" I said incredulously. "Who sent a bounty hunter?"

"My parents."

My face fell. I had a whole bunch of questions, but Lance went back to digging, and I took that to mean he didn't want to talk about it. I joined him after a few seconds, but I felt like I needed to say something because the silence was too heavy.

"Is that when you came to Bletchleysbum?"

"Yeah. I was hoping that by going that far away, I'd be able to start a new life." He stopped digging and wiped his nose on his sleeve. "But on my way home after the snowball incident, I saw that same bounty hunter talking to old man Hibbert, showing him a drawing. I knew my time in Bletchleysbum was up. So that's why I turned myself in to Smythe. Now here I am, hoping to start over again."

"Is Lance Hightower even your name?" I asked. I thought back to how much I hated his name. It was just too perfect.

"Nah, I just wanted something manly. But I've grown to like it, so let's just keep that pretense going, shall we?"

I looked at him in amazement. I had hated this poor sod, not just because I was jealous, but also because he had seemed so phony. And now that I knew that he really was a phony—and why—I couldn't help but have a whole new level of respect for him.

But there still seemed to be so much about him that I didn't know.

"So, we're still friends?" he asked before I could get in any more questions.

"Of course we are," I said. And I smiled for the first time since I'd been dragged to this school. "In fact, Gay Lance, I'd like to think we're best friends."

We shook hands.

"Please don't call me that."

"OK, Glance."

"I've made a huge mistake," he said, smiling.

We kept digging until Staff Sergeant Pip told us to stop.

"All right, ladies," Smythe said to our group the next day, "listen up."

"Do you have a problem with women, sir?" I said.

Smythe glared at me. I took that as a sign that maybe I'd hit a nerve. *Here's my chance to really infuriate him*, I thought. He strolled over to me. I was looking forward to engaging him in a philosophical discussion about gender identity.

"What's that, Maggot?" he asked.

"It's just that you often insult us by using various terms for women, including 'ladies,' 'girls,' and 'girlfriends,' and I wonder if it's because you don't have a healthy relationship with, or respect for, women. After all, some of the strongest people I've ever known are women, including my dear old mom, who—"

"You don't ever want to stop digging latrines, do you, Maggot?"

"Ah! Another one of your fine rhetorical questions, sir!"

"I love sending you to LD, Maggot. You know why?"

"I'm sure you will tell me, sir!"

"Because the more latrines you dig, the less you know about actual warfare. And you know why that makes me happy?"

"Because you have a cheery disposition, sir?"

"Because," he said, and he got right up to my face as he said this, "I'm going to insist that you are first in line for battle, and I shall weep nary a tear when you are cut down in the first five seconds of the war."

He could tell by the look on my face that he had gotten through to me.

"You think I don't know what you're doing, Maggot?"

He paused, waiting for me to make a snide remark, but I just gulped and stared at him.

"You're not the first coward who has tried to get thrown out of military school. It won't work. We don't throw cowards out of military school. We make their lives miserable. And if you think LD is as miserable as I can make your life, you're gravely mistaken. Cadet Blythering!" he said, suddenly turning to the chap standing next to me, "You're in charge until I get back." It figures Smythe would put Blythering in charge. Blythering had what I liked to call "Resting Sneer Face."

Smythe turned to me again. "Why don't you and your *boyfriend* accompany me for a little stroll." He turned and marched us towards a small stone building at the far northern end of the bailey.

"Unfortunately for you, Maggot," said Smythe without looking at me, "you've dug so many latrines we don't have room for more. So you're officially off latrine duty. For now. That leaves me with only one other option. And it's a doozy."

I glanced at Lance, but he didn't acknowledge me.

We arrived at the building, which was guarded by a sentry. The man came to attention when Smythe approached him. "At ease, son. I just want to show my friends here our accommodations."

The guard nodded and fished out a key, which he used to unlock the heavy wooden door.

"Follow me," said Smythe. Once inside the building, Smythe grabbed a torch and lit it. He led us down a flight of stairs. Then another. And another. We kept descending into the damp, moldy, darkness for several minutes. We arrived at the bottom, and Smythe led us down a tight passageway. At the end of the corridor were four doors with heavy locks on them. Smythe unlocked one door and opened it.

"After you," he said, gesturing for us to go inside.

Lance and I shot each other nervous glances. I peeked into the room but couldn't see anything.

"Now!" said Smythe loudly enough to startle us. I followed Lance into the room, and Smythe joined us.

It was a jail cell, five feet square. The walls and floor were made of clay. On one wall, I could see that someone had attempted to claw their way out to freedom. Intellectually I understood that to be a fool's errand, for we were at least fifty feet underground, but emotionally I agreed with the impulse.

"This room has been reserved for you, Maggot," Smythe said, his face all orange and red from the torchlight. "And the one next door is for your girl—I mean, boyfriend. After all, I wouldn't want to disparage women, now would I?"

He walked around the room, running his hands along the walls until he got to the claw marks. "You see these marks? A cadet who, much like yourself, tried to get thrown out of the military made these marks last year. You know how long he was left alone in this room before he started screaming and tried to claw his way out?" Smythe looked at us to give us time to ponder the question. "Six hours. Six hours in the blackest darkness you have ever experienced. That's all it took before he lost his mind."

And with that, Smythe took one hand and closed it over the torch, putting out the flame.

Chapter Nine

I DON'T KNOW IF I can adequately explain to you how terrifying it is to be engulfed in total darkness. Maybe you think you could handle it. I certainly would have thought the same thing. But until Smythe put out that torch, it occurred to me that I'd never experienced total darkness before. And, unless you've been trapped in a cave, you haven't either.

Think about nighttime. You're in bed. Your mom tucks you in, blows out the candle, and says good night. Your room is dark. And maybe you find that a bit scary. But it's not completely dark, for the moon and the stars give you some light. It takes your eyes a minute to adjust, but eventually, you can see. Once, when I was little, I got locked in a closet by my mean cousin Ronald. I thought that was dark, but even in there, light managed to seep in through the cracks in the doorframe, and after a while, I was able to see a little.

But in that underground jail cell, there was the complete absence of light. It took a few seconds for that to sink in, for my eyes still held the afterimage of the torch flame. But then total darkness set in. In fact, though I may be remembering this incorrectly, I think it was lighter when I closed my eyes than when they were open.

Panic set in almost immediately, though I tried to control myself.

"Drill-Sergeant?" I said after a few seconds.

He didn't respond, but I heard him leave. I tried to run to the door before he could shut it and lock us in, but I merely ran into Lance.

"It's OK," he said. His voice sounded huge. "He didn't lock us in. Hold on to me, and we'll feel our way out of here."

Now as far as mazes go, this was about as easy as it could be. After all, on our journey down here, we had merely descended a few flights of stairs, traveled through a straight hallway, and made a right at the first room. So, finding our way back shouldn't have been that hard. But it's amazing how not being able to see can throw a sword in the works. Even just leaving the cell proved to be harder than one would have thought. But with some teamwork and patience, we managed our way out of the room, down the hall, and back to the stairs. Walking up the stairs proved challenging because they were uneven, which I hadn't noticed during our lighted descent. But again, with patience, we were able to climb up without injury. About three flights up, we could start to see some light, which made our ascent even faster.

We arrived at the top of the stairs. Smythe had left the door to the building open. Even though our eyes had slowly been adjusting to the presence of more light during our ascent, once outside, we were blinded by the sunlight.

When our eyes finally adjusted and we could see without too much trouble, there was Smythe, standing at-ease, rocking back and forth on his feet.

"You cowards took your sweet time getting up here."

"Sir, sorry, sir," said Lance. He snapped to attention. I followed, though I was still a bit traumatized from the ordeal, so my form may not have been exactly by the book. Luckily, Smythe didn't seem to care.

"Let this be a warning to you both. Next time you screw up or talk back or even so much as blink in a way I don't like, there won't be any more latrine digging. I will simply lock you up in one of those cells. Do I make myself clear?"

"Sir, yes, sir!" said Lance.

"And how about you, Maggot? Do I make myself clear?"

"Crystal, sir."

He stared me down for a second. I guess he was hoping I'd do something he didn't like, but I remained at attention.

"Dismissed," he said finally.

"So much for your plan, eh, comrade?" said Lance as we entered our barracks.

I didn't respond.

I was unnerved. Smythe had merely left me in the dark for a few minutes, and that had been enough to force me to surrender. What kind of a man was I?

"You girls enjoy your make-out session in the dark?" said Cadet Blythering. A few of the other cadets sniggered.

"Shut your bleeding trap, you cussing cusswad," I said. I launched myself at Blythering and would have punched him in the face if Lance hadn't held me back.

"Easy, Nibes!" he said. "Don't give Smythe a reason to lock you up."

I couldn't believe myself. I had never been enraged like that before. Angry, yes. But enraged? I knew I wasn't mad at that idiot Blythering. I didn't care if he insulted me. I was just angry because Smythe had won and I was taking it out on anyone I could.

"Aw, isn't that sweet," said another cadet, whose name was Pierbright. "He's protecting his girlfriend."

I relaxed a bit, and Lance let me go. I shrugged my shoulders and cracked my knuckles and forced myself to smile. I wanted to say something snappy, but nothing was forthcoming, so I turned around and climbed onto my bunk and lay down. I stared up at the ceiling, plotting my next move, but after a few minutes, I realized I had no move.

I was stuck here for the rest of my short life.

The next few days were horrible. I did my best to follow Smythe's every order, even when he specifically tried to mess me up. One morning, he told us to do a hundred pushups. We dropped and started doing them. Two weeks ago, I wouldn't have able to do even twenty pushups, let alone a hundred. But thanks to all the exercise I had gotten digging all those latrines, I was in the best physical shape of my life. I knew none of the other cadets could make it to a hundred, but I also knew that Smythe didn't care about them. He walked over and stood right in front of me, watching me as I struggled.

"Eighty-eight, eighty-nine," he counted.

I was slowing down.

"Ninety," he said. "Come on, Maggot. Give me a reason to lock you up. Ninety-one. Ninety-two."

My arms were giving out on me, but I willed myself to keep going.

Just one more, I thought.

"Come on, comrade!" said Lance.

"You're pathetic," said Blythering.

"Give up, Sally," said Pierbright.

"Ninety-eight," said Smythe, leaning in low.

My arms were shaking. I stopped at the top.

"Keep going!" shouted Smythe.

I lowered myself down and pushed with all my might and somehow got to the top.

"One more, Maggot."

I dropped to the ground and took two deep breaths. And I pushed.

"You can do it, Nibes!"

"Loser!" said someone else.

My arms were screaming at me.

Come on! I thought. *Do it!*

"Ahhhhhhhh!" I shouted, hoping my voice would propel me up.

I summed every last bit of strength I had. It was just enough. I reached the top of my hundredth pushup, still screaming.

"You did it!" said Lance.

I collapsed on the ground and didn't move for several minutes.

Smythe walked away, shouting for us to get cleaned up for dinner.

Lance gave me a hand up and draped my arm around him. "Come on, mate." He walked me back to our barracks.

"Aw, look!" said Pierbright as we entered the room. "How romantical!"

We ignored him, and Lance let me sit on his bed, which was the lower bunk.

Blythering kneeled next to me. "Do you two want to be alone so you can make out in peace?"

"That sounds lovely," I said, "but I've already got plans with your mother."

His face clouded over.

Frankly, I never understood why mother jokes tended to drive people crazy. Had some idiot made a similar comment about my mother I would have shrugged it off. But I knew Blythering was one of those fools who couldn't bear to hear another bloke even say the word "mother" without him totally losing his mind.

"You take that back!" he said, grabbing me by my leather vest.

"Gentlemen!" said Lance, hopping down from my bunk. "Let's all just relax, shall we?"

Blythering let go of me and stood up. Pierbright joined him.

"Standing up for your girlfriend, eh?" said Blythering.

"I just don't want anyone to get into trouble."

"You think we don't know about you?" said Pierbright, poking Lance in the chest.

"Know what, old chap?" said Lance.

"We know all about you, fairy boy."

"Funny, your mother—" began Lance. But he didn't get to finish that sentence.

In hindsight, I know that Blythering and Pierbright were just trying to insult Lance the only way they knew how. At an all-male institution such as this military school, where being gay was strictly forbidden, the first insult most boys tended to hurl was an accusation of being gay. It was a stupid and mindless insult. I knew this. But ever since Lance had confessed to me that he actually was gay, I was very sensitive to anyone accusing him of that, for I knew if he were found out, the administration would do far worse things to him than to lock him up in that dungeon.

But I wasn't thinking. I simply heard what those idiots were saying and I lost my mind.

I leapt off the bunk and punched Blythering in his stupid face. Then I launched an elbow at Pierbright and caught him off-guard. Unfortunately for me, that was the end of my attack, for both cadets were bigger and stronger than me, and they soon began pummeling me into submission. Lance did his best to fend them off, but it was no use.

I guess another cadet had run to get help, for only a few minutes into our fight, Smythe burst into the room and yelled, "Enough!"

After Smythe had settled us down, I confessed to being the instigator, saying that I was tired and that I had let my temper get the best of me. Smythe's right eyebrow shot up. I think he was surprised that I would admit to doing anything, but at the same time, I could tell he was delighted to be able to deliver me to that dungeon. Lance tried to claim guilt as well, but the other cadets in the room said that it was me who had started the fight.

Smythe marched me across the field. "I have been looking forward to this moment, Maggot," he said. "I can't wait to see what this does to your spirit."

Minutes later, Smythe shoved me into the cell and slammed the door shut. I found a corner and sat down while he locked the door. I sat in that damp, oppressive blackness for hours.

Had I only been worried about myself, I think it would have been more of an ordeal. But I was worried that my idiotic attack had perhaps given away Lance's secret, and I didn't want to be responsible for anything that might happen to him.

So focused was I on trying to improve my attitude and vowing to protect Lance that it seemed like only a few minutes had passed when Smythe came back down to release me.

"Well," he said, seeing me stand up and brush myself off, "You're not a screaming madman."

"No, sir," I said.

"Next time I'm going to leave you in there for a few more hours, do you understand?"

Over the next two weeks, I tried to follow every rule and ignore every insult hurled at either Lance or myself, but I still wound up getting into trouble. Smythe had what a crossbowman would call an itchy trigger finger. If I so much as turned left when he said to turn right, he would lock me up. And each visit to the dungeon was longer than the previous one. My last visit I was locked up for ten hours. And I'll tell you, that room does things to you.

It's not just the dark that gets you; it's the total lack of sound. It's so quiet you can hear your blood pumping through the blood vessels in your ears.

During my last stay, I fell asleep, and when I awoke, I didn't know where I was for a few minutes.

That was terrifying.

But I refused to give in to madness the way that other cadet had. I wasn't going to give Smythe the pleasure.

At the same time, after that last visit, I vowed that I wouldn't let myself get locked up again.

I didn't think I could take it.

Chapter Ten

I SPENT THE NEXT week being the perfect soldier. I followed Smythe's every command and managed to turn the proverbial cheek whenever an insult was directed at Lance or me. I did more pushups than anyone else. I marched longer, faster, and with more precision than my fellow cadets. I even managed to learn how to properly defend myself with my sword. In fact, I got so good, Smythe seemed to forget that I was there, which was perfect. He started yelling at other cadets, including Blythering and Pierbright.

I started to feel like myself again. I even managed to crack a few jokes—in private, of course. I was almost beginning to enjoy military life.

Almost.

One morning Smythe marched into our barracks. We jumped to attention.

"Guess what, maggots?" said Smythe, smiling. Whenever Smythe smiled, it meant pain and torture for us, so I was a bit concerned about where this conversation was headed. "I've got a project for some of you."

Smythe picked up a huge bag and told Lance, Blythering, Pierbright, and me to grab our backpacks and some flasks of water. We jumped to. "Follow me," he said when we were ready.

He led us out of our barracks, across the bailey, and through the barbican. As we were crossing the bridge over the moat, Lance leaned towards me.

"Listen, comrade. I never properly thanked you for sticking up for me."

"Think nothing of it, mate!"

"No one's ever stuck up for me before." He paused to make sure I was looking at him. "Ever." The way he said it stung. I could only imagine the kinds of things people had said and done to him over the years.

"You can count on me, comrade."

We marched past the field where I had dug so many latrines and stopped in front of a copse. "See that?" Smythe asked.

He pointed through the trees to a picturesque clearing, the kind for which northern Amerigorn was famous. It had all the tropes art students feel compelled to paint in their impressionistic landscapes: a babbling brook, moss-covered trees, a horse-filled stable, and even a half-built barn. The only detail that seemed out of place was an old shack that looked like it had seen better days, but aside from that, it was the kind of place you'd take a girl for a romantic picnic. I briefly pictured Melissa and me, stretched out and lazy after having eaten our fill.

"That's where you're going to be digging our new latrines."

Well, so much for the picnic.

Pierbright and Blythering sighed. I don't know what they were sighing for; they'd never had to do any LD. Lance and I had dug every single latrine for the school. And from the look of the tools Smythe had supplied us with—he'd brought gloves, brand-new shovels, and even two axes to help cut through any stubborn roots—this was going to be a piece of pie.

"New latrines, sir?" Lance asked.

"You know that stomach bug that's been tearing through the school?"

We did. It was a nasty one, too. Gave you diarrhea and nausea something fierce. Thankfully, no one in our squad had gotten sick yet.

"Thanks to that, we've run out of latrine space," Smythe continued. "And it's an emergency. I've seen whole regiments decimated by illnesses like this. And since we're set to deploy for the front in a couple of days, we can't afford to have any more soldiers or cadets fall ill. So, we need two hundred feet of latrine, and I expect you to finish it by noon."

He walked up to me and stood uncomfortably close. "If you fail this mission, Maggot, you'll be looking to set a new record for time spent in that cell of yours. Do I make myself clear?"

Crystal.

We grabbed our shovels and began digging. Smythe started walking away, "Oh, I almost forgot," he said. "This land belongs to Old Mrs. Halloway. She lives in that farmhouse over there. She has generously donated this bit of land to us to do her part for the war effort. But given that's she's an elderly lady, I don't want her startled by the sight of you maggots mucking about on her land. So, one of you needs to go tell her what you're doing."

"Old Mrs. Halloway!" I said when Smythe was out of sight.

"You know her?" asked Lance.

"She's an old family friend. I've known her since I was a toddler. She moved away from Bletchleysbum years ago. I didn't know she moved here."

"How do you know it's her?" asked Pierbright. "There's got to be tons of Mrs. Halloways around here."

"Yes, but there is only one Old Mrs. Halloway," I said.

"Well, why don't you go tell her what we're up to?" said Lance.

"I will!" I said, happy to get a late start on the latrine digging.

I walked several hundred yards up to her front door and knocked. I could hear a faint "Coming!" and, after a few moments, she opened the door. She looked the same as I remembered her, though her hair was a touch grayer, and she had a few more wrinkles.

"Hallo, Mrs. Halloway!" I said—one did not call her Old Mrs. Halloway to her face. "It's me, Nigel!"

"My word! So it is!" her face lit up. What a pleasant sight that was. I can't remember the last time someone had been excited to see me. "Nigel! Won't you come in for some tea? I'd love some company."

"Would love to, Mrs. H, but I'm with the military school and I'm supposed to be digging some latrines on your property today."

"Military school?" She tutted. "Oh, you must've gone and done something dreadful to deserve that."

"It's a long story," I said, not wanting to ruin the moment.

"How's your mother?"

"Same," I said.

"Poor thing," she said. "Your father was such a lovely man."

I smiled. What I wouldn't have given to be able to sit and hear stories of the good old days.

"Well, I won't keep you," she said. "But please do come back when you have time. And thank you for stopping by, Nigel."

"I will, thanks. Great to see you!" I waved and turned to go.

"Oh, Nigel!" She said. "I just remembered. Are you boys digging over in the woods by the brook? Well, would you do me a small favor? I hate to ask, but my builders have abandoned me to go help with the war."

"Sure thing, Mrs. H. Anything for you."

"Well, there's an old shack next to where they are building my barn. It's rotted out, and I'm afraid it's going to attract carpenter worms. And, well, with my new barn going in, I don't want a colony of those creatures taking a hold on my land. I've spent way too much money on that barn as it is. I'd hate for them to destroy it before it got built. Would you mind tearing that shack down for me? I'd be ever so grateful."

"Uh, well, sure."

"You don't mind? It won't take you but a moment. It's so old. But it would save me a lot of worry."

"Like I said, anything for you."

"Here! Please take some cookie cakes for your trouble."

I tried to refuse, mostly because that's the sort of thing you're supposed to do in that kind of situation, but she would have none of it. So, I trudged on back to the boys with a handful of warm, delicious cookie cakes in my backpack.

I reached the top of one hill and saw the shack in question. She was right. At first glance, you might not know it was in trouble, but as I approached, I could see the telltale signs of rotting wood. I was surprised carpenter worms hadn't taken up residence already. Once those worms get on your property, you might as well move away, for they are impossible to eliminate. They eat anything and everything made of wood, whether it's in bad shape or not, but rotting wood attracts them in droves.

As I got closer to the boys . . . well, I don't know where my dumb ideas come from, but one such idea grabbed hold of me and refused to let go. And I laughed. And whenever I laugh at my one of these ideas, I know it's something I'm going to do.

A week earlier, I wouldn't have dreamed of doing what I was about to do, but I was feeling cocky. And, well, I couldn't help myself.

I did my best to look angry, and I stormed down the hill towards the boys, muttering a few curse words as I went.

They stopped digging.

"Took you long enough!" said Pierbright.

"Son of a dungbeast!" I said, throwing my backpack in anger, hoping I didn't smash the cookie cakes.

"What's up, comrade?" asked Lance.

"Gimme that axe!" I shouted at Blythering. I grabbed it from him and stormed up the hill towards the shack.

The boys looked nervously at each other.

"What's wrong?"

"What's wrong?" I said. "That old bat said we couldn't dig our latrines, that's what's wrong!"

"She what?" said Pierbright.

"She said to hell with our war effort and to hell with our school and to hell with us!" I stopped and turned around to face the boys. "She even said she didn't care if Smythe kept me locked up in that cave for a whole week; she wasn't letting anyone touch one grain of dirt on her precious property."

I turned and stormed back to the shed.

"What are you gonna do?" asked Lance. The three of them were racing to catch up with me.

"I'm gonna tear down her shack, that's what I'm gonna do."

"What?!?" said Pierbright. "You can't do that! We'll get in trouble!"

"I don't care!" I said. "I've known that woman for years. I've done all sorts of favors for her, and this is how she repays me?!?"

I swung the axe.

"You're a lunatic!" said Blythering.

"Stop!" said Pierbright!

"Never!" I screamed, slamming the axe, easily splintering the rotting wood.

"I'm not staying for this," said Pierbright.

"Me either!" said Blythering. And the two of them ran off.

SMASH! I swung the axe once more, and the whole shack came tumbling down.

Just then I heard the sickening sound of another axe smashing into wood. I turned and saw Lance delivering a crushing blow to the main support beam of the barn—the new barn that Mrs. Halloway was still building and that had cost her so much money.

"Wait! No!" I said, but it was too late.

I stared in horror as the entire barn came crashing down.

"Let's do her stable, comrade!" Lance said with a beautifully evil smile on his face. "That'll teach her to mess with us!"

Chapter Eleven

"I AM SO SORRY," I said to Lance. We were in adjoining cells our that damp, dark dungeon. "I am so, so, so sorry."

"I know, mate," he said. I could barely hear him through the thick walls. "It's all good."

"It's not all good. I've royally screwed up this time."

Boy had I. Not only had we destroyed that barn—the cost of which to repair was more money than either Lance or I had ever even conceived of—but we had also lost the school's ability to dig latrines on Mrs. Halloway's property. And during this time of crisis, that was no small matter.

Smythe had already screamed at us. He had been so mad there was more spit flying out of his mouth than words. I tried to shield my eyes, but that just made him madder. All I could do was stare at the bulging veins on his neck and hope he didn't die of a stroke or heart attack, because that would be my fault as well. Finally, he finished his wrathful, spit-filled message and had us locked up in these cells.

"How long do you think we'll be down here?"

Before Lance could respond, I heard someone unlocking my cell. Torchlight momentarily blinded me, but once my eyes adjusted, I could see Staff Sergeant Pip holding open my cell door.

"Well, lad," he said gravely, "you've gone and done it this time."

Pip led us outside and across the bailey to the Great Hall. I gazed up at the enormous building. Even though I was profoundly terrified about what was going to happen to us, I couldn't help but be a little curious as to what the interior looked like.

A guard saluted Pip and opened one of the two giant wooden doors. We followed Staff Sergeant Pip inside.

We walked down a long hallway and came to a bench, parked next to another set of enormous doors. Pip instructed us to sit. He took a deep breath and walked over to the heavy wooden doors. He raised his hand to knock but paused.

"I know you've caused lots of trouble, lads," he murmured, "and I'm sorry for what they may do to you, but I think you're both good souls, and I wish you the best." He saluted us and knocked. A voice told him to enter. He did so, closing the doors behind him.

Smythe was yelling. He sounded far away, but I could hear echoes of his angry voice reverberating through the doors. Neither of us had the slightest idea what kind of punishment was awaiting us, but judging from Smythe's unbridled anger and the sympathetic looks we were getting from passersby, I gleaned that whatever it was, it was going to be even worse than the dungeon.

I gulped.

I gulped and once again apologized to Lance.

"I'm not gonna lie," he said. "Screwing up seems to be the one thing you are startlingly efficient at. But, you didn't ask me to destroy that barn."

"That was brilliant. I mean, totally misguided, but I'm glad you've got my back."

"Always," he said. And we shook on it.

"I hope you two will be inviting me to your wedding," said Smythe, who had appeared out of nowhere. "Get inside!" he said.

We got.

We followed him into the actual hall part of the Great Hall. True to its name, the room was vast. And the sound. The room amplified and multiplied our footsteps, so we sounded like a herd of noceros. I'd never heard anything like it. Sunlight streamed in through large windows near the ceiling, so I had to squint as we marched. Usually, the hall was reserved for official ceremonies in which up to a thousand people would sit on long benches, but that was not on the agenda for today. Instead, someone had shoved all those benches up against the walls and placed a single table in the middle of the enormous room. Behind that table sat three men—captains from the look of the gold badges pinned to their chests. I'd never seen two of the captains before, and I was glad for that, for they looked like the kind of chaps who, decades ago, had decided that smiling was overrated. The third man was Captain Phoughton, who did smile as we came into the hall.

"Ah. There we are. Have a seat, boys," he said.

We sat down on the only two seats available to use, across the table from the captains. Smythe walked around to the other side and stood next to the other officers.

"Well!" said Captain Phoughton, drumming his fingers on the table, "You two have caused an awful amount of commotion and damage, haven't you?"

"We're awfully sorry—"

"Silence!" Smythe cut me off.

"Ah," said Captain Phoughton. "There's no need for shouting Smythe. I can see how sorry the boys are. Let's move on to the reason we are here, shall we?"

Smythe, who didn't look very happy at being muzzled, stepped back and sulked.

"Right," continued the captain. "There has been quite a lot of discussion as to what to do with you boys. We certainly can't keep you here as there seems to be no end to your creative and destructive talents. And we can't very well send you back home because that would send the wrong message. After all, you were both sent here as a punishment for your previous misdemeanors. And if every boy knew he could simply misbehave and be sent home, well, where would we be?

"But," he continued—and I have to say, I noticed that when the captain asked a rhetorical question, it was immediately apparent he was doing so; he didn't prolong his pause the way Smythe did— "my colleagues and I have reached a verdict."

He stood up. The others followed suit. He cleared his throat, took a deep breath, and said, "We are sending you off on an adventure."

"A what?" I said.

"A quest."

I nudged Lance, totally surprised by this turn of events, but happy to go along with it. An adventure! That meant no fighting in the war! And no more having to deal with Drill-Sergeant Smythe!

"Fantastic, sir!"

"What have you got for us, then?"

"We want you to retrieve the mythical Relic of the First Age," said the captain to the left of Phoughton.

"Sounds bloody brilliant!" I said.

"Did you say 'mythical'?" asked Lance, with ever the keen eye for detail

"Did I?" said the captain. "I meant magical. The magical Relic of the First Age."

Magic? I couldn't believe it. The rumors were true!

"Even better!" I said. "A quest for a magical relic! Just like in the tales of old! Do we get some weapons or some such?"

"Here you go," said Smythe producing two small swords—the kind we'd been using for drills.

"What, these?" I said, gazing with disgust at the rusty swords. "I mean, no offense, sir, but these are some crap weapons. We're off on a quest! We need weapons with storied histories and majestic names!"

"Exactly!" said Lance, "Something like Auroman, the mace that slew Grudnok."

"Oooh!" I said. "That sounds incredible. Or maybe a famed war hammer from an epic poem!"

"You've got two standard-issue swords," said Smythe. "You can give them names if you like. How about Wilma and Nancy? Will those do?"

"Hello, Wilma!" I said, holding my sword aloft—well, as aloft as a short sword can go. "How's tricks?"

"I think mines' more of a Wilma, mate," Lance said. "See the curvy lil' bob on the handle? Definitely more of a Wilma. Whereas yours is a Nancy if ever there was one."

"Behold! Nancy!" I struck a heroic pose. "Fear not, ye maidens! For I wield the famed Nancy of yore!"

"Ooooh, I like that!"

"It's good, right?" I said. And then I faced Lance square on. "Now tell me—and be brutally honest with me. If you were a damsel in distress and you saw me rising out of the mist, swinging good ol' Nancy here, would you swoon? I've always wanted to make a gal swoon."

"Depends," Lance said, thinking it through. "What's attacking me? Because if it's a gork or a—"

"I hope this is the last bloody time I ever have to say this," interrupted Sergeant Smythe. "But are you two maggots finished? Because I bloody well hope so!"

"Well then, gentlemen," said Captain Phoughton, "If you would please hold out your right hands and place them on the Great Book."

"Oooh!" I said, winking at Lance. "This is the bit where we swear a Royal Oath! I've always wanted to swear one of those."

"Ditto," said Lance. "It's the only kind of swear my mom would let me do."

Smythe and the third captain held out copies of the *Illiyorad*, the book that contains all the ancient stories of the gods of Amerigorn, and we duly placed our right hands on them, ready to swear away. Had we been paying closer attention, we might have noticed that both Smythe and the other captain were holding something behind their backs.

"Are you ready, gentlemen?" said Captain Phoughton.

"Sir! Yes, s—"

Before we could finish, Smythe and the captain revealed two small iron gadgets that glowed a bright red, and they slammed these bright, red, glowy things onto on the backs of our hands, pressing down hard for a good second or two, so we couldn't pull away.

The pain was severe. My nostrils filled with the scent of burning flesh—a smell I can still remember to this very day. Finally, Smythe pulled the gadget off me. I yanked my hand back to try to rub the pain away.

I was unsuccessful.

"Do you swear to . . ." began Captain Phoughton.

I swore all right. I swore swears my mother would be shocked to hear come out of my mouth. Lance and I swore right through the captain's little speech.

Finally, when I pulled myself together, I managed to say something along the lines of "what the bloody cussing hell?"

I looked at my hand and saw a black, raised letter B.

"What is this?"

"That," said Captain Phoughton, "is a Royal Mark, letting everyone in the world know that you are on a Royal Quest for the mythical—I mean, magical—Relic."

"Couldn't you have just given us a ring or something? This looks awfully permanent."

"What does the B stand for?" said Lance.

"Is that a B?" said Phoughton. "It's supposed to be an R for 'relic.' You must have moved."

That hardly seemed plausible, but my hand was throbbing, and my head was spinning. Everything was happening so fast.

"Where is this Relic?" Lance said, shaking his right hand as if that would make the pain fly off. I tried it. It didn't work.

"Therein lies the quest."

We waited for him to give us more details.

"You have no idea where it is?" I said, finally.

"Give us something to go on," said Lance. "Tell us it's in a distant cave guarded by a fierce dragon or something."

"That could very well be the case," said Captain Phoughton.

I couldn't wrap my head around what he was saying. "Is that all you've got for us to go on? It's somewhere?"

"Ah . . . well, I should clarify. It's somewhere *outside* the kingdom."

I glanced over at Lance, who looked back at me.

"Outside . . . are we being banished?" I asked, looking at that B on my hand.

"Banished?" said Captain Phoughton as though we had just asked him to model a pair of fuzzy bunny slippers.

"We're not allowed to do that anymore," said the third captain, sniffing with disgust. "Had we banished you, we would have branded a B on your hand so everyone would know you are not welcome in the Kingdom ever again."

"Quite right," said Captain Phoughton. "As it is, we have branded you with a smudged R, which means that you are hereby formally sent out on a Royal Quest. It just so happens that this quest takes you outside of the kingdom."

"But this R looks just like a B," I said, wanting to make a point. "People will think we've been banished."

"Huh," said Phoughton. I expected him to elaborate on this, but Captain Phoughton was one of those chaps who was not keen on doling out information, being quite content to let you fill in the blanks.

"What is this relic, exactly?"

"Good question!" said Phoughton. "We can't wait for you to tell us."

"So . . ." said Lance, "we don't know what we're looking for . . ."

"Or where it is," said Captain Phoughton. "Quite right."

"I don't think I want to go on this quest," I said, feeling sick to my stomach.

"It's either that," said Smythe, "or we 'lose' you at the bottom of the Pit of Scarlic."

I'd never heard of this pit before, but it sounded bloody awful. Are there any pleasant places—or parts of the body, for that matter—that have the word pit in their name?

"Well, Lance!" I said, trying to make the best of this, "I guess we're off to find a magical relic."

"And don't come back until you find it!" said Smythe, slamming his hand down on the table.

"Just a Q before we go," I said. "How many blokes have been sent out looking for this magical-mythical-thingamajimmy?"

"'Twelve."

"And have you ever seen any of them again?"

Smythe smiled his ugly smile.

I trembled.

"Tell you what," Drill-Sergeant Smythe said. "You find that bloody thing, and we'll throw you a parade."

"And all our sins will be forgiven?"

"Sure."

"What's so special about this thing?"

"It's one of the original artifacts of the First Age," said Captain Phoughton. "Older even than the Cufflinks of Doom. And more powerful. It may very well be the only object in the world that still has magical powers."

"What can one do with this relic, exactly?"

"One can bring it back here, that's what!" said Sergeant Smythe.

"Well, there you go, Lance!" I said, trying to make the best of it. "It's as good as gold! We just nip out of the kingdom, run about the world, fending off thieves and gorks and whatnot, find this blasted thingamajig, and Bob's your uncle, we come home heroes. Whadd'ya say?"

"I'd say we have no choice."

"That about sums it up," said Smythe. "Now, get lost."

"Would a 'please' kill you?" I said.

"Guards!" Smythe shouted. "Escort these two imbeciles out of the kingdom!"

Two guards seemed to materialize out of nowhere. They grabbed us—rather roughly, I should note—and escorted us out of the room. (When I say "escorted" what I mean is they carried us over their shoulders, like sacks of potatoes.) They proceeded to "escort" us out of the building, towards City Gate, the only entrance from the school into the city of Shropsfordshire. From there, they carried us into the marketplace.

It was rather humiliating, to say the least. Hundreds of people stared at us, smirking and pointing.

I tried to make the best of the situation. "We're on a quest!" I said to one lovely maiden, who quickly averted her eyes. I nudged Lance and said, "She was impressed."

"Is that what that look was?"

"Do you gentlemen have to be so rough?" I asked, for my escort was digging his fingers into my legs. Their pace slowed not one step, nor did they loosen their grip. I was getting so little blood flow in my right leg I thought I was going to lose it.

At long last, we approached the famed structure that was Newgate.

Now Newgate, as you may or may not know, was built on the ruins of Oldgate, which was destroyed in the last war. Oldgate, of course, wasn't originally called Oldgate. Being the northernmost gate to the city of Shropsfordshire, it had been called Northgate. But after the new gate had been built there was resistance to calling the new gate Northgate; after all, people had fond memories of the original Northgate, and they felt like calling this new gate Northgate would be like erasing history. So people started calling the new gate New Northgate, but that turned out to be rather a mouthful, and we humans are nothing if not lazy. So, some bloke came up with the ingenious idea of calling the new gate Newgate and everyone rejoiced.

But there was a problem.

You see, if you wanted to refer to the old gate, you couldn't call it Northgate because then people would get confused since Newgate was still the northernmost gate in the city. People would ask if you meant Newgate, to which you would have to say, "No, the old Northgate." Once again, someone—and I can only imagine it was the same bloke who had come up with Newgate, his creative juices flowing—came to the rescue of the people and declared, "Let us now and forevermore refer to the old Northgate as Oldgate.

And let us ne'er speak the word Northgate again, lest ye be flailed a thousand times." I could be making that last bit up.

And so it seemed the city's naming crisis was at an end . . . until they built a newer gate on the western wall of the city.

Well! That threw everyone into a tizzy. And if you've ever seen a city full of people running around in a tizzy you'd know to get out of the way.

"'Ang on a second," someone said. "How can we still call Newgate Newgate when it's no longer the new gate?"

A terrific debate spread across the land. We couldn't very well call the new gate Westgate, for we already had a Westgate. Someone suggested Northwestgate, but that idea was tossed out because the new gate lay in a more of a west-north-west part of the wall. (One bloke suggested we call it Westnorthwestgate, but he was stoned to death.)

Finally, it was decreed by the king that the new gate would be called Newergate.

To say that there was much rejoicing through the land would be stretching the definition of the word *rejoicing*. But no one griped about it, either, which is basically considered a victory in today's political climate.

Of course, the trend didn't stop there, for we humans seem rather fond of building gates. Newgate and Newergate were soon followed by Newishgate, which was given that name because before it could be completed, we had already started building another gate, which is now known as Newlynewgate.

(We've rather smartly avoided using the name Newestgate, for that would mean we couldn't build any more gates. Score one for human ingenuity!)

Of course, no one dares point out the fact that since none of our new gates have any directional names, it's almost impossible to remember where any of these gates are. But I digress. (Try asking directions for Newlynewgate, and you're likely to start a half-hour discussion group.)

Anyway, back to Newgate, which is not only the most iconic entrance to the city of Shropsfordshire, it also marks the northernmost and busiest entrance to the Kingdom of Amerigorn. On this side of the gate's portcullis was civilization. On that, the Great Beyond. I had only briefly glimpsed the Great Beyond from the castle drawbridge. I certainly had ever gone into that wilderness, though I had always dreamed about it. Now it seemed that the moment was finally about to come.

I started to get a little emotional.

"Gentlemen, if we could pause for a hot second," I said as we arrived at the border. "I just want to say a few words."

They tossed us out on our butts.

"Or," I said, standing up and rubbing my sore backside, "we could skip that part."

Part Two

Chapter Twelve

WE STOOD ON the famed Bridge of Sighs, pausing to have our first up-close look at the Great Beyond.

Frankly, we were disappointed.

It was immediately apparent that calling this side of the gate "the Great Beyond" was false advertising: with all the traffic coming and going from the city, this side of the gate looked a heck of a lot like the other side of the gate. Nevertheless, I took a deep breath and said, "Get a load of that fresh air!"

"I feel like a changed man," said Lance.

"Well! We have the entire globe to cover and some unknown thing that does who-knows-what to find. Which way shall we go first?"

Lance smirked at me. "Well comrade, given that we're on a bridge and we're not allowed to go backwards, that doesn't leave us a ton of options."

"Quite right! Tally ho, as they say."

Thus, we began our quest.

Now I don't know about you, but when I imagined blokes out on a quest for a magical relic, I pictured a group of adventurers, boldly striking out into the wilderness, hacking away at vines, and fighting off beasts and villains and all that sort of thing.

That was pretty much exactly how it was for us, except instead of the wilderness we were on a crowded highway, and instead of hacking away at vines we were mostly coughing our way through an interminable amount of dust. And instead of fighting beasts, we were mostly dodging an obscene amount of horse poop.

It was not terribly romantic.

We wandered down the road, passing building after building of smithies, markets, inns, dry goods shops, and taverns. This road looked no different than any main thoroughfare in Shropfordshire.

"So far, I'm not impressed."

"With the world?"

"Yeah, I mean I signed up for adventure. This is just . . . shopping."

"I'll bet we could get some good deals over there." Lance pointed to a shop with a sign out front that said "The Thrill of the Hunt."

After about an hour more of walking, my stomach started to rumble.

"I'm getting a bit hungry. You?"

"I can always eat," Lance said. "Do we have any food?"

"Just that lelthbread Smythe tossed in our bags."

"Hmm . . ."

"Hmm?"

"That's gone," he said with not even a trace of sorrow.

"Gone? That was supposed to last us a whole week!"

"Huh," said Lance. "No wonder my stomach is upset."

"Do we have any money?" I asked.

"Not unless you brought some."

"This is ridiculous! How do they expect us to scour the globe for this thing if we don't have any supplies?"

"They don't expect us to scour the globe. They just wanted to get rid of us. We're dead to them."

"Seems a bit harsh. I mean, it's not like we destroyed a finished barn."

We came up to a tavern.

"Maybe we can offer to do some work for food?"

We walked inside. It was packed, which surprised me, given that this was the eighth tavern we'd passed. We made our way through the crowd to the bartender.

"What can I do for you . . . gentlemen?" said the portly man behind the bar.

"We're looking for something to eat, but we have no money."

For the second time that day, we were tossed out onto the road.

"Is it just me," I asked, "or did he have amazingly quick reflexes for a man of his size?"

We dusted ourselves off (again) and sallied forth.

The two of us walked for hours, and we were no further from civilization than when we began our journey. Dusk approached. We were tired, hungry, and dirty.

"This is the pits!" I said.

"I thought we'd be camping out under the stars, with a campfire, and some food roasting over it, relishing about how we spent the day vanquishing trolls . . ."

"And saving ladies! Don't forget the ladies."

"You're obsessed with girls."

"Aye."

"I mean, if we could just get out of this strip, we could maybe find some woods to sleep in. That would be an improvement."

It started to rain.

"This whole banishment thing just keeps getting better and better."

We walked a little further in silence.

"Maybe we can go back, hat in hand, and beg him to throw us into that pit thingy?"

"Right?" I said. "What I wouldn't give for a little eternal damnation."

"Or a sandwich."

"Those are good, too."

"Remember the good old days when Smythe merely locked us up in that dungeon?"

"Like it was yesterday."

"It was four hours ago."

We walked . . . and walked.

Finally, Lance stopped.

"What's up, comrade?"

"We've got to find a place to sleep," he said, looking around. Then he smacked me on the arm and said, "Come on."

I followed him to a stable. The owner, rather than throwing us out on our behinds, actually said we could sleep in his stable if we did a little work in the back. He told us to see Old Joe.

We walked around to the back. The smell of horse poop was positively deafening. We saw a dozen stalls, each one housing a horse. In the middle of all the stalls stood an old-timer, leaning against a post, lost in thought, and drinking what I could only assume was a rather potent alcoholic beverage of some sort. We approached him.

An old brown mare whinnied at me. I shivered. The last time I'd seen a horse of her color, I'd hit it with a snowball. I walked up and gently stroked the side of her face. "I'm sorry I hit your friend," I whispered to her.

She snorted at me.

The snort startled the old man. "Hey there, youngins!" he said with a crazy laugh. "What can I do ya fer?"

Lance stepped up. "The owner said we could sleep out here in the stable if we did some work?"

Old Joe looked at Lance's hand and laughed. "You've been banished! Me too!" He showed us the back of his right hand.

And there it was. The same mark we had. I paled a bit at this realization, knowing that we were destined to have this mark on our hands for our entire lives.

"When were you banished?" I asked him.

"When I was about your age. Ah, but don't worry. Being banished isn't all that bad. Look at me!"

We did look at him. He looked bloody awful. He had ragged clothes and was covered in scabs, and his tooth-to-tattoo ratio was totally wrong.

"Is this where you live?" I asked.

"Live? Oh no! I tend not to stay around in any one place too long. I've been here for a few weeks, but I'll be moseying on my way soon enough."

"How do you earn a living?"

"I shovel poop!"

"How long you been shoveling poop, comrade?" Lance asked.

"I'd say about forty years or so. That's the good thing about poop: There's always plenty to shovel!" And then he let loose with that insane laughter of his.

"Good talking to you!" Lance grabbed my arm, dragging me away from Old Joe.

"Come back!" Joe said. "There's plenty of poop for all of us!"

We kept walking.

"I am not going to spend my life shoveling poop," Lance said.

"Agreed."

"Nige, I know you and I are total screw-ups."

"Mostly me."

"Yes, mostly you. But look," he took a deep breath, "we need to find that darned relic. I don't care what it takes, but we have to get back to society."

"Agreed."

"Where do we start?"

"I have no idea. But!" I said, "We can go do some research at the library."

"The library is in the kingdom."

"Exactly!" I said. And then I said, "Oh. Right. In the kingdom where we can't go because we've been banished."

He looked around, scanning the area for ideas. His eyes lit up. "But! I know where we can go! The library at Riverfell." Riverfell was the name of the famed Elvish city where the Group of Nine had gathered to begin their quest to destroy the Cufflinks of Doom.

"Elves!" I said. "I've always wanted to see an elf! I hear they're the world's most beautiful creatures."

"Then we're off!"

"Excellent!" I said, clapping my hands together.

We stood there in the rain, which was now coming down even harder.

"Are we really going to sleep in the rain?"

"If we catch a cold and die we'll never find that relic," Lance said.

"My point exactly."

We walked back to the stable, picked up a couple of shovels, and got to work.

"It feels better shoveling poop when you've got a purpose," I said.

And so, dear reader, yours truly and his trusty friend spent the first night of our epic quest for the Magical/Mythical Relic of the First Age shoveling horse poop. It was about as exciting as you'd think it would be.

When we finally finished, we settled in for the night under a cozy layer of warm hay.

"Night comrade," I said. And then I sneezed.

I sneezed again.

"I forgot you were allergic to hay."

"Me, too."

Sneeze.

"You gonna be able to sleep?"

Sneeze.

"Eventually." Sneeze. "I hope."

I sneezed a few more times.

"Listen, mate," said Lance. "I hate to abandon you to your problems and all, but I'm going over there."

"It's just as well," I said. Sneeze. Lance gathered his things and bid me good night.

I must have passed out at some point, for I remember dreaming of Elvish women, and of living in a world in which I never had to shovel poop again.

Chapter Thirteen

THE NEXT MORNING, Lance and I started down the road, which we hoped would eventually lead us to the library at Riverfell. (Smythe never gave us a map, and our fellow travelers were not exactly willing to chat with two boys who smelled like horse poop.) We walked past more taverns and gazed longingly through the windows, watching people eat enormous breakfasts. My stomach growled with a painful intensity I still remember. I didn't know it was possible to be so hungry.

Plus, my eyes were still puffy from sleeping in hay, so not only was I hungry, I was half-blind.

"So this is what rock bottom feels like," I said.

"What makes you think things can't get worse?"

"Whatever happened to 'chillax, comrade'?"

"I ate all the chillax yesterday," Lance said with a sniff.

Half an hour later, we came upon a postiary. I had an idea. A long shot, but I thought it would at least be something. And besides, it would give us a few minutes' rest from walking. I told Lance I wanted to make a brief stop.

We entered the shop. A middle-aged man was busy sweeping feathers into a dustpan. "Be right with you, gentlemen," he said. Having the word *gentlemen* aimed in my general direction made me feel better already. The man finished sweeping and picked up the dustpan. He cracked open a heavy wooden door behind him. As soon as it opened, the sound of a hundred squawking birds filled the shop. No wonder he used such a heavy door. There was no way I could work with all that racket. He dumped the contents of the dustpan into a rubbish bin and closed the door. Blissful silence returned.

He walked behind a counter and clapped his hands. "How can I help you?"

"I'd like to send a raven, please."

"That'll be 20 gilders."

"Twen—that's highway robbery! I could eat for a month on 20 gilders!"

"Well, we do have a cheaper option."

"Oh. All right, then. What's that?"

"A titmouse."

I couldn't tell if I misunderstood the man, or he if was simply having me on, for I had never heard of such a creature. Lance, though, seemed to know all about them. "Tufted or un-tufted?" he asked.

"What are you going on about?" I murmured.

"There are two kinds of titmouses," Lance said.

"Is it titmice?"

"Good question." Lance turned to the shopkeeper, "Is it titmouses or titmice?"

"Birds," the man said, cutting right to the chase. He had clearly been asked this question before and was not about to go there. "Titmouse birds. And it's two gilders for a tufted titmouse and five for an un-tufted titmouse."

"Now that surprises me," I said. "I would have thought the tufted titmouse would be more expensive. After all, you're getting more bird. And, I can only assume, they're prettier."

"Do you care how pretty your delivery bird is?" the shopkeeper asked me. He said it like he thought I was some kind of weirdo.

"Well, I guess so. After all, this bird is going to be delivering a letter to my mom. I don't want some ruffian to do it and give her the wrong impression."

"You've been banished from the kingdom and sent on a hopeless quest," said Lance, "What sort of impression were you hoping to give?"

"Fair enough," I said.

"Un-tufted titmouse birds are faster," said the shopkeeper. "They don't have a tuft, so there's less wind resistance."

I tutted. "Says a lot about our fast-paced world when people would rather pay for speed than beauty."

"You've clearly given this some thought," said the shopkeeper. "Have you given any thought as to how you're going to pay for this beautiful tufted titmouse?"

"Ah!" I said. "Yes, I have. I have given it some serious thought, indeed."

"You don't have money."

"Not as such," I said. "But! I am willing to work for it!"

"Is that right?"

"Quite right."

"Are you a hard worker?"

"Not even slightly."

"Well, you're honest," he said with a sniff. "Tell you what. Hear all those birds in the back? Those birds produce an amazing amount of . . ." he paused, sensing that he should perhaps adjust his language for us, ". . . poop. If you and your friend shovel all that bird poop and bring it down the road to farmer Malvern, I'll consider your debt paid."

"How about that, Glancey old boy?" I said, smacking him on the arm. "We'll get to put our highly developed skills to work after all."

"Great," he said.

Dear Mom,

I have been banished from the kingdom and sent on an impossible and pointless quest that I will never complete, and so I will probably never see you again.

How are you?

Apparently, I have a real knack for shoveling poop. Who knew all those years of schooling would pay off so handsomely?

I love you very much. Don't worry about me. I am with my friend Lance. You remember him, the chap with the nice ears? Did you know he was an ace at destroying barns? I am sure this will come in handy on our meaningless quest.

Love,

Nigel (your son)

"Is that really the letter you want to send to your mom?" Lance asked me.

I read it through. "I think that sums everything up rather nicely."

"Aren't you concerned she'll be worried about you?"

"I'm counting on it." And then I launched into my infamous Mom impression. "'Banished? My son says he's been banished!' And then she'll scream bloody murder all the way up the chain of command. 'We don't banish children! Now you bring my son and his friend back here right this minute!'"

"Do you think it'll work?" Lance asked.

"Not a bit. But it'll give her something to do. OK, my good man," I said, handing the letter to the shopkeeper.

"Which bird do you want?"

I looked over the flock of tufted titmice (titmouses?) and spotted a lanky one in the corner.

"How'bout him. He looks like his life could use some purpose."

"That one?" said the shopkeeper. "That's Gerald. No one ever picks Gerald."

"Then he's the bird for the job."

"I dunno, Nibes," said Lance looking Gerald over. "Seems a bit scrawny."

"That's what I like about him. Besides, it'll do 'im good to get some fresh air."

The shopkeeper shrugged, tied the message to Gerald's leg, and set him free.

The bird flapped his wings mightily and rose into the air. What a sight he was! Right up until he smashed into the side of the building, tumbled down an awning, and plopped on to the ground with a faint "fffffphth."

"Or," I said, "Maybe we could send that bird over there."

Two minutes later, a healthy bird soared into the air to deliver my message.

"I don't know," I said, watching the bird fly away, "he doesn't have the drunken panache Gerald brought to the act of flying."

"Or 'crashing,' as some of us call it," said Lance.

"Speaking of whom, what are you gonna do with ol' Gerald?" I asked. I couldn't help but feel sorry for the poor thing. He didn't look at all well.

"Probably feed him to the cat," he said.

I looked at Lance. He looked at me.

"We'll take him off your hands, comrade," Lance said.

"It'll cost ya," said the shopkeeper.

"Really?"

"Nah, I'm just kidding. But," he added, "I'm not kidding about shoveling that pile o' poop."

He pointed to some shovels. And we got to work.

We shoveled away. It took us about twenty minutes, which almost seemed like a vacation, considering we were used to shoveling for hours on end. Then we delivered the poop to farmer Malvern, who had a stand half a mile back towards Shropsfordshire. When we brought the wheelbarrow back to the shopkeeper, he gave me a little cloth hammock that contained my new wounded friend Gerald. He pinned the hammock to my vest and even handed me a scoop of birdseed, which I placed in my pocket. We shook hands with the shopkeeper, and Lance and I started on our quest once again.

My stomach roared at me, and I noticed I was now shaking from hunger.

"Do you think we can eat birdseed?" I asked.

"I was thinking of eating the bird," said Lance.

I placed a protective hand over Gerald. "Never!" I said. My stomach rumbled. "Although, ask me again in a half hour."

We walked for maybe twenty minutes when we heard a voice call out.

"Oy!" it said.

We looked around, but we didn't see anyone trying to get our attention.

"Oy! You two!" said the voice.

"Say, Comrade Nigel. Am I so hungry that I'm now hearing things?"

"Up here, cadets!" said the voice. We shielded our eyes from the sun and looked up to see a soldier on the top of a small tower. "You two! Stay right there!" He turned and ran into a doorway, which, presumably, took him to a flight of stairs.

"Should we run?"

"Probably," Lance said. "But frankly, I'm so tired of all this walking I welcome any change of pace. Even if it means a swift death."

"With our luck, this guy'll bore us to death by telling us about his dreams or something."

"We could pick a fight with him."

"Oooh! I like the sound of that!" I pulled out my sword. "Ready to get to work, Wilma?"

"Wait," said Lance. "I think mine is Wilma."

"Oh, right. I keep forgetting. Sorry, Nance."

"You two! Come here!" said the soldier, who was now standing at an open gate. Now that he was at eye level, we could see he was a lieutenant.

"Wouldn't do well to pick a fight with a superior officer now would it?" I asked Lance. I slid Nancy back into my scabbard.

"Maybe he's got a pit to throw us in."

"One can dream."

We walked over to the lieutenant.

"Come on, come on!" he said. "We haven't got all day!"

He pulled us into an antechamber.

"Right!" he said. "State your names."

"Well, I'm—"

"YOU ARE IN THE PRESENCE OF A SUPERIOR OFFICER!" screamed the lieutenant.

We snapped to attention. We had completely forgotten ourselves.

"Now!" he said, "State your name."

"Sir! Cadet Lance Hightower, sir!"

"Sir! Cadet Nigel Pipps-Schrewsberry-Billingsbottom III, sir!"

"Much better!" he said, calming down. That's the thing with these military chaps. Most of them are rather chill individuals as long as you follow the rules. The minute you get a little lackadaisical, though, they let you know what's what. "What are you two doing out here? Get yourselves banished?"

"How—I mean, Sir! Yes, sir!"

He leaned in close to me and peered at Gerald. "You have a bird pinned to your chest."

"Sir, yes, sir!"

"Very good," he said, standing upright and clearing his throat. "Right. Well, I'm hereby giving you new orders."

"Sir?"

"You are now in charge of prisoner transport."

"Sir! But we are on a quest—"

"Yes, I bloody well know the drill, cadet. The Academy sends all their hooligans out on this quest. That quest can wait. This is an urgent matter vital to the success of the war effort. And as a special officer in His Majesty's service, I am authorized to draft any soldier—or cadet—for my purposes, do I make myself clear?"

"Sir, yes, sir!"

"Follow me."

"Sir?" I said. "I'm not saying this out of any sign of disrespect, sir, but out of a sincere effort to ensure the success of your mission."

"Go on."

"You don't want us to transfer a prisoner, sir."

"He's right, sir," said Lance. "We're awful."

"The worst. Heck, we couldn't even manage to dig a latrine without destroying an entire barn."

He sighed, which made me like the man. Smythe would have simply screamed at us. I looked the lieutenant over a bit more closely. He was unshaven and looked rather tired. Clearly, the man had not gotten a night's sleep in a good long while. I would soon understand why.

"If I had any soldiers I could spare I would. But it looks like we're stuck with each other. Besides, our prisoner shouldn't give you any problems." He gave us the once-over. "Looks like you two could use a meal and a night's sleep. Tell you what. We'll give you a hot-cooked meal and a bed and tomorrow we'll outfit you with some supplies and send you on your way with my prisoner. Agreed?"

Food! A bed! An easy mission! How could we say no?

"Sir! Yes, sir!"

The lieutenant led us into the bailey of the fort, which was tiny compared to our school's courtyard. The whole fort looked like it was maybe one-twentieth the size of that castle. But then we followed him past a small stable to a tiny shack. I couldn't figure out how the three of us would be able to fit in there until he opened the door, revealing a spiral staircase.

We walked down one flight and entered a surprisingly large mess hall, maybe fifty feet square. As we walked to a table, I could see hallways and other rooms, and I realized that the basement of this place was far more extensive than the outside of the fort.

We sat down and the lieutenant, whose name was Thuffsbury, had a seven-course meal brought out to us.

I scarfed down every last bite and asked for seconds, which, to my surprise, were brought straight out to me. I have never eaten so much so quickly in all my life. The food was probably somewhat on the disgusting side, but neither Lance nor I cared one bit. It was food. And it was hot.

"Look, Nige," said Lance with a full mouth. "I know you can't help yourself, in terms of being a bumbling idiot and all."

"No argument there."

"But we really have to complete this mission. I can't spend another night without food or shelter."

"Agreed. Besides, I rather like the lieutenant. He only screamed at us once. Makes me want to make him proud or something."

"I'm sure that feeling will pass."

"OK, so we deliver this prisoner, and then we resume our quest."

"Agreed."

Once we had eaten our fill, we took a little tour of the place.

The lieutenant had his own quarters. Next to that was a large room with thirty bunk beds, which was where the rest of the men slept and where we were to bed down for the night. The room was quite smoky, owing to the six torches needed to light the place, and it made me curious about the design of this bizarre fort. Why build everything underground? Surely the military could have commandeered more space above ground and built a bigger fort.

As we walked around, I noticed the soldiers here wore the strangest uniforms I'd ever seen, which is saying something, since I've been around soldiers my whole life and knew in great detail pretty much everything there was to know about uniforms and armor. But these chaps weren't dressed for battle. They didn't wear chain mail or leather padding. Instead, they wore black cloth brigandine vests, with black sleeves, and black trousers. And they wore a type of black leather footwear that I'd call boots, except they didn't make the noises that boots make. Frankly, these silent, black-uniformed chaps gave me the heebie-jeebies as they tended to sneak up on you.

The lieutenant caught up to us as we were getting ready for bed and told us more about the place, and how there was another level below this one that consisted of nothing but jail cells.

He told us they were currently housing seventy-five prisoners here and had the capacity for another twenty. These weren't regular prisoners like the kind you might find in the jail of your local village; they hadn't committed pedestrian crimes like theft or murder. This prison housed war criminals.

"War criminals," I echoed, with no small degree of awe in my voice. The very phrase conjured up the most fearful images of bloodthirsty monsters, foaming at the mouth, ready to rape and pillage. "Do you mean gorks?"

"Mostly gorks," he said.

Suddenly I felt less than safe for several reasons. A of all, I was bloody terrified of gorks even though I had never seen one. B of all, the word "mostly" left me rather cold. What other kinds of creatures could be holed up below my feet? Who else were we at war with? And C of all, was he actually expecting us to transport a gork? The very notion was too frightening for words. The lieutenant sensed my unease and reassured me that everything was OK.

"These gorks have all been subdued. Besides," he continued, "our intelligence officers are just getting ready to go to work on them again."

Intelligence officers! That would explain the odd uniforms. Clearly, this must be a new branch of the military; after all, our army had been happily intelligence-free for two millennia.

Before I could ask what he meant by his last statement, he said some rather chilling words. "If you have any earplugs, you may want to use them. Goodnight, gentlemen. Try to get some sleep." And he left with a queer look in his eye.

Lance and I looked at each other, wondering what we were in for when we heard the most ungodly, ear-piercing, soul-shattering scream come from below. It went on far longer than I would have imagined possible. Lance and I tried to cover our ears, but the sound cut right through us and even rattled our beds. No earplugs in the world would have been able to muffle that sound. Lance said exactly what I was thinking: "What the hell have we gotten ourselves into?"

The screams continued throughout the night.

Chapter Fourteen

I MUST HAVE DRIFTED off at some point, but I can't imagine I got more than an hour of sleep. I awoke to the sound of Gerald chirping at me. I had pinned him to the side of my mattress so he could sleep without fear of being crushed by me rolling over on him. I sat up and dug some birdseed out of my pouch and fed him some. I wondered if he had been able to sleep at all.

"What do you think was going on last night?" Lance asked me as I climbed down from my bunk.

"Our intelligence officers were questioning the prisoners," said the lieutenant, who had appeared out of nowhere. "Come on, cadets. Breakfast time and then you're on your way."

"Questioning?" said Lance once the lieutenant had gone.

"Is it too late for us to run away?"

I pinned Gerald's sling to my vest, and we somberly walked to the dining hall and sat down for breakfast. The food wasn't bad: eggs, beans, toast, and tea. But it was hard to have an appetite. I couldn't imagine what they'd been doing to the prisoners all night long to make them scream like that, nor could I imagine they'd gotten any useful information out of them. To further confuse my brain, I was having a hard time coming to grips with the fact that I was feeling empathy for gorks. After all, gorks were our enemy. Had been for over two thousand years. I knew what they were capable of. I knew the atrocities they had committed during the Really Big War. I knew they were somehow responsible for the destruction of Fell's Palace. And on top of all of that, my father died fighting the gorks in the Seven Day Skirmish. But still. It didn't seem right to torture anyone like that, gorks included.

"All right boys," said the lieutenant as we handed in our empty food trays. "Time to go."

We followed him up the stairs to the courtyard. There, right in the middle of the yard, was a cage on wheels, not unlike the one I had been carted away on. This one was covered by a tarp so we couldn't see who or what was inside.

"Here's a map of where you're going. It's a straight shot. You'll be staying off the main road you were on yesterday. People are a bit touchy about gorks these days, and you don't want to find yourselves having to defend your prisoner against vigilantes. There's a trail out from our back gate that leads straight to your destination."

"Where are we taking him?"

"This prisoner is of no more use to us, so you're going to our easternmost outpost, Fort Phipps, where the prisoner may be exchanged for one of our boys." He pointed on the map to the trail he wanted us to take. I took it and studied it for a few seconds. Beyond Fort Phipps lay the Gorkish Empire. I couldn't believe we were supposed to walk towards that hellish place.

The lieutenant grabbed a couple of heavy bags and loaded them onto an ox. The ox was then hooked up to the cage.

"Boys, this is Arthur. He's a good ox. He's done this journey, back and forth, several dozen times, so he practically knows the way. You have plenty of supplies: a tent, food, and more. If you stick to the path, you should be there in about four days. You'll be fine. The road to Fort Phipps is clear of danger. You'll receive new orders from the commanding officer when you get there."

"Four days?" I said. I thumbed at the cage. "Do we need to feed him or—"

"No," he said bluntly. He bent down slightly to address us directly. "We have put plenty of food in the cage. Do not worry about the prisoner. Do not even look under this tarp. And most importantly, do not speak to the prisoner. Gorks are very tricky creatures. You cannot believe a word they say. Just keep moving and you'll be fine. Good luck, cadets."

And with that, he hit the rear end of the ox, which started to walk towards the gate. It was all happening so fast, but Lance instinctively grabbed the ox's reins and I walked beside him. One of the intelligence officers opened the gate for us. A minute later, we were on the road, walking further and further away from home.

It was astonishing how quickly we entered the wilderness. Five minutes into our new journey, we could see no sign of human habitation. Just trees. Mile after mile of trees. For the first time since we began our journey, we could hear birds chirping and bugs buzzing. The air was noticeably fresher.

The world suddenly felt very, very large.

"It's hard to believe," I said. "Only two months ago, we were at peace and I was living the life of a no-goodnik causing trouble in a small village. Now, we've been banished from the kingdom and we're transporting a dangerous gork through the wilderness during wartime."

The cart hit a rather deep pothole, causing the prisoner to cry out in pain.

Lance and I glanced at each other.

"Should we see if he's all right?" I asked.

"No. But that's probably not going to stop us."

"Oy!" I said. "You all right in there?"

There was no reply.

"Do gorks speak our language?" I asked Lance.

"Dunno."

I whipped out Nancy and tapped on the cage.

"You alive in there?"

Still no answer.

"You know, Nige," said Lance, "I know we're really good at screwing up, but can we go more than five minutes before totally disregarding the one thing the lieutenant said not to do?"

"I know he told us not to look inside the cage, but I want to know if this thing is alive. I don't want to go all the way to that blasted fort only to find out we've delivered a dead gork when the customer has clearly ordered a live one."

"Fair enough," said Lance. "I say we pull apart the covering and have a look."

"Great," I said. "I'm right behind you."

"Oh, I'm supposed to do it? I'm not getting that close to a gork!"

"Tell you what," I said. "You do this one and I'll do the next one."

"You're all heart," said Lance.

He edged closer to the cage as the ox kept pulling it along down the path. I followed closely behind him, sword at the ready. He looked at me and nodded and then he grabbed the cloth and pulled it apart to reveal the creature inside.

"Eeek!" I shrieked.

The thing was hideous. Huge and misshapen. It was vaguely humanoid in the same way that a child's pottery creation is vaguely an ashtray. Sure, it had two arms, two legs, a torso, and a head, but all of the parts were the wrong size. And its skin was a sort of puke-green color. And slimy. Did I mention it was slimy? Slimy. I was afraid to go near it lest some slime get on me.

"Sweet butter crumpets!" said Lance, who was clearly on the same page as me. That's why I like Lance. We both feel the same way towards slime creatures.

"Got a problem?" it said.

"Er. Ah. No."

"Not us."

"Uh . . . hang on," I said, for the timbre in the gork's voice sounded different from what I was expecting, "are you a girl gork?"

"No," it said.

"Ah. Right."

"I am a woman."

"Really? Are you sure?" I said.

"I didn't know gorks had girls," said Lance.

"Women."

"Right. Sorry. Women."

"Well, it stands to reason, mate," I said. "Propagation of the species and all that."

"Thank you for planting that image in my head, Nibel."

"You're quite welcome, Glancey, old boy."

"I'm actually considered quite beautiful, thank you," the creature—she—said.

"Oh. Ah. Well. Er. Um. Congrats on that," I said. (I mean, what are you supposed to say in that situation?)

"You know I could crush both of your skulls with just one hand?" she said.

"Really? One hand, you say?"

"You know what I always say, Nibes: Beauty is in the eye of the one whose skull is about to be crushed."

"Why, I remember you saying that very thing just the other day."

"Can you close the curtain?" she asked. "I've already been tortured enough. I don't need the sight of you two cussing idiots tormenting me for the next four days."

I looked at her more closely. She wasn't kidding about being tortured. She had dried blood everywhere, even on her face. And what I had assumed was a misshapen arm now revealed itself to me as a broken arm that had been set at the wrong angle.

"Your arm all right?" I asked.

"What do you care, you cussing cusstard?"

"I don't care," I lied. It was hard to look at someone whose arm was so clearly mangled and not want to see it fixed. I had broken my arm once a couple of years ago. I'd been trying to escape from my room late at night and the vine I was clinging to broke off from the tree. My arm was broken in exactly the same way as hers and the doctor had needed to set it. The pain I experienced when he set it was positively unbearable. I'd needed to clamp my teeth down on a wooden board so I wouldn't bite my tongue off. That, my friends, is a lot of pain.

"But," I said, "your arm isn't set properly. It won't heal right."

"You wanna come here and fix my arm, lover-boy?"

I shivered a bit at that suggestion.

"Coward," she said. And then she did the most dashed-crazy thing I've ever seen anyone do. She rose up on her knees (gasping a bit, for she must have had a shattered rib or two), looked me straight in the eye, grabbed her arm at the wrist, and pulled it until the break straightened out. She didn't even utter a groan, though I could tell it must've hurt like a bear. I could even see a tear form in her yellow eye. It was the single most astonishing display of strength and courage I'd ever seen. Lance and I stood there with our mouths agape—literally. We were so startled, we stopped walking altogether, and we watched her in her cage, slowly rolling down the path.

"You two look like you're about to faint," she said.

Her remark broke the spell, and we caught up with the cart.

"Do you have a name?" asked Lance in what I'm guessing was a desperate attempt to change the subject.

"Cuss you, you stinkin' cussing poor excuse for a cussing-cusswad with a cuss-filled cussing cuss," she said.

"Is that a family name?" I asked.

She stared at me for a moment. Then she reached through the bars of the cage and pulled down the tarp, thus ending the interview.

"I like her," I said as we continued our journey. "She's got spunk."

Chapter Fifteen

LANCE AND I continued on our journey, ate lunch, chitchatted about this and that, and tried to ignore the fact that we were escorting a female gork in the middle of the wilderness. Mostly I tried to pry more information out of my new best friend.

"Where's your home?"

Lance tightened up his mouth a bit and decided how much he wanted to tell me. I wasn't quite sure I understood why he was reluctant; after all, he had told me what I could only assume was his most dangerous secret. And here we were, banished from Amerigorn for the rest of our lives. If he couldn't completely trust me, we were in trouble. But I decided I wouldn't press the subject.

"Mezic," he said after a bit. And that seemed to be all he wanted to say on that subject.

The Mezic Kingdom lay to Amerigorn's south. While that answer didn't totally shock me—after all he had the dark features and strong accent of someone who was from that region—I was surprised to learn that he wasn't an Amerigornish citizen. Frankly, it never dawned on me that one could simply leave one's country and move to another. I was simultaneously impressed and sad at how far Lance was from his home.

"Think your parents are worried about you?"

"Ha! They disowned me. The only reason they sent that bounty hunter after me was to see me punished."

Well, what can you say to that?

"I'm sorry, mate. That's rough" is what I said, though that felt hollow.

"It's been an adventure."

We heard some mumbling from the cage.

"What's that?" I said. "You want to curse at us some more?"

"I said how typical it was for humans to turn on their own. All they know is destruction and torture."

I whipped open the tarp. She glared at me.

"OK, we're not perfect," I said. "But we're not all awful. Lance here is one of the good ones."

"And you?"

"I'm just kind of a screw-up."

"And ugly," she added.

Lance laughed. I turned to him. "Oh, I see. The truth comes out."

"What's your name?" he asked her. "We have a few more days' journey in front of us, and I refuse to call you 'the prisoner.'"

She looked at him for a second.

"Please? Look, I'm Lance, and this here is Nibel."

"Nigel."

"I'm Eldrack," she said.

"El—" I swallowed. "That's . . . pretty."

"I don't care if you think my name is pretty."

"Oh. Well, good. Because I don't. I was just being polite." I sniffed loudly to let her know I was annoyed.

"Eldrack is a very common female Gorkish name."

"How very nice for you." We rode in silence for a bit, but then, because I can't help myself, I said, "Elves have pretty names."

"Elves? Elves are disgusting."

"Dis—did you hear that, Lance?" I asked, turning to my friend. He shrugged and pantomimed a gesture that clearly stated that he wanted no part of this discussion.

"What's an Elvish name that you consider pretty?" she asked.

"Theowyn," I said.

"Gesundheit," she said.

"Ha!" laughed Lance.

"You're taking her side, are you?"

"Well . . . I'm not as big a fan of elves as you are. I've always sort of fancied dwarves, though of course they're all gone."

"You people are both loony. Elves are widely regarded as beautiful creatures."

"Meh," said Lance.

"Ooh, I like him," said Eldrack. "Maybe the only human who doesn't disgust me."

"Oh, come on, we're not all that bad," I said.

"You treat the rest of the world like your playthings. You run around conquering everything and taking prisoners of everyone you don't like."

"Look who's on her high horse. Well, you're a bloody terrorist, now aren't you?"

"A terrorist?"

"Yeah. A terrorist."

"I am not," she said.

"Oh, really? Then why the bloody hell did Lieutenant lock you up? What were you doing, picking fleerflowers?"

She stiffened. "I got abducted from my home. I was cooking dinner when suddenly I heard a noise, and before I could react, someone hit me in the head with a hammer. When I woke up, I was in a cart like this one, on this very road, going in the other direction."

"Sure," I said. "Cooking dinner."

"It's the truth."

"We wouldn't have grabbed you if you were only cooking dinner. You must have been doing something wrong. After all, we're the good guys."

"You?" she said, genuinely horrified. "The hell you are! You humans are the scourge of the planet!"

"Ha!" I said. And I meant it to sting. "You're delusional. Everyone knows you gorks are the baddies. Right, Lance?"

She stared at me for a good second or two, her yellow eyes boring into me. I expected her to yell at me or something. Instead, she leaned back against her bars. "See this?" She gestured her arms around, pointing at the scenery. "All of this? This road, this forest, those hills, all the land as far as you can see . . . all of this belonged to the gorks until just a few years ago."

"That's not our fault. You gave this land to us in treaties."

"Treaties? You mean treaties like the Great Doozy Treaty of 4073 and the Hey That's a Beautiful Hill You've Got there, Mind if We Have It Treaty of 4079? Those treaties?"

"Those aren't real treaties," Lance said. I was glad for some backup, for clearly, Eldrack knew more history than I did.

"They certainly are," Eldrack said.

"Why would you be so foolish as to sign a treaty called 'The Great Doozy'?"

"We were threatened with war. And no gork was ready for another war."

"You mean another butt-kicking?" I said, and I held up my hand to high-five Lance.

He wasn't going for it.

"Let me ask you this," she said, changing tactics, "what is on your banner?"

"Our what?"

"Your banner. The banner of your Kingdom. The one your generals carry into battle. What's on it?"

"A sword."

"Going through a skull," said Lance.

"It's very snappy."

"A sword going through a skull," she said. "And you don't think that says something about you?"

"It says we have a great graphic designer."

"What's on your banner?" asked Lance.

"A flower."

"See," I said, "that's why your side will never win. A flower is a rubbish symbol to rally your armed forces behind."

"You're missing the point. We stand for nature and beauty. You stand for destruction. And skulls."

"I'm not quite following you," I said.

"I think she's saying," said Lance, "that her graphic designer has a more effeminate worldview and that somehow makes her side the superior one."

"Ah. Yeah. Well, I appreciate all things effeminate," I said. And then I looked at her, "Well, most things effeminate. But I fail to see how—"

"Bad guys have skulls. Good guys have flowers. Period, end of discussion."

"You're forgetting that whole period of history when you gorks tried to destroy the entire world."

She sat down, looking slightly defeated. "Smoron did that to us."

"Oh, well, isn't that bloody convenient? It wasn't your fault . . ." and even as I said this, I remembered saying the same thing just a few weeks ago. It wasn't my fault the Eternal Flame got extinguished. It was. And yet it wasn't.

"Hang on a second," said Lance peering down the road. "Nibcs, I think we should pull the covers down around her cage."

"Jail cell," she said. "I'm not an animal."

Lance pointed up ahead at a group of humans, camped out along the road.

"He's right. We don't want any trouble." Lance and I made sure to cover Eldrack up.

We arrived at the camp a few minutes later. There were four men sitting around a campfire. To say that they were not shining examples of humanity is an understatement. These men wore suspicion the way I wear underwear. I felt something I had never felt before.

Dread.

I found myself stroking Gerald's head to help calm my nerves.

As we approached these men, I realized what a sheltered life I had led, for I had always lived in a well-organized and safe kingdom. Yes, our village has petty crime from time to time, and sure, sometimes people hurt other people. But what we don't have in our civilized world is a brutal disregard for everyone who isn't you. And I think it comes down to one thing: in the kingdom, there are always other people around.

People do funny things when no one else is looking. And by *funny*, I mean awful.

So here we were, two tweens and a gork prisoner, at the mercy of these four rugged hoodlums, on a road in the middle of the wilderness, with no one else around.

It occurred to me that Lieutenant Thuffsburry was an irresponsible ass, not to mention Sergeant Smythe and the rest of those cowards who had banished us to begin with.

And to be clear, these rogues by the side of the road hadn't done anything. Yet.

But it was very clear that they could do whatever they wanted.

I glanced at Lance. "I got this," he murmured.

That was fine by me.

"What 'av we 'ere, Roger?" said the tallest bloke. He was a mean-looking individual with a large build and who clearly hadn't bathed in over a month. He had a crazed look in his eye, like he had gotten his head smashed by a bottle in one too tavern fights. He hopped up with surprising agility and sauntered over to us.

The bloke he was talking to, who, I am assuming, was named Roger, was even more frightening in that he didn't move a muscle. Just his eyes. He lay back against a tree, with a long piece of grass hanging from his mouth and a cockeyed hat obscuring part of his face.

"Looks like another prisoner transfer," Roger said. He had a reedy voice that was unsettling in a way that hadn't occurred to me before. His voice had a slight waiver that implied that he had gone off the deep end.

The other two stood up and walked to the opposite sides of our cart.

We were surrounded.

"I wouldn't get too close if I were you," said Lance. He said this very calmly. Almost matter-of-factly. Like he was doing these chaps a favor. "This one's diseased."

"Zat so?" said Tall Bloke.

"What disease has he got then, eh?" said Roger, who still hadn't moved.

"Pox."

"Right. The pox," said Roger. He sniffed and tilted his hat back. "Funny. Every gork prisoner who passes through here seems to have the pox. And yet . . . none of the guards ever seem to have it."

Huh. That surprised me. I was actually pretty impressed with Lance's quick-thinking. But apparently, others had tried it, too. And failed.

Roger stood up. Slowly. "Here's what's going to happen next," he said. "You two are going to walk away. And the good news is you will get to live out the rest of your sorry lives with all of your limbs intact."

"What are you going to do with her?" I asked before I could stop myself.

"Her?" said Tall Bloke. "Look, Rog, we got ourselves a she-gork!"

"Even better," said Roger, pulling out a large knife. The difference in size between his blade and my short sword was only a few inches. He gazed lovingly at his weapon. He even stroked it. Then he looked at me. "We're just gonna talk is all. Now buzz off."

While I was distracted by Roger and his knife, Tall Bloke pulled away the cover. Eldrack was crouched in the front right corner of the cage—jail.

"Pretty," Tall Bloke said, revealing several missing teeth in his smile.

Eldrack said something along the lines of, "Cuss you, you ugly cusswad. Your face looks like a cuss stepped on a cuss and cussed out a cuss," which drew a laugh from the four villains.

I don't know why I cared what happened to Eldrack. After all, she had been nothing but mean to me. And she was a gork. Our enemy. But I did care. And not because it was our sworn duty or any of that nonsense. I just felt the need to protect her. I believed her story. She hadn't done anything wrong. And she had already suffered enough at the hands of man.

While the men were laughing at Eldrack's insults—and again, I don't know where these ideas come from—I whipped out Nancy and poked Arthur the ox right square in the butt.

This had the desired effect. The poor ox had been quietly munching on some hay. And then suddenly his eyes grew wide and he sprang to life, and sprinted down the path, pulling Eldrack's jail with him.

The thing about oxen: They aren't fast. But they are almost impossible to stop.

He ran straight at Roger, who had to dive out of the way. The other men were too startled to realize what was happening, so Lance and I—and thank goodness Lance was on the same page—took off after the cart.

The chase was on.

I'm not particularly fast, but I was scared, and that counts for something.

The good news was that, because the woods were so thick, the ox didn't have any choice but to run down the road. The bad news was we had nowhere else to go. So it was quickly becoming a question of who would get tired first.

Lance was doing a rather good job of keeping up with the cart. I, however, was starting to get winded. I could hear Roger gaining on me. Gerald bounced around in his little hammock, clearly not pleased with the whole situation. I was a bit concerned for him, but there wasn't much I could do about it at the moment.

Gerald! That reminded me!

I could almost feel Roger's breath on my neck he was so close. In another second, he would be able to reach out and grab me.

I reached into my pocket and grabbed a handful of Gerald's birdseed and threw it into Roger's face.

It worked.

He clearly wasn't expecting that and, given that he was running at full speed, and it seems that a seed or two got him in the eyes, he stumbled and fell, and rolled to a halt.

That gained me some time, but I was quickly running out of air. I could see Tall Bloke and one of his friends—the fourth villain had given up a while ago—were still coming after me. I turned around and tried to keep going.

Then I noticed that the cart was slowing down. Clearly, our ox had had enough of this nonsense.

This was a problem. I suppose I could have run up and poked it in the rear again, but frankly, I didn't know how much more of this running I could take.

Lance had a better idea.

He and the cart were several dozen yards ahead of me. He pulled out his sword and smashed the cart's lock open. Eldrack bounded out of her cell and ran towards me. I threw my sword to her and she—rather amazingly—grabbed it, jumped in the air past me, and slashed at Tall Bloke.

Luckily for him, he was too startled by what was happening and too winded from having run for several minutes, that he stumbled and fell before she could strike him.

"Don't!" I yelled, for it looked as though she was going to stab the fallen fellow. She glanced back at me, turned the sword upside down, and conked him on the head. She stood there, swinging her sword, staring down at the last remaining assailant, who decided that perhaps he had better things to do than mess with an angry, armed gork. He came to a stop several yards away from her, held up his hands, and backed away.

We had won!

I fell to my knees, gasping for breath. Eldrack came walking back to me, swinging the sword.

She stood over me for a second.

I looked up, honestly having no idea what she would do next.

She swung the sword around, causing me to flinch. Then she grabbed it by its blade and thrust the handle down to me.

"Your sword sucks," she said.

"Don't say that," I said in between gasps. "You'll hurt poor Nancy's feelings."

She helped me stand back up, and we walked to the cart.

"We'd better keep moving," Lance said.

Eldrack made ready to climb back into her jail cell.

"Hang on," I said. I climbed in and lay down. "I need the rest."

"God, you humans are pathetic."

"You're welcome," said Lance. He climbed on top of the cage—just like when we were carted away to school—and also lay down. Eldrack sighed, took up the reins, and led us on our way.

Chapter Sixteen

I MUST HAVE DOZED for a while. When I came to, I was in one of those states when you're not sure if you're awake or asleep, because this was the second time in two months I had awoken in a jail cart. When I finally collected my thoughts, I realized where I was, but not quite sure why we were all where we were. I sat up and turned to see if Eldrack was still with us. I wouldn't have blamed us if she had fled for the hills. But she was there, guiding the ox, with Lance walking beside her. I crawled out from the jail cart and caught up to them.

"Comrade Nibel!" smiled Lance. "So glad you could join us!"

"Why are you still here?" I asked Eldrack. And then I immediately realized how rude that sounded. "I mean, we're only taking you to another jail, aren't we? I'm sure I speak for Lance when I say we don't care if you escape."

"I already offered that route to her, old thing," said Lance.

"I appreciate that," said Eldrack. "But these woods are swarming with human scum—no offense."

"None taken," I said. I thought about my own recent encounters with humans—those hooligans, the intelligence officers, Smythe. I wasn't so sure I really was on the side of the good guys.

"If I were captured again, they would just bring me back to be tortured. But if I play it straight and go with you guys, they'll exchange me for a human prisoner, and I'll get to go home and see my parents. I haven't seen them in two years. They probably think I'm dead."

"Two years?" I swallowed. For some reason, I had assumed she had been taken after the attack on the palace. My thoughts turned to the screams I had heard last night at the fort. The idea that Eldrack had been tortured like that—for two years—made me sick to my stomach. "I had no idea," I said meekly.

"How old are you, Eldrack?" Lance asked.

"Fourteen," she said.

"You mean humans kidnapped a twelve-year-old?" said Lance.

"I thought you said you were a woman?" I said, trying to change the subject.

"What do you call a fourteen-year-old human?"

"A teenager. Like us."

"Hang on," said Lance. He was peering down the path. For a moment, I was scared we'd see another band of bandits, but I could make out what looked like soldiers and some horses, a couple of tents.

"Must be coming up to a patrol."

"Uh," said Lance looking at Eldrack. "You might want to climb back in the cart."

She sighed but nodded. "I guess it wouldn't look too good for you to have the enemy walking freely beside you, huh?"

"Sorry," I said, helping her back into her cell. I closed the gate. I went to lock it and was startled to see the lock had been smashed open. Then I remembered Lance's bold move with Wilma when those ruffians had been chasing us. "What are we gonna do about the lock?"

"Hope no one looks too closely?" said Lance.

"You guys are pathetic," said Eldrack. She reached through the bars, grabbed the lock, and squeezed it really hard with her hands. Slowly but surely she bent it back into shape. Or, at least something that looked passably good. The fact that she had done this with a broken arm made me blanch.

I lowered the tarp and joined Lance up in front of the ox.

As we neared the patrol, a soldier stepped out in front of us and held up his hand. We pulled the ox to a stop. The soldier—a sergeant—approached us.

"Cadets?" he said.

Lance and I looked at each other.

"They must be desperate back there to be sending cadets on prisoner transport."

"Awfully desperate, sir," Lance said.

"Let's see what you got."

He lifted the cover and inspected Eldrack.

"Sir?" I said, trying to distract him so he wouldn't notice the lock. "We were attacked."

He looked sharply at me. A few other soldiers took notice and approached us.

"Where?"

"A few klicks back," I said, relishing to use of the word klick. It had always sounded so manly whenever my dad would say it. Even Lance gave me a surreptitious thumbs-up.

"How did you escape?"

"What's up with your lock?" said another soldier.

"Well, that happened during the attack," I said. And I launched into a somewhat-true version of events, minus the whole part about letting Eldrack out of her cell.

"Birdseed?" laughed the sergeant. "That's the greatest thing I've ever heard!"

The rest of the troop laughed as well. One soldier even smacked me on the back, sending me flying forward a few steps and sent Gerald flying out of his little hammock. He fluttered dizzily into the air, which elicited more laughs. The soldiers laughed even harder when plopped back on to my shoulder, clinging on for dear life.

"Awww, 'ees got a wittle girlfriend," laughed one soldier.

"Simmons!" snapped the sergeant to the laughing soldier. "Hook these gentlemen up with a fresh lock. And make it a good one."

"You don't know how lucky you gents are," he said to us. "If this thing," he pointed at Eldrack, "had known how badly damaged your lock was, it could have ripped open the gate in no time at all and eaten you."

I glanced at Eldrack, who gave me a surreptitious eye-roll.

Simmons pried off the old lock and put on a fresh one. He tossed the key to the sergeant, who then handed it to me.

"The way up ahead is totally clear," said the sergeant. "We're actually on our way back to the kingdom, so we'll track down those bandits of yours and punish them. Good work, cadets."

He pulled down the cart cover and smacked our ox on its rear end. We were on our way once again.

We walked in silence for twenty minutes or so to get away from all the soldiers, then I reached over and pulled up the cover to let Eldrack out of her jail cell. She looked like she had been mulling something over in her head, and she spoke up before I could let her out.

"What are you going to do after you drop me off? More prisoner transports?"

"Not us, Comrade Eldrack," said Lance. "We're on a quest!"

"You two?"

"You laugh at us?" I said. "Didn't you see how we took care of those villains back there?"

She laughed. "Oh, I saw all right. I hope you don't run out of birdseed. What are you questing for?"

"The mythical Relic of the First Age," said Lance.

"Or," I said to Lance, "was it the magical Relic?"

"The Amulet of Ashokenah?"

"The what?"

"Good luck finding that. We gorks have been looking for that for ages."

"The what of who?" I said. I'm not good with names. Or words, for that matter.

"The Amulet of Ashokenah. An amulet is a magical object. Like a pendant or a ring or something."

"What is with all this magical jewelry and panties? Why not magical swords, or daggers, or meatloaves?"

"A magical meatloaf?" said Lance.

"I'm hungry."

"Anyway," said Eldrack, "This amulet was a gift to the gorks from Ashokenah, back in the First Age."

"Who?"

"Ashokenah?" she said. "God?"

"Gorks have gods?"

"One God," she said.

"Oh," I said. "How come I've never heard of him?"

"Because you're a heathen idiot?" she said.

"That sounds about right."

"What was this chap's name again?" said Lance.

"Ashokenah the Almighty! Ashokenah the Terrible! Ashokenah the All-Seeing! Ashokenah who spake 'Go forth and smite all who would deny me!' Ashokenah The One True God." She said all of this with no small amount of . . . well, let's call it anger, in her voice.

"I feel like I've heard that name before . . ." said Lance.

"He sounds like a buzz kill," I said. "Say, Lance. If we ever get around to throwing a party, let's make sure we don't invite that guy."

"Are you defiling the name of Ashokenah who begat Meblechtick?" she said. "Ashokenah who begat Kustarrich? Ashokenah who begat Arafenna and Dromona and the mighty Abzanenka?"

"Wow," Lance said, suddenly impressed. "That is a lot of begetting."

"Now he definitely can't come to our party," I added. "He'll steal all the girls."

"You dare mock our God, human scum?" said a deep voice from behind us.

To say that we were startled is an understatement.

I jumped and turned around. Three gork soldiers emerged from the woods, fully armed, and looking none-too-pleased with our recent comments. Their sheer size surprised me. Eldrack was only maybe six inches taller than me. And because she called herself a woman, I had assumed every gork was roughly her size. But these blokes were each two feet taller than me, and their shoulders were a foot wider. Muscles bulged out from, well, from everywhere. Even their ears had muscles.

"Bleeding bells!" I said, stumbling backwards and falling to the ground. The force of the impact sent Gerald flying off of me.

"Don't kill us!" I tried to crawl away as fast as I could.

The gorks were in no rush. The leader quietly strode forward and planted his foot on my left shin, pinning it to the ground and preventing me from squirming away. One of the other gorks grabbed Lance by the throat. The third gork grabbed Arthur's reins to stop him.

"Why should we spare a couple of insulting heathen idiots who are holding a fellow gork prisoner?" he said.

"We're cute?" I offered, trying to flash a winning smile.

"Don't kill them," said Eldrack. "They're bumbling, blithering, heathen idiots, but they're OK."

"And why should we care what you think?" said the leader. "You who have allowed yourself to be taken prisoner by humans?"

Eldrack looked down at the floor of her cage in shame. I know I should have been worried about my own destiny, but I couldn't help but feel bad for her. She had only been twelve when she was captured. I couldn't see how that made her weak or shameful.

"No," said the leader. "We will kill them, just as Ashokenah commanded us to."

And with that, he grabbed me by my vest and picked me up off the ground. It was such an effortless motion on his part. He wasn't struggling under my weight at all. I couldn't help but wonder just how in the bloody hell humans had ever won any battle against them, let alone two wars.

He slammed me down on a large rock.

"Ashokenah! I sacrifice this infidel in your name—"

"Oh! Wait! Ashokenah!" said Lance, who had clearly not been paying any attention to the fact that his best friend was about to be murdered. "I knew I'd heard that name before! I saw a necklace that belonged to him once."

"Necklace?" said the gork leader, suddenly paying attention to something other than killing me.

"Lance," I said as gingerly as possible, "Not to quibble in the middle of your distraction, but were you really thinking about necklaces in my time of need? I am about to be sacrificed here."

"Oh! Quite right. Sorry, comrade. You now have my complete attention. Proceed, gork person. And Nigel, I am deeply moved and sorry about what is about to happen to you."

"Thank you."

But the gork leader let go of me. He grabbed Lance and picked him up off the ground and held him there, shaking him so that Lance's legs flailed about like a ragdoll.

"You've seen the Amulet of Ashokenah?" demanded the gork.

"Is that what that was? It was all the rage a few years back. Some bloke named . . . uh . . . Quiggly or something—"

"Quint the Defiler?"

"The very fellow, although I don't remember that being his last name. Anyhoo, he discovered the thing—"

"You mean he stole it from the Lost City of Anafenza?"

"As you like. He brought it back to the kingdom and took it on a national tour, passing through all the museums—"

"Museums! Our sacred relic is being defiled by your people!" He shook Lance as he said this.

"I think I'm going to vomit," Lance said.

"Where is the amulet now?"

"Oh I say, I don't know. Do you, Nige? Nigel?"

"I was not sneaking off just then," I said from behind a large bush. "I was only coming around this way to get a better view of your imminent death."

The gorks were not amused. One of them picked me up and slung me over his shoulder.

"Oooof!" I said, which is about the only thing you can say when a gork throws you over his shoulder. The gork leader threw Lance onto his shoulder, too.

"Where are you taking us?"

"Back to our people. We are going to torture you until you tell us the location of the Amulet."

"Oh, no need for all that, my good man," I said. "It's in the National Museum."

The gork leader dropped Lance and grabbed me from the other gork's clutches.

"Where is this museum you speak of?"

"Don't tell him, Nigel!"

"In our capital. Right next to Newishgate, on the corner of Dryde Park."

"I can't believe you just told them!" said Lance.

"I don't want to be tortured!" I added, "Who cares? Let them get their sacred relic back."

"But that's the magical Relic of the First Age we were sent to recover!" said Lance.

"Oh, right! Sorry. I got a bit confused back there when I thought we were about to die."

"We will attack your city and destroy every building," the gork leader said, pulling me close to his face as if to drive these points home. "We will slaughter your people and defile your monuments. And then, and only then, will we recover our sacred relic. The power that resides in that relic will enable us to destroy humanity once and for all!"

"Way to go, Nigel."

I shrugged. The other two gorks cheered.

"And now we have no further need for you two," said the leader.

"Just when I thought this day couldn't get any worse," I said.

The gork leader slammed me down on a rock.

"Ooof!" I said.

"I sacrifice this infidel in the name of Ashokenah," the gork leader said. Then he raised a sharp, gleaming sword—the kind of sword that looked like it had a hard-won name, like Scumslayer—and brought it down towards my head.

And then, he just fell over.

On me.

"Ooof!" I said again.

The gork was dead. He was dead, and he was on top of me, his face pressing up against mine, his blood dripping onto my cheek.

I was a tad bit conflicted about this sudden turn of events. On the one hand, I was happy it was the gork who was dead and not me. But on the other hand . . . having an enormous, dead gork lying on top of you is no picnic.

I was about to scream—mostly because I didn't know what else to say— when I noticed a crossbow bolt sticking out of the dead gork's head. So, instead of yelling, I twisted my head to see where the bolt had come from. I saw the sergeant we had recently passed on the trail, striding towards me, loading another bolt into his crossbow.

I pushed the deceased gork off me and started to get up, when another dead gork landed on me, pinning my arms to the ground, and covering me with more gork blood. This time I did scream. I mean, a bloke can only take so many dead gorks falling on him before he snaps. And in my case, that number of dead gorks was two.

I squirmed around for a moment until I could finally free my arms, at which point I was able to get enough leverage to be able to shove the second gork off of me. I scrambled out of the way before any more gorks could fall on me.

The last remaining gork picked Lance up to use him as a human shield, and he was able to buy enough time to push his way to the tree line, where he threw Lance at the soldiers and dashed off into the woods.

"Ooof!" said Lance, which made me feel a little less like a wimp.

"Get him!" shouted the sergeant, and a couple of men sprinted into the woods.

"You two OK?" said the sergeant.

"Ow," said Lance, lying in a heap on the ground.

"I never want to have another dead gork fall on me, if that's OK with you," I said. And then I said, "Thank you for rescuing us."

"How did you know we were in trouble?" asked Lance as he slowly rose from the ground.

The sergeant whistled sharply. At first, I thought this was some weird military way of answering questions, but then Gerald flew down and landed on my shoulder.

"Gerald!"

"Pesky little bugger came flying over to us, all agitated, so we figured you chaps were in the soup."

OK, I'll admit it, a wee little tear welled up in my eye. This little bird had saved our lives! I stroked his head and fed him some birdseed. "Thanks, mate," I said quietly.

The two soldiers who had gone after the gork came back to us.

"He was too fast for us, sir."

"Never mind," said the sergeant. "He can't hurt us now."

I blanched and looked at Lance, who eyed me back, clearly thinking the same thing: That gork, thanks to me, now knew where to find the Amulet of Ashokenah, Last Relic of the First Age. And while neither Lance nor I knew exactly what this amulet could do, we knew that both the humans and the gorks wanted it. Badly.

I gulped.

Chapter Seventeen

THE SERGEANT GAVE us a two-soldier escort for the rest of our
trip to Fort Phipps, and, perhaps because of their presence, our journey
was uneventful.

Each day we walked at a steady pace, though mostly in silence. Each
night we set up camp, cooked our food over a roaring fire, and slept under
the stars. Our two soldier friends generally kept to themselves. I could tell
they thought of this as the military version of babysitting, but that was fine
by me. At least they weren't jerks to us like every other soldier had been.
And they completely ignored Eldrack, which was also a welcome change.

As comforting as it was to have professional soldiers watching over us,
on the downside, we couldn't speak to Eldrack. This felt surprisingly weird.
Surprising, because we had only gotten to know her over a single day. But
what a day that had been. Eldrack had gone from being a complete mystery
to someone I could have almost seen as a friend. And yet, as the attack by
her fellow gorks—as well as the brutal response by our countrymen—had
shown, we were destined to be enemies.

I certainly didn't think of her as an enemy.

There were a lot of things I wanted to say to her, although frankly, even if the soldiers hadn't been around, I'm not sure I could have put my conflicting emotions into words. I was sorry she was being borne away in a jail cart that I knew from personal experience was not comfortable. I was sorry two of her fellow countrymen had been killed right in front of her. And I was sorry about this whole bloody stupid war that was brewing because I knew it was only going to get worse. There would be more bloodshed, torture, pain, and misery.

I couldn't say any of that, which was doubly frustrating because she was only a few feet away, and I had to pretend as though I had never spoken to her before.

At least I had Lance. The soldiers didn't pay us any mind, so we had some freedom to speak, though we tried to keep things on the quiet side. We didn't want the soldiers hearing about how I had just sealed humanity's fate.

"You're an idiot," said Lance.

"I know."

"You've completely ruined everything."

"I can only say I'm sorry so many times."

Lance sniffed. "I don't know that that's true."

We walked a bit. And then, while the soldiers were busy arguing over some girl, he leaned in and mumbled, "Quite ironic them sending us off on a mission to find this magical thing when they've had it sitting in their own museum all this time."

"I know, right?" I said, perhaps a wee bit too eagerly, but I was just happy he wasn't mad at me. "How could they not know?"

"I guess they just thought it was some ancient treasure."

"But hey, let's look on the bright side. At least we've found the bloody thing. I say we send a raven to Captain Phoughton, tell him where it is, and ask him if we can come home."

"Sounds like a plan," said Lance, before adding: "But you're still an idiot."

We were so engrossed in our conversation we walked into our soldier friends.

"Oy! Watch where you're going, cadets!" said one soldier.

"We're here," said the other.

There it was. Fort Phipps. Spread out before us like a grand buffet. The word fort had led me to think that this would be some puny wooden structure, not unlike that prison outpost, but Fort Phipps was a castle, maybe a third the size of the Royal Academy. Its walls were twenty feet high, and I spied dozens of archers patrolling the battlements. Outside the castle, hundreds of soldiers ran drills and marched in formation. To the west of the castle stood several buildings and even a market.

One of the soldiers nudged me with an elbow. "See those woods?" I looked where he was pointing. There, 200 yards to the east, stood a vast, ancient forest. "That is the Gorkish Empire." A brilliant, beautiful ruby maple tree caught my eye, and I found myself wondering if that tree knew that it lay inside the most-evil empire known to man.

No wonder this fortress was built like this. Should the gorks decide they wanted to invade, this would be the first place they would attack.

"Right," said the other soldier. "Our orders were to deliver you to Fort Phipps. We've done that. So we'll be on our way. Good luck with everything."

"Do you know where we can send a raven?" I asked.

"First, you need to deliver your prisoner."

I had been so gobsmacked at seeing the Gorkish Empire that I had utterly forgotten about Eldrack.

"Where do we take her?"

He pointed at a wide brick building outside of the castle. The soldiers gave us a salute, bid us goodbye, and headed straight into the nearest tavern.

I looked at Lance. He shrugged. I wanted to speak to Eldrack, but there were too many people around, so we led the ox in silence.

As we approached the building we could see a sign over the entrance that said "Gaol."

"What's a gaol?" Lance asked, mostly to himself.

"It's a jail," sneered a passerby. "A jail. You never heard of a jail before, you dumb skug?"

"What's a skug?" I asked.

"Boy, you two are idiots, ain't ya?" The passerby, who was no longer passing by, began waving his arms in the air. "Hey, everyone. Look at the two idiots who ain't never heard of no jail or no skug!"

People mostly ignored him, but that didn't stop him from sneering at us and giggling.

"Yer boot's untied," he said to me with a dopey grin on his face and drool coming down the side of his mouth. Now, I'm no stranger to the whole "your boots untied" trick, whereby you tell someone their boot is untied and then pop them in the face when they bend down to look, so rather than fall for that, I bid him a good day and proceeded to walk towards the "gaol."

And I promptly tripped on my untied bootlace and fell on my face.

In the mud.

That set the pesky peasant laughing all over again and saying things like, "The idiot can't even tie his bootlace!" Thankfully, he didn't stick around.

"Stupid boots," I said. Lance led the ox towards our destination while I attended to my laces.

At the jail's entrance, a beefy guard sidled up to us.

"Prisoner?"

Lance uncovered the cart. The guard said something disgusting about Eldrack being a female that I won't repeat here and told us to take the cart inside and meet up with the warden.

We entered the building, and I braced myself, expecting to hear howls of pain like we did back at the fort. But I didn't. Instead, I saw room after room of gorks chained to tables, sewing leather. Lance and I exchanged looks as we continued down the main hall. I glanced down at Eldrack. She seemed even more puzzled by the sight than I was.

"Are they sewing?" she murmured.

"Looks like it," I whispered.

A look of disgust crept over her face. "Gorks don't sew."

A tall, rotund man with a curly-white mustache strolled on over to us and held up his hand. We pulled Arthur to a halt.

"Howdy, boys. Name's Jessep. I'm warden here." He had a strong Western accent, which was rare this far to the east.

He didn't wait for us to introduce ourselves. He knelt and inspected Eldrack.

"Oooh-wee, we got ourselves a fine, strong, young female, now, don't we?" He was practically drooling as he said this. "What are you, darlin', 'bout fourteen years old?"

"Eat mud," said Eldrack.

"Well, now! Feisty!"

He stood up. "Y'all can hand me the key. I'll take real good care of her."

"How long before you exchange her for a human prisoner?"

"Human? Ha! Naw, see, we don't do that no more. This here's a work camp."

"But we had been told . . ."

"Yeah, I know the drill. But there ain't been no human prisoners to exchange since the war." He held out his hand for the key.

"How long do they stay here?"

"Oh, they ain't leaving, son, don't you worry about that. Naw, see, they's here for life."

I gulped, remembering the moment when Eldrack could have run away but chose instead to come here to be exchanged.

The warden continued, "Used to could punish them and do a little torture and such." He sighed, thinking about the good old days. "But we ain't allowed anymore. Naw, now all we can do is crush their spirits with endless menial labor."

"Well, that's still pretty evil," I said.

"Yeah? Thanks for saying that. But it's not the same. I like getting my hands dirty, know what I mean?" He sighed. "Nowadays I mostly sit around filling out paperwork."

"What are they making?" asked Lance.

"Boots," he said. He pointed at my feet. "The kind you're wearing, in fact."

"They made these?" I felt sick.

"Sure did. How do you like 'em?"

"They're terrible."

"Yeah, ain't they? Cheap, though. Anyways," he said, once again holding out his hand for the key, "You can turn her over to me. I'll put her to work straightaway, I promise. She won't never see daylight again." He even winked at me as he said this.

My mouth went dry. I could feel Lance and Eldrack's eyes drilling into me, but what choice did I have? I grabbed the chain around my neck, lifted it over my head, and handed him the key.

"I guess you'll wanna be reporting for duty back at the gatehouse," he said, thumbing in the direction we needed to go.

I looked down at Eldrack and could feel a tear welling up in my eye. I turned away so the warden wouldn't see me.

"Thanks," I said.

And I started walking away. Lance paused a second and then followed me.

"Guards!" the warden said. And two enormous soldiers walked over to the back of the cart.

"Hey now!" said the warden. "Don't forget yer ox. They'll be wanting him back at the gate."

He unhooked Arthur from the cage and led him over to me.

I took the reins and watched the guards as they tried to coax Eldrack out of her cage. They did so by poking her with their swords. One of them must have poked her hard, for Eldrack let out a curse word.

"Don't be damaging the goods, now," said the Warden, turning back to his prize.

The guards kept prodding Eldrack until they eventually got her out of the cage. I couldn't look at her; but then I made the mistake of looking at a cell on my left. Inside were two gorks, who paid no attention to Eldrack. They just kept right on sewing. They looked older than Eldrack. Way older. They had a greyish pallor to their skin. I gathered that they had been captives so long that a new prisoner didn't interest them in the slightest.

I shivered. That was about to be Eldrack's fate.

A horrible idea came to me. I tried to push it away because it meant ruining Lance's and my chance at returning home, but it wouldn't let go of me.

"Forgive me, comrade," I mumbled, "I'm about to do something really stupid."

Chapter Eighteen

"RIGHT BEHIND YOU, mate," said Lance.

I looked back at Eldrack. The guards were trying to attach a huge iron to her leg, but she wasn't giving up the fight.

One guard slowly uncoiled a long whip.

I drew my sword.

"Do it, brother," he said.

"Sorry, Arthur, old pal." And then I took my sword and poked him in the bum.

"Oooooo!" said the ox, for I think I must have hit the same spot I had poked the other day.

But, like a dependable friend, he jolted forward and charged straight at the guards. I yelled to Eldrack to get out of the way, but she was way ahead of me. Seeing that the guards were distracted by the onrushing ox, she punched one of them in the jaw, knocking him down. Then she leapt out of the way— just in time to avoid being run over—and started sprinting towards us.

"Look out, kids!" said the Warden.

We spun around and bolted for the exit. Eldrack was right behind us. As we ran past jail cell after jail cell, a wave of shouting followed us. Every gork in the place was inspired by the sight of one of their own running for freedom.

We were forty feet from the exit when that beefy guard poked his head around the corner to see what was causing all the ruckus. I can still picture the look on his face at the sight of the three of us charging at him. I guess in all the years that this place had been open no gork had ever escaped.

"Save the kids!" shouted the warden.

The guard whipped out his broad sword and struck his battle stance. He made for a very imposing figure.

"Duck, cadets!"

He sliced through the air, about chest high—a move Lance and I knew well from our training in military school. We both fell to our knees onto the wooden floor, and our momentum allowed us to slide under the sword. Gerald flew up in the air, over the sword, and Eldrack took that same route with a great leap. She landed on the other side of the soldier and kicked him, sending him flying back into the jail.

"Where to?" said Lance as we hopped back up and started running again.

I reached up and grabbed Gerald and tucked him into my arm. I knew he wouldn't be able to hang on to me for an extended run. I looked for the nearest tree line and dashed towards it. Lance and Eldrack followed.

At first, I was afraid all the people in the market would get in our way, but that changed the minute one merchant looked up from his work, saw a rampaging gork coming right at him, and screamed. The rest of the crowd panicked and dove out of our way.

So far, so good, I thought. I figured we'd be at the trees in two minutes.

I heard a whistle coming from the jail, and the warden's high voice carrying across the field, "Escapee! Heading west!" He blew the whistle several more times.

To our left, I saw an entire regiment jump to life. Their sergeant shouted orders, men scrambled into formation, archers nocked arrows, and crossbowmen cocked their bows. Their actions were so frenzied I got the distinct impression these chaps had never had anything so exciting happen to them before.

The sergeant raised his sword. Fifty soldiers launched themselves straight at us. I knew we would make it to the woods before they did, but after that, I didn't know how long I could keep going. My legs were already starting to burn.

"Hold your fire!" shouted the warden. "You'll hit the kids!"

Hit the kids? I thought. I mean, that was awfully nice of him and all, but we had just committed treason. We were fair game.

And then it hit me: They didn't know we were helping Eldrack to escape. They thought she was chasing us!

"Split up, cadets!" one soldier from the regiment shouted to us. "She can't chase—"

That was all he could say before the three of us plunged into the thick forest.

"Where to?" said Eldrack.

"Just keep going. They're gaining on us," huffed Lance.

"Ohmygods," I said, "I'm gonna die."

"You're going to die if you don't keep running," Eldrack said. She wasn't out of breath at all.

Running through woods was a lot harder than I thought it would be. I don't know how we didn't trip, with all the vines and dead branches reaching up to entangle us.

"This way, sergeant!" said one soldier, who was a lot closer to us than I thought was possible.

I heard a distant, familiar sound.

"Over here!" I said, darting left under a fallen tree.

The woods thickened to the point where running was impossible, which made me start to panic a bit.

"Where are we going?" said Lance. He unsheathed Wilma and started slashing at the growth.

Duh! Why didn't I think of that? I drew Nancy and began chopping away, too. We made swifter progress. Eldrack followed behind me.

"I hear a river up ahead."

"I can't swim," said Eldrack.

"Time to learn."

We hacked and pulled our way through an especially dense copse. We finally broke out into the open, and there it was: a beautiful, wide, slow-moving river.

"I can't go in there! Gorks can't swim!"

A bolt flew past her right shoulder.

We spun around. The regiment was almost upon us.

"Back away from those cadets, gork, or we'll shoot!" said one soldier.

"You already shot!" she said, which was a fair point.

A crossbowman took aim.

"I'm sorry," I said.

And then I tackled Eldrack into the river.

I was not prepared for how bloody cold the water was going to be. I should have been, given that we were still in the middle of winter, but, in all the commotion, I hadn't had time to think things through. The water was so cold it made me gasp, which is precisely the wrong thing to do when you're underwater. So I tried to swim to the surface to get some air, only that was a lot harder to do than I was expecting, which brings me to the second thing I noticed:

A cadet's military uniform is a terrible bathing suit.

Not only was my uniform heavy, but my sword and backpack were dragging me down. I started to panic a bit, fearing I'd never get back up to the surface. I let go of Nancy and pulled my way up. Frankly, if it hadn't been for all those pushups Smythe had made me do, I'm not sure I would have made it.

I finally broke the surface, gulped some air, and that's when I noticed the third thing: this river wasn't so slow moving after all. I couldn't even see the soldiers or the spot from where I had jumped.

Lance surfaced next. Apparently, he had needed to ditch Wilma, too.

"Eldrack?" he said.

"Blast it all!" I said.

I took off my backpack and vest and threw them at Lance. Then I dove down to see if I could find her.

The visibility was awful. I swam around looking and grasping for her but came up empty. I resurfaced, looked at Lance, who shook his head, and I dove down again.

I was starting to panic. How long had it been since we jumped in—or rather, since I had pushed her? How long could a gork hold her breath?

Then I saw her, trying in vain to swim.

I was almost out of air myself, so I had to swim back up. I tried to keep my bearings so I wouldn't lose her. I surfaced, took a deep breath, and dove down where I thought she had been. It took longer to find her than I would have liked, but I did find her.

She was flailing about in a total panic.

I tried to move into position to save her, but she did what every drowning person does: She grabbed on and pulled me down.

I'm a good swimmer. It's one of the very few things I've ever been good at besides getting into trouble. My dad taught me how to swim when I was a wee lad. He also taught me how to save a drowning victim. But, he told me, the hard part isn't towing a person to safety, it's knowing how to deal with panic. People who are drowning aren't rational. They're not even thinking. They are just doing everything they can to try to get up to the surface. And if that means trying to use the rescuer as a ladder, then that's what they do. Even though Dad had told me this very thing would happen, I had forgotten, so Eldrack's actions took me by surprise.

Now I was panicking because Eldrack wouldn't let go and I was starting to run out of air myself.

Then I remembered, you have to shock a drowning person out of their panic just long enough for you to get a proper hold and save them. Pinching them is a good thing—the pain is usually enough to startle them. So I tried to pinch Eldrack, but her tolerance for pain is way higher than a human's, so that didn't work.

Now my lungs were starting to burn.

This is it, I thought. *Eldrack and I are going to drown, and it's all my fault. Everything that's happened to Lance, Eldrack, and me is all my fault. If I hadn't been such a mess-up, none of this would have happened. I wouldn't have even been sent off to military school. Instead, I'd still be at home trying to snog—*

That's it!

I reached up behind Eldrack's head and pulled her into me.

And I kissed her. On the lips.

She stopped flailing and looked at me like I was insane.

This was my moment.

I swung around behind her and slipped my left arm under her chin. And I pulled on the water with my right arm and kicked as hard as I could.

It felt like I wasn't getting anywhere.

I kicked and pulled and struggled, hoping against hope, my lungs searing with pain . . .

And then I surfaced and pulled Eldrack's head out of the water. We gasped for air.

So far, so good, but I was getting tired. It was hard enough for me to keep myself afloat, let alone a heavy gork as well.

"Lance!"

I felt myself starting to go down again when a hand grabbed my hair.

"Ow!" I said.

"Shut it, ya sissy!" He pulled us over to a log, and we grabbed on to it and pulled ourselves far enough out of the water where we could rest and finally catch our breath.

After a moment, I felt something land on my head. It was Gerald. In all the flurry of activity, I had completely forgotten about him. I had tossed him into the air when I shoved Eldrack into the river. He pecked at my head in annoyance.

"Sorry, old friend."

The current took us around a bend, close to shore.

"Over there," said Lance, pointing to a sandy beach. We kicked our way over until we were close enough to crawl onto the bank. We collapsed on the sand and just lay there, panting, for several minutes.

Eventually, Eldrack sat up and slapped me. Hard.

Chapter Nineteen

"YOU KISSED ME!"

"Let's not shout that out to the world, shall we?"

"On the lips!"

"You kissed her?" said Lance.

"It was a strategic decision; one I'm starting to regret."

"I'm curious, mate. How do you strategically kiss someone?"

Eldrack reached down and picked me up as though I weighed nothing.

"What are you, some kind of sicko?" she said.

"Was there tongue?" said Lance.

"Sue me, all right! I didn't know what else to do! We were both drowning."

"You have a thing for gorks?" she said.

"You're welcome for saving your life!"

"You mean you want me to thank you for saving my life after you tackled me into the river when I specifically told you gorks can't swim?"

"They were shooting at you!"

"Look, if you two are going to be boyfriend and girlfriend, I'm gonna leave," said Lance. "I didn't sign up to be a third wheel."

Eldrack looked at Lance and snorted. She dropped me.

"Well, now what?" said Eldrack.

"I need to put on some clothes, that would help," I said. And I wasn't kidding, either. Now that I wasn't exerting myself anymore, I was starting to shiver.

"But what is our long-term plan?" said Eldrack. "After all . . ."

My teeth started to clatter.

"What's wrong with you?"

"I'm freezing, that's what!"

"Yeah, I'm a bit cold myself," said Lance.

"You humans are pathetic."

"At least we can swim," I said.

"And, apparently, kiss at the same time," said Lance.

"Prison is starting to sound really appealing," said Eldrack.

We split up to collect firewood, and before long we built ourselves a roaring fire. I was a bit concerned the smoke would attract soldiers, but we had to risk it. Our need to not freeze outweighed our need to not get caught.

Eldrack proved to be rather adept at hunting, and she soon caught us three squirrels. I was a bit squeamish about eating one, but I was ravenous from all my exertion. I devoured the cute little thing the minute it was cooked. I fed Gerald some wet birdseed. He was not happy, but he ate it nevertheless.

After we ate, we warmed ourselves by the fire and discussed our options.

"Even if I could get back to my homeland, chances are pretty good I'd be ostracized for having been caught by humans in the first place. They'd see me as a disgrace to gork-kind. Then again," Eldrack said with a sigh, "there isn't any place in all of Esteria where I'd be welcome. We gorks have made a bit of a nuisance of ourselves."

"What's wrong, Nige?" asked Lance. A good bloke, that Lance. Always looking out for everyone else.

I sighed. "I just realized I'm never going home again."

"What? Now? Now you're realizing this? Didn't this occur to you when you were sent off to spend the rest of your life in the military? Or when we got permanently banished from the kingdom?"

"Yeah, but at least I had hope. I always thought I'd be able to find a way out of whatever predicament I'd gotten myself into. Even when we got banished from the kingdom, I still had hope of finding that amulet and returning home a hero. But now? Now there's no bloody hope at all, is there? We've just committed treason. That's a crime that is literally punishable by death."

"Maybe Captain Phoughton would forgive us if we told him where that amulet is?"

"What?" gasped Eldrack. "After everything you've seen of humankind, you'd still give them the most powerful weapon on Earth?"

"Well it's better than if the gorks get it," Lance said. "And unfortunately, thanks to your boyfriend, they know where it is now."

"What does that blasted thing do, anyway?" I asked.

Eldrack's anger softened a bit. She stirred the flame for a second before admitting: "No one knows. It's been thousands of years since anyone has even seen it. We've all heard the legends: that it can move mountains and level cities. But who knows? It may—and my brethren would call me a blasphemer for saying this—but it may just be a myth. For all we know, it's just a pretty necklace. Personally, I think when Elbo destroyed the Cufflinks, he destroyed all the magic in the world. Certainly, everyone else seems to think so."

"Well, both the human and gork authorities think it has magical powers, so we need to act like it does."

"And do what, exactly?" said Lance.

"Destroy it," I said.

"Are you insane?" Eldrack said.

"He is," said Lance. "He's bloody insane. I've been following a lunatic. And now look where it's gotten me."

"Look," I said. "Let's go over our options. One: We do nothing. We just drift along and scrape a living on the edges of civilization . . ."

"Sounds romantic," said Lance.

"Right, but the gorks are going to invade our kingdom. Thousands of humans and gorks will die. And if the gorks get their hands on it and it really is magical . . . well, history has shown us how that goes."

The two of them shrugged.

"Option two: We send that raven to Phoughton. And let's say they figure out how to use it. What then? I mean, we humans are no better than the gorks! Remember that prison warden? How creepy was that guy? Imagine him with the world's most powerful weapon? Or worse: Imagine Smythe with it."

Lance mumbled a bit, but he nodded and shrugged in agreement.

"What about the elves?" he said. "There are still a few of them left. We could give it to them."

"I'd rather die," said Eldrack. "I'd rather you humans had it than those cussing elves."

"You're forgetting how King Selron helped Stephanus hide the Cufflinks rather than destroy them so he could enjoy his magical panties. No. We have to take it to Mount Boo-Boo and destroy it. If it's half as powerful as Eldrack says we can't let anyone use it."

"All right. So what's your plan? How are we gonna break into the kingdom? In case you haven't noticed we're both marked," he held up his hand to show off that branded B, "and she isn't exactly going to get a welcome parade. Then, assuming we do get in, how are we going to steal it from the National Museum, which I don't need to remind you, is heavily guarded?

Then we have to take it through the Gorkish Empire, over the Mountains of Death, across the Sea of Destruction, through the Forest of Terror—"

"You're totally making those names up," I said.

"Actually, he's not," said Eldrack. "We gorks figured out a long time ago that if you give everything an awful name, you're less likely to be invaded. Although, it's not an empire. It's a kingdom. You humans love to call it the Gorkish Empire because you love to make us sound all scary. But we're just a kingdom. Like you."

"Even assuming we can do all of that," said Lance, ignoring Eldrack's little diatribe, "then what? We'll be on the other side of the Gorkish Emp— Kingdom. You'll be farther from home than ever. We'll still be traitors. And we won't even have a magical amulet to save us."

"I like to live by a code, comrade," I said. Lance huffed at that, but at least he cracked a smile. I continued in my best Lance impression. "I believe one has to do the right thing, even if it means making the ultimate sacrifice."

"That's rich," he said, but he could tell I was serious. He took a deep breath. "Listen, comrade, it took Elbo months to travel through all those places, and he had the help of a warrior king, an elf, a dwarf, a Wizard, and a giant eagle. And even with all of that he almost didn't succeed. What makes you think we can do it?"

"Gumption?" I said.

Lance sank his face into his hands.

"Look, I understand it sounds psychotic when you spell it all out like that. But if we just take it one step at a time, it won't be so bad. So for now, let's focus on step one. All we have to do—for now—is break into the kingdom. That shouldn't be so hard, right?"

Actually, it was surprisingly easy. I don't know what your kingdom is like, but it's not like there's a big wall up around our country. Yes, we have walls around our cities, but it's pretty easy to enter our kingdom without anyone knowing about it. We simply hiked west for a few days through the woods, until we came to the Moor River, which as I mentioned earlier, forms the Northern border of Amerigorn. We were a few klicks to the west of Shropsfordshire in a densely wooded area that seemed to be seldom traveled.

We waited until nightfall to make sure no hunters or fishermen spotted us. Then I stripped down to my underwear, handed Gerald over to Lance, and swam across the river. I towed a rope behind me that the lieutenant had included in my backpack. The water was freezing, but it was less swift than that last river had been, so I was able to make it across with little trouble.

I brought the rope over to a massive tree and tied a knot that Lance had taught me. I yanked on it three times. Lance and Eldrack pulled themselves across the river, along with a makeshift raft they had built to carry our equipment. Once they were across, we changed into dry clothes. We decided to leave the rope in place, in case we needed it for a quick getaway. Hopefully, someone wouldn't come along and take it.

We spent the rest of the night walking eastward through the Grand Woods until we could see Shropsfordshire. We crouched down behind some tall, leafy bushes and spied on the city, taking notes, and trying to come up with a plan. We were only a hundred yards north of the road where we had hiked to Fell's. It felt weird to be here: Last time I had seen the city from this angle, I'd been making plans to escape. Now I was trying to break back in.

To our left, we could see the walls of our school. To the right, at the other end of the city, stood the king's new palace. (After the earthquake had damaged Fell's, this palace had served as the king's temporary headquarters. Now, in the wake of the attack, the king was living there on a more permanent basis.) In between these two landmarks I could make out three of the city's famed gates: Newergate, Westgate, and, to the right, Newishgate, which was our target, because that would take us to the National Museum.

Dusk approached, so after getting a lay of the land, we backtracked deep into the woods and set up camp so we could hide during the daytime.

Eldrack managed to catch two squirrels and a fleetfox. Her reflexes were amazing. Faster than Prindella, even! A fleetfox is one of the fastest animals in Amerigorn, but Eldrack managed to snag one on her first try. We skinned the animals and cooked them over a small fire. Now that we were in the kingdom, we really didn't want to draw any attention to ourselves, but we needed to eat. The fleetfox was especially delicious.

"Well," said Eldrack, leaning back after finishing her meal, "we managed to accomplish step one, breaking into the kingdom. Now what?"

Just then a bird flew overhead. I blanched.

"Raven," I whispered.

Eldrack acted quickly. She grabbed a burning log and started waving it in the air.

I had forgotten ravens could be used to find us.

I know ravens aren't used everywhere as a means of communicating, but here in Esteria, we use them all the time—so much so that we take them for granted. But whenever someone from Wosteren visits us, they are amazed at this, and they always ask how it works. After all, it's not like you can give a bird an address and expect them to find it.

So: How do ravens and the other messenger birds of Esteria deliver messages? By smell. When I sent that letter to my mom, I wrote her name on the note and told the postiarian she lived in Bletchleysbum. The postiarian had a swatch of clothing with a specific smell for the postiary in Bletchleysbum, and the bird (a tufted titmouse, in my case) flew towards that smell. Once the bird arrived, the Bletchleysbum postiarian gave the bird a waft of my mom's swatch. The bird then, presumably, flew straight to her.

Most message birds, like the titmice (or is it titmouses?) and starlings of Esteria, don't have keen senses of smell. They're fine for messaging between postiaries, but not much else. But the Royal ravens of Esteria have a fantastic sense of smell. They can track down recipients no matter where they are. Those are the birds King Olerood and King Skidmark used for the Butt Declaration. They're also used by the military and local sheriffs' departments to search for wanted criminals.

Like us.

Eldrack kept waving the burning log to help mask our scent, and eventually, the raven flew away, but we weren't sure if the bird been able to identify us.

"That complicates things," said Lance.

"Could be unrelated to us," I said.

"We can't take that chance."

"How did you elude the ravens when you ran away from home?" I asked him.

"I burned everything I owned before I left, so they had nothing to give the birds."

Smart. We hadn't had that luxury when we got banished from the kingdom. We had left dozens of items behind at school that the military could use to track us down.

"Do we abort our mission?" asked Lance.

"No," I said. "If they're looking for us by raven, they're going to find us. We just need to get to that amulet and hope we can figure out how to use it before they capture us."

Chapter Twenty

SPOTTING THAT RAVEN changed things, but in a way, changed them for the better. Before that bird had shown up, we'd been suffering from what my dad used to call "analysis paralysis." We had come up with so many different strategies for busting into the city we couldn't decide which was best. We were going around in circles, arguing for and against each one. What's more, each option required us to do reconnaissance, which would take time and place us in danger.

The raven forced our hand. We had to make our assault that night.

We chose the most straightforward plan because it was something we could with little or no prep work: Eldrack would go to Westgate where she would cause a diversion, and hopefully, that would be enough to allow Lance and me to enter Newishgate. Then we were to meet at the museum. That was it.

And after that . . . well, we had no idea. We didn't know how many guards would be there waiting for us. And if we did manage to get into the museum, we didn't know where the amulet was. And, assuming we were able to find it, we didn't even know how—or if—it worked. And if any part of this ridiculous plan failed, we would be captured. Lance and I would be tried for treason and sent off to death row, and Eldrack would either be put to death or sent off to that jail in Fort Phipps, which was probably worse.

But we were committed. And we kept to our simple philosophy: One step at a time.

"How do I look?" asked Eldrack after putting on Lance's helmet. We hoped his uniform would better hide her most gork-like features.

"Like a gork," I said. "But hopefully no one will notice until it's too late."

"You look beautiful, my dear," said Lance. He even brought up her hand and kissed it.

I think she blushed. "This is why he gets all the girls," she told me.

"Does he now?" I said, smiling.

We bid her good luck and sent her north, to Westgate. She had practiced how to walk like a human, but she couldn't quite get it right, so we fashioned a cane for her, hoping people would take her for an elderly, wounded veteran.

"This will never work," I said, watching her hobble away.

"It only has to work long enough for us to get close."

We double-checked our outfits. Lance was dressed in Eldrack's leather vest, which didn't fit him very well, but it was good enough to keep him from freezing.

I sighed. "I miss Nancy."

"That crap sword?"

"She was my crap sword."

He patted me on the shoulders. "We should go."

No one looked at us twice as we emerged from the woods. I kept scanning the sky for ravens, but Lance told me to stop. "There's no hiding now, mate."

We soon joined the main thoroughfare and within minutes were surrounded by merchants, musicians, peasants, and others as they made their way towards the city.

The B that had been branded on my hand suddenly felt like a brightly lit beacon. I kept trying to find ways to casually hide my hand, but that seemed to be having the opposite effect—that of a person pretending to be someone who wasn't acting suspicious—so I stopped and tried instead to focus on Lance. But I was feeling paranoid. I even suspected that people had noticed the B, but were trying to remain quiet until they could alert the guards as to my presence.

Lance seemed perfectly at ease with the whole situation. He strolled along, casually nodding and winking at ladies as he bid them a good evening. And they all sighed and giggled and smiled and paid no attention to his hand or, thankfully, me.

The line moved steadily towards the gate, faster, in fact, than I was comfortable with. I worried we'd get to the guards before Eldrack could create her distraction. After all, the guards were sure to check our hands, and the minute they did that, the jig, as they say, would be up.

I was about to suggest to Lance that we find a reason to let people go in front of us, so we could buy some time when I heard a voice say, "What're you doing with gork armor?"

I looked around to see who had said this rather startling thing.

"Down here," said the voice.

Sure enough, there between us walked a person no higher than my waist.

It was an honest-to-gods halfling. I stared in amazement, for I had never seen one before. Height-wise this chap was the size of a four-year-old human, but whereas the bodies of human kids are proportioned differently than adults, with larger heads and such, this halfling looked like an adult human who had been shrunk half-size. Given that halflings were called halflings, this should not have been a surprise. But I found it hard not to stare.

Lance took it all in stride, as though he ran into halflings every other day. He smiled broadly, "I won it in a whist game."

"Oooh! You like to play whist, do ya? Funny, you showing up in gork armor only a few days after a gork escaped from Fort Phipps."

Honestly, there was nothing funny about that at all. Lots of kids our age wore equipment from the Really Big War—especially if it was from the Gorkish Emp—I mean Kingdom. It was cool. A friend of mine cherished a mace his grandfather had gotten off a dead gork. So, this halfling was just making trouble as halflings were known to do.

Still, I froze.

Well, I didn't exactly freeze—I kept walking—but the rest of me froze. And the halfling noticed.

"Ha!" said the halfling, "I knew—"

"My coin purse!" said Lance, searching his person. "My purse!"

I was baffled by this reaction from Lance. He didn't have a purse.

"You!" he said, pointing with his left hand at the halfling (to hide the B on his right hand). "Give me back my coin purse, you fiend!"

"I didn't take your purse!" said the halfling.

A crowd gathered. We were fifty yards away from the gate, which was not where we wanted to be causing a scene.

"What's all this then?" said a lanky merchant guiding an ox.

"This little imp stole my coin purse! And I want it back!"

"He's lying!" said the halfling.

"Sure 'e is," said the merchant, as he picked up the kicking and screaming little man. "That's what the last 'alfling said when I caught 'im stealing me pots and pans. Now 'and it over to 'im!"

"I'm the victim here! You people are stereotyping me!"

He wasn't wrong. Halflings were well known as the second most annoying creatures in the entire world (behind the mosquito). They were always making a nuisance of themselves. They were known to be drunkards, liars, and thieves. And every one of them claimed to be the nephew or niece of Elbo the Great. (In fact, when the world learned that it was a halfling who had destroyed the Cufflinks of Doom and saved the world, the collective response from humans, dwarves, and even the elves, was, "Great. Now we'll never hear the end of this.") Of course, these were broad stereotypes. Most halflings were wonderful, law-abiding citizens. (In fact, my father told me he knew several halflings he was proud to call friends.) So I felt terrible that we were doing this to this poor halfling . . . right up until he said:

"How could you do this to the nephew of the Elbo the Great? Remember when he saved your lives?"

Well, that was all the crowd needed to hear. They probably would have torn him asunder, were they not interrupted by a loud gong.

Everyone stopped.

GONG!

"That came from Westgate!" said the merchant.

"Must be the gork!" said another

"I told you!" said the halfling. But no one was paying any attention to him.

GONG!

"Safest place is in the city!" I said.

That started a stampede of humanity, all rushing towards Newishgate.

"It's a diversion!" said the halfling, his voice growing ever more distant. "You're being tricked!"

The gonging of the emergency bell continued.

The crowd bore down on the poor gate guards, who looked like they desperately wanted to be elsewhere.

One guard tried his best. "Please stay in an organized line—" but he was quickly and ruthlessly trampled.

We followed the horde in through the gates just as the other guards managed to lower the portcullis, thus stopping the crowd behind us. I looked back and saw the guards attending to their fallen comrade, who seemed to be OK.

"We did it!" I said.

"Let's just hope Eldrack made it through."

"This way to the museum."

We swam our way through the crowds. Clearly, the city had not done an adequate job of practicing emergency drills, for people were running in every direction.

"One gork caused all this panic," said Lance. "Crazy."

We arrived at Dryde Park and saw the museum on the left.

"Oh cuss," I said. Why did I say this? Because the museum was huge. Maybe half the size of the Royal Academy. It was three stories high and looked like it had a hundred rooms.

"How on earth are we going to find the amulet in that place?"

"One step at a time, comrade," Lance said with a wink.

He was right. First, we needed to get inside the blasted place. Then we would worry about finding the relic.

As we approached the museum, we scanned the entrance to see what we'd be dealing with. It looked like there were only two guards.

"This shouldn't be too hard," said Lance.

I hoped he was right. Something in the sky caught my eye.

A raven.

Well, as Lance said, there was no hiding now.

We sprinted up the stairs and ran over to the huge, wooden doors. The guards approached us.

"Tally ho, my good men!" said Lance with a huge smile.

"Museum's closed," said a guard.

"So it is. And with good reason, too! There's a gork on the loose."

"Please leave," said the same guard.

"Would do, would do," said Lance, "But my friend here thought that hiding in this well-protected fortress would be the best way to stay safe from that gork menace."

"Sod off," said the other guard. He even drew his sword out a few inches to let us know that he was not in a jovial mood. I briefly thought about trying to overpower them, but then I almost slapped myself for thinking such a silly thought. These guys each outweighed us by fifty pounds. We needed another tactic.

"Do you have a code?" I said to the first guard.

"I said, sod off!" said Angry guard.

"I live by a code," I said, focusing on the less-angry chap. "I believe water is wet." I even squinted my eyes a bit at the word *wet* to, you know, imply stuff.

It didn't work.

"Of course water is wet," he said. "That's the stupidest thing I've ever heard."

"Ha! You simple-minded fool!" said Lance jumping to life. "Are you a total stranger to metaphor?"

"Uh . . . maybe?" said the guard.

"Look, if you two don't move along—" began Angry guard. But Lance wouldn't be stopped.

"Only an idiot would think we were talking about water."

"But he said water. Isn't that right, Neville?"

"I don't know anything," said Angry guard, whose name, apparently, was Neville, and who clearly didn't want to commit himself.

"We're talking about life, man. LIFE!" Lance said that last word with such ferocity, it was as though he had grabbed the man's chain mail and yanked him up a foot or two.

"So you're saying life is wet?" said the guard.

"Wet?" I said, trying to go with the spirit. "Lift your thoughts out of the mundane!"

"Don't make me run you through with this sword," said Neville, wanting to get back to the point.

"So . . . life is . . . not wet?" said the first guard, struggling to keep up. I felt bad for him, for he really seemed to want to understand.

"Precisely!" said Lance. "Not wet. And of course, you know what that means."

"Yes," said the guard with a secret smile. "I sure do."

"Very good, man!" said Lance, grabbing him by the shoulders in a brotherly embrace. "I knew you were a poet. A warrior poet!"

The guard stood a little straighter. "I do feel rather poetical sometimes."

"Hang on a second," said Neville. "Let me see your hand . . ."

Oh no! He had spotted Lance's brand!

Just then Eldrack bonked him on the head, knocking him out cold.

"Oy!" said the first guard. But before he could pull out his sword, I ran up and kicked him in the you-know-what. He collapsed to his knees. Eldrack finished him off by slamming her helmet on top of his.

"You made it!" I wanted to hug her but thought better of it.

Lance dashed over to open the museum doors, but they were locked.

"Search the guards. They have to have the key."

"How did you get through Westgate?" I asked Eldrack as we searched. That part of our plan had been even fuzzier than the rest of it. Mostly it consisted of "Eldrack will figure something out."

"It was the weirdest thing," she said. "I was in line with dozens of other people, waiting to be searched before I could go into the city. And I did what you had suggested and hid my face and coughed a lot, so it looked like I was sick. People pretty much gave me room and didn't get too nosy.

"Anyway, I got up to the gate, and there were three guards there; one to check incoming visitors and two to, I guess, beat up anyone they didn't like. And I thought, how in the world am I going to get through this? So when it was my turn, I walked up to them and pulled off my helmet, thinking I would scare the poop out of them. I even said, 'boo!' But these guys? They weren't scared in the least. The guard who was checking everyone simply pulled a cord and sounded the alarm. The other two jumped forward and grabbed me. And these guys were massive and strong.

"I tried to fight my way out, but they had me, plain and simple. No way to escape. But get this: Just as I was about to give up, a knight—in shining armor, no less—fell from the sky and landed on the guards."

"Huh?"

"How did that happen?"

"I didn't ask. I just seized the opportunity, leapt over the guards, and ran into the city, growling at anyone who came too close until I caught up with you losers."

"Got it!" I said, holding up the key.

"Let's go," said Eldrack.

"Comrade!" Lance said. "Catch!"

He tossed me the guard's sword and scabbard. I caught it and looked at it in wonder. It felt wonderfully heavy in my hands. I placed my hand on the grip and slowly unsheathed the weapon. I was holding a proper, double-edged arming sword. I swung it around twice, marveling at its balance. This was the kind of sword I'd always dreamed of wielding.

I held it aloft and turned to Eldrack.

"Behold, fair maiden! I have come to save thee!"

"Can we get going?" she said.

"Are you swooning?"

"Sure."

"I knew it!" I sheathed my sword. "Thanks, comrade! Now it just needs a name!"

Lance winked and unlocked the door.

We entered the museum.

Chapter Twenty-One

THE PLACE WAS dark, but Eldrack spied a lit brazier across the great hall. She and I ran to it while Lance locked the doors.

We lit three torches from the brazier and looked around. Lance caught up to us, and Eldrack handed one to him.

Museums were fairly new to the human world. Elves had had museums for hundreds of years, but humans had never had much call for them until after the Really Big War when King Olerood decided he wanted to have a place to display his booty. "What's the point of being insanely rich if I can't show off how insanely rich I am?" he reasoned. So, he converted this old, unused temple into our first museum. Other cities have since followed suit, but this was still Amerigorn's largest museum.

Because museums were so new, no one had put any real thought into how to best organize the treasures inside. They just grabbed some stuff, filled up a room, and then went on to the next room. So we literally had no idea where to begin looking.

"Let's split up to cover more ground," I said.

"Bad idea, comrade," said Lance. "We need to all be together when we find this blasted thing so we can make a quick getaway."

"He's right."

"OK," I said, scanning our surroundings. "Then let's start with that wing."

We ran across the hall and down the first hallway. There were a dozen rooms on each side.

"Oh my gods! We'll be here a year!" I said.

"Shut up and start looking," said Eldrack.

Now we did decide to split up, and each of us took a room. We reasoned that as long as we were within shouting distance, we would be able to quickly regroup if need be.

I bolted into the first room on the right, which was filled with ancient statues dating back to the First Age. They were incredible, and I wished I had time to marvel at them, but I didn't. I saw no jewels or jewelry, so I ran to the next room.

Weapons! Maces, swords, daggers, spears, shields, crossbows, etc. etc. It seemed like there was more organization to this museum than I had initially thought. *Why didn't they just put a sign outside the door?* I thought. *Would have saved me thirty seconds.*

On to the next room.

I won't bore you with the details. Simply put, we examined with every room in the wing and came up empty, so, we ran back out to the hall and headed down another.

Four more rooms for me and still no luck. Same with the others.

"Upstairs!"

We ran back out to the hall and over to the giant, spiral staircase.

When we got to the top of the stairs, we heard a sound that made my stomach drop: the deep squeaks of the front door opening. Then footsteps. Many footsteps.

Eldrack pointed down the west wing of the museum. We did that half-run-half-tiptoe maneuver that every mischievous kid has mastered and made our way down the hall.

I entered the second room on the right and was surprised to see that it was full of jewelry. A lot of jewelry. Hundreds of pieces.

I gulped.

This was going to be even harder than I thought. I headed over to an area that had a lot of necklaces, hoping that the amulet would be attached to one. There were a ton of beautiful pendants, charms, and the like, but none of them screamed out at me "Most Powerful Weapon in the Universe!"

I was about to get the others to help when I heard someone on the stairs. Rather than panic, my brain did a surprising thing: it started thinking. Lance had said this thing had gone on a national tour. This amulet, being such a big deal, would have its own display. No piece of jewelry in this room had been given any special treatment, so I decided our amulet was not here. I sprinted to the doorway—quietly!—and peeked around the corner.

Still no soldiers or guards in sight, but I could hear them advancing up the stairs.

Lance appeared out of his room.

He shrugged.

I looked down the hall. We still had more than a dozen rooms to cover, and we were rapidly running out of time. Then I saw a big room way down at the end of the hall. That had to be it.

I pointed. Lance nodded, and we ran down the hallway. Gerald did not care for my running. He pooped on my shoulder and took flight, trying to keep up with me.

Eldrack came out and followed us.

"Your bird pooped on your shoulder," she whispered helpfully.

"I heard something over here, sir!" said a voice near the top of the stairs

This was our last chance. That blasted amulet had better be here or we were dead.

We burst inside, and I immediately knew we were in the right place. Whereas the other rooms contained scads of unnamed items, this one featured just nine—each one showcased in a fancy display, complete with a sign and even a couple of paragraphs detailing its history. I saw an ornamental vase that looked to be thousands of years old, called the "Urn of Philipanny." Next to that was the "Zepta Stele," a stone tablet covered with hundreds of chiseled characters from a long-dead language. But then, in the far right corner of the room, I saw it: The Amulet of Ashokenah.

"Here!" I gasped as I rushed over to it.

It was beautiful.

Well, sort of. The amulet itself was a plain round silver disk, about three inches in diameter, with faded writing etched around the perimeter, and attached to that was a tarnished silver chain. But in the center of the amulet lay a large, multifaceted violet stone that seemed to bend the light, making it hard to focus on it. Although I wasn't trying to read the display text, the phrase "over three thousand years old" popped out at me.

"OK! Now what?" I said.

"Down here!" came a voice from the hall.

We could see a dozen soldiers running towards us.

"Eldrack!" said Lance as he pushed at a tall iron display case. She sprinted across the room to help him.

A guard lunged forward, yelling, "Stop in the name of His Majesty—" BAM!

Lance and Eldrack knocked the case over, blocking the entrance.

I grabbed the amulet. It didn't feel magical.

"How does it work?"

"I don't know," said Eldrack, struggling to keep the barricade in place. "Uh . . . uh . . ."

"Put it on!" said Lance.

"Hurry!" said Eldrack.

I did.

"Now . . . I don't know, say something magical!" said Lance.

"Abra Cadabra!"

"Seriously?" said Lance.

"Wait! Give it to me! It's Gorkish!"

I tossed it to her. She slipped it over her head and said, "Abrack Cadabrack!"

"Oh come on," I said, "You can't tell me that you speak Gorkish by adding 'ack' to the end of every word."

Lance grabbed it and put it on. He looked like he was struggling to think of something. "Hocus pocus!" Nothing happened.

"Lance!" said Eldrack as the soldiers on the other side of the iron cabinet began pushing in earnest.

He tossed the amulet to me and then turned around so he could concentrate all of his strength on holding the cabinet in place. Even with his help, he and Eldrack were losing the battle. The case moved back six inches. Then eight.

"Now or never, mate!" yelled Lance.

I put the necklace on and tried to calm down, thinking that I just needed to breathe and focus. It was hard, though, knowing I was about three seconds away from being captured. It was also difficult, given that I had no idea what this thing could do. I mean, it's one thing to tell yourself to focus, but it helps if you know what to focus on.

With one last heave-ho, the soldiers pushed the case back far enough that they were able to break into the room.

Eldrack and Lance ran to my side and grabbed on to me in a protective gesture.

"Anything?" said Eldrack.

A dozen soldiers poured into the room and surrounded us, pointing their swords and spears at our faces. I expected them to advance and grab us, but they held their position. And waited.

"Hi, guys!" Lance said with a wave. "What's up?"

In sauntered Drill-Sergeant Smythe.

He smiled.

"Well, well, well," he said. "Look at what we have here. And oh look, you're stealing a national treasure. Let me add that to your list of crimes."

He cracked his big ugly knuckles.

"Come along, Maggots. Or do I get to drag you out?"

At that moment, the only thing that occurred to me was: *I wish I was home.*

And suddenly, that's exactly where we were.

Part Three

Chapter Twenty-Two

THERE WAS A lot of screaming.

The second person to scream was my mother. This was understandable, given that two people, a gork, and a dizzy, tufted titmouse had suddenly appeared in her kitchen, not two feet in front of her. Add to that insanity the fact that said titmouse promptly pooped on her prized cutting board, and, well, it was simply too much for the poor woman to handle.

My friends began screaming, mostly because of the unexpected change of scenery and the fact that my mother's screams are of the shrill and piercing variety. They've been known to cut through schools. Plus, my mom threw a wooden spoon at Eldrack's face, which is undoubtedly the kind of thing that would startle anybody. (Hats off to my mom's quick reflexes!)

I mentioned that my mother was the second person to start screaming. I was the first, but I was doing so for an entirely different reason.

For my friends, the trip from the museum to my mom's house had been instantaneous. For me, it was anything but. One second I was standing in the museum about to be nabbed by Drill-Sergeant Smythe, and then BAM! I was plunged into a void.

A void is nothing like darkness, although it is completely dark. Being in a void is like being in a vast black emptiness, with no sense of up or down, no sense that you have a body, no sense of time, and absolutely no sense that this torment will ever end. It was way worse than being locked up in the hell that was the dungeon at the academy.

But the void wasn't entirely devoid of everything. There was . . . well, I couldn't see it all that clearly, but I saw an object way off in the distance. And I could hear something that was too far away to identify but which I found unsettling, nevertheless.

In real time, my leap from the museum to Mom's had taken but a second, but in the void, it seemed to last just long enough for me to think that I had somehow died. I opened my mouth to scream, but no sound came out, which only made me panic and scream my silent scream with even more gusto. Just as I started to think I was trapped for eternity, I appeared in Mom's kitchen only to assaulted by her screams.

So, I was screaming, the loudest.

"Are you a ghost?" my mom said after we all stopped screaming.

I finally caught my breath. "Yes, Mom. I'm a ghost. You sent me off to military school, and now I'm a ghost who will be haunting you for the rest of your days."

She looked at the three of us for a second, trying to soak all of this in.

"Boo!" I said, thrusting my hands at her.

She collapsed on the floor.

"I'm starting to understand why your mother sent you away," said Lance.

"How did we get here?" said Eldrack.

"Oh that's easy," I said, "I just thought, I wish I was ho—"

I disappeared and reappeared right where I was. Gerald, who had settled back onto me, and thus had vanished and reappeared with me, let me know how he felt about all of this teleportation nonsense by pooping on my head.

"Ahhhhhh!" I said. But I didn't say that because of Gerald's poop.

I said it because of that object in the void.

I tore the amulet off. "Get that blasted thing away from me! I don't want to go back there!"

My friends had no idea what I was going on about. Lance calmed me down and suggested we carry my mom over to her bed, so she wasn't just sprawled out on the kitchen floor. Once that was accomplished, we settled down in her room, I explained about the void and that mysterious object to my friends. "The second time I used the amulet I saw and heard the same things, BUT THIS TIME THEY WERE CLOSER!"

"Closer?"

"Yeah. And I got scared."

"Could you see what it was?"

"Well, this is going to sound silly, but . . . it looked like a . . . well, it looked like a nose."

"Oh, come on!" said Lance, leaning back in his chair. "You didn't see a nose, Nigel. You only thought you saw it."

"Let me guess," said Eldrack, "the sound you heard was sniffing?"

"You laugh!"

"Because you're putting us on, mate!" said Lance. "Everyone knows Smoron is dead!"

"Is he?" I said.

"Yeah," said Lance. "He is. I read Elbo's blasted book. All four thousand pages of it. Elbo killed him when he destroyed the Cufflinks."

"A gork!" screamed my mom. "There's a gork in my bedroom!"

We were so caught up in our conversation we hadn't noticed my mom had come to.

"That's right, Mom. And she's here to eat you for putting me in that blasted school!"

She fainted again.

"Seriously, comrade. Let it go. Your poor mom can't handle this."

I sighed. "Sorry. I'm flustered."

"Anyway," Eldrack continued, "Smoron didn't have anything to do with the amulet. Ashokenah gave it to the Gorkish people a thousand years before Smoron was even born."

"Look, guys, I know a nose when I see one!"

"It's true," Lance told Eldrack. "He can recognize body parts."

Perhaps I should explain the whole nose thing.

It goes back to the Cufflinks of Doom.

I mentioned before that the Cufflinks secretly controlled the magical panties. And this was true, but only Smoron knew how to wield that power. The Cufflinks did have another, more immediate effect, however, and it was one that anyone who wore the Cufflinks experienced. Once you put on the Cufflinks, people found you irresistible. Everyone loved you or wanted to serve you. That was how Smoron was able to make the gorks follow his every whim.

But there was a downside. When Elbo wore the Cufflinks, he spoke of a nose that followed him and got closer and closer each time he put them on. He called it the All-Smelling Nose of Smoron, and according to him, that nose was the spirit of Lord Smoron, trying to come back to the real world and reclaim his Cufflinks. Luckily, we never found out if that was true because Elbo destroyed the Cufflinks before Smoron could return and commence his plan of world domination. But the Nose legend took on a life of its own. As a younger child, I lost more than a few nights' sleep, thanks to various spooky campfire stories about the Nose of Smoron.

"Well if it is Smoron," said Eldrack, "Then we really need to get to Mount Gash and destroy that thing."

"Mount Gash?"

"Yeah, you keep calling it Mount Boo-Boo, but its real name is Gash."

"I definitely don't want to go to Mount Gash," I said. "That place sounds horrid."

Lance nodded. "Agreed, whereas Mount Boo-Boo sounds kinda cute. Like a nice place for a picnic, even."

"All in favor of going to Mount Boo-Boo?" I said, raising my hand.

"A gork!" shrieked my mom, coming to, once again.

"Mother, I'd like to introduce you to my new wife, Eldrack."

And she fainted.

"You really are the worst, comrade," said Lance.

Eventually, my mom did emerge from unconsciousness and stay that way (in spite of my best efforts). She was generally unhappy about everything: the fact that her son had stolen a national treasure, committed high treason, and, perhaps most offensive of all, brought a real live gork into her house.

Frankly, she still hadn't gotten over being mad at the fact that I had gotten banished from the kingdom. She spent a good two minutes giving me grief over the letter I had written her.

"And to send it by titmouse?" she said, "Is that what you think of your mother?"

"At least it was tufted," I said with a smile.

"Tufted or not, a titmouse is not a proper messenger bird. And, speaking of titmice, why do you have one on your shoulder?"

"So it is titmice!" I said. "Thanks for clearing that up."

"So, not only are you are a banished thief and traitor to your nation, but you don't even know the plural of titmouse? Is that right?"

"I'm starting to get the feeling you're not happy to see me," I said.

"Nigel, I sent you off to military school because you were a no-goodnik. Has that changed?"

"No. Frankly, I've only gotten better at no-goodniking. One might say I am now a master no-goodniker. Plus, now I have a magical artifact, so there'll be nothing to stop me and my no-goodniking ways."

"You return that item at once!"

"Would love to, Mom, but I can't. It's too powerful."

"Actually, Mrs. P," said Lance, "we're off to destroy that thing, so it doesn't fall into the wrong hands."

"And yet you're letting my son hold it."

"I like her," said Eldrack, nudging me with her elbow. "She has you down to a T."

"OK, Mom. We won't stay—"

"Good."

"Mrs. P, ma'am," said Lance, who knew just how to charm my mother, "would you be so kind as to furnish us with some food for our trip? We promise not to bother you again."

She sighed but then said, "OK, Lance. For you."

I ignored her and leaned over to Lance, "Why do we need food? I can just zap us right there."

"You might be able to zap us over to Mount Boo-Boo, but after we destroy that thing we're gonna need to walk back. And it's a long way."

"Mount Boo-Boo?" said Mom, "Oh, that sounds dangerous. Be safe, dear. And have a good life. You know, away from here."

In spite of her sarcasm, she did spend the next hour helping us gather supplies, including blankets, clothes, and food. She handed me a towel. "You need a bath, dear. You smell like bird poop."

When we were ready, we gathered in a small circle. My friends held on to my arms. I grabbed the amulet in my right hand, closed my eyes, and thought: *I wish I was standing at the foot of Mount Boo-Boo.*

And before I knew it, nothing happened.

"Great," said my mom.

I tried several times to make it work, but the blasted thing wouldn't send us to Mount Boo-Boo.

"Figures," said Mom. "Perfectly good magical amulet. Survives for three thousand years, and then my son gets his hands on it."

"Wait, I know!" said Eldrack, "Maybe you need to be scared to make it work. You were scared at the museum."

"OK. Scare me."

"Boo?" said Lance.

"But wait, that isn't it. Because I used it here a second time and I wasn't scared at all."

"You used it a second time, dear?"

"Yeah, I simply thought, I wish I was ho—"

I vanished and reappeared. Again.

"OK, that's totally a friggin' nose!" I said once I found my bearings. "It's a big smelling nose, and it's getting closer each time."

"Maybe it only works if you want to go home?"

"That would be annoying, so it's probably true," I said.

"Now I'll never get rid of him!" said Mom to the ceiling.

"Give it to me!" said Eldrack, holding out her hand. "Maybe I can bring us to my home. That's a lot closer to the Mountain, at least."

I moved to give it to her but paused for a second. I have to say I was a tad hesitant to give it up.

"Nibel?"

I shook my head and pulled the necklace off my head and handed it to her.

Reluctantly.

Lance and Eldrack looked at each other.

"That can't be good," Lance said.

Eldrack donned the amulet. We held on to her arms, and she closed her eyes.

Nothing.

"Wait," I said. "I think you have to hold it while you're wishing yourself home."

She did. Still nothing.

"Oh, for crying out loud," said my mother.

We ignored my mother and were about to try again when Gerald started chirping and fluttering about. We heard a sound over by the open kitchen window.

There, standing on the windowsill, was a Royal raven.

"Oh thank heavens," Mom said. "Now you really do have to leave."

Chapter Twenty-Three

"OUT YOU GO!" she said as she shooed us through the door. "Goodbye!"

"Is it me, or do you get the distinct impression my mom wants to get rid of us?"

She slammed the door shut.

"Well, comrade Nibel," said Lance, slapping me on the shoulder. "You finally made it home."

"Yeah, yikes. Had I known my mom's true feelings for me, I could have saved myself a lot of trouble with all of that wishing and hoping."

"You OK?"

"Well, the good news is I have other pressing matters to worry about like that raven. Maybe if we can escape danger I'll have time to sob about how my mother doesn't love me anymore."

We walked towards the market. From there, I knew we could turn north and eventually make our way back to that rope we had left ourselves to cross the Moor River. The only problem was that trip would take at least a day, and I was doubtful we'd get that far now that the raven had spotted us. Surely Smythe and his thugs would catch up to us before then.

The night was cloudy, which provided us with some cover to move about town and avoid Nektor, the village watchman.

The night bell rang ten times.

"Seems like only yesterday, eh Lance? Sneaking into Blyburn's . . ."

"Why isn't it working?" asked Eldrack, clearly uninterested in taking a walk down memory lane.

As we walked, we tried everything we could think of to make the amulet work. Eldrack tried using the amulet to wish that she was back in my home but to no avail. We even let Lance have a go, thinking that if we could get transported to his house that would be some sort of progress.

Still nothing.

"You're the only one who's made it do anything, comrade," said Lance, tossing it back to me. It felt good to have it back in my possession.

We entered the market square. The villagers had long since repaired the damage from the snowball incident. All the carts and stands were back up and looking splendid. They even had a new Phoenix Tree decorated and blazing away.

I was musing on how normal everything was here, and how unhinged my life had become when I heard a familiar voice call out.

"Halt!"

We halted and turned to see who was speaking to us. I was expecting to see old Nektor, even though the voice didn't register as his. But it wasn't him. It was my old friend Nate. He stood facing us, holding a lantern and a spear, with a watchman's badge pinned to his left jacket lapel.

We gaped at him. He stared back at us. I don't know if he was more surprised to see Lance and me or Eldrack.

"I'll take care of this punk," said Eldrack, cracking her knuckles.

"No," I said. "He's a friend." Funny how that word slipped out. After all, it had been Nate who had doomed me to this life I now led.

"What ho, Nate?" said Lance as though it was just another night on the town. "I see you have a new job. Good show, old man!"

"It's true what they said," said Nate, unable to take his eyes off Eldrack. "You've gone and turned traitor."

"Oh come now, Nate old boy," reassured Lance. "No one is a traitor."

"Oh, no? What about . . . that . . . thing?"

"Nate," I said, "Let me introduce you to my good friend Eldrack. Eldrack, Nate."

"Oh, you're the scum who turned on his best friend. Nice to meet you," she said with a curtsey.

"Oh. I see," said Nate, getting uppity. "You extinguish the country's oldest Phoenix Tree, steal an ancient amulet from the national museum, and free an enemy of the state from prison, but I'm the bad guy?"

"He's got a point, Comrade Nibel," said Lance. "You are officially a bad boy!"

"You're right! I didn't even realize it! You think the girls will, you know, swarm and swoon?"

"Quite possibly, my good man."

"Listen, fellas," said Eldrack, ever the party-pooper, "there's an armed watchman here. Can we focus on how to get out of this situation?"

"It's no use," sneered Nate. He always was an excellent sneerer, but I had never been on the receiving end of his sneering before. It made me want to smack him. "I've already alerted the authorities. An entire regiment is on their way."

"The fun never stops, does it?" I said.

Eldrack lunged at Nate and said, "Boo!"

"Ah!" he said, and he ran away. I don't blame him. Eldrack could be downright scary when she wanted to be. Even Gerald was startled enough to fly off my shoulder.

We could hear marching feet from around the corner.

I grabbed the amulet. My friends held on to my arms.

"Now or never, Nibes," Lance said.

A troop of soldiers rounded the corner and came charging at us. This time they weren't going to stop and talk to us. I could tell by the looks on their faces that they planned to slaughter us and deal with the paperwork later.

The first soldier was only two feet from impaling Lance with his spear.

I panicked and thought of the safest place I knew—the last place I had felt any kind of warmth and welcome.

There was another round of screaming as we popped into a quaint sitting room, scaring the sweet jeeblejuice out of an old woman, who promptly fainted.

"Good job, Nibel," said Lance after he recovered from the trauma of almost being killed. "You've dropped another old woman."

"Where are we?" asked Eldrack, looking around in wonder and suspicion.

"Give us a hand, mate," I said to Lance. He helped me lift our victim and carry her over to her bed. "This is Old Mrs. Halloway, the kind old bird whose barn we destroyed . . . wow, was it only last week?"

"Sorry ma'am," said Lance with a nod.

"You two are impressive devils, I'll give you that," said Eldrack. "Heck, the gorks don't need to invade your kingdom, they could just let you two roam around and destroy the place."

Lance gave her the backstory about the barn while I checked Mrs. Halloway's pulse. She was still alive. I breathed a sigh of relief. I mean, I don't mind destroying buildings and trees and stealing the odd priceless artifact or two but had we accidentally killed this poor woman, I would have never forgiven myself.

"OK," I said, once I was satisfied Mrs. Halloway would be all right, "we're a little too close to the school grounds for me to feel especially safe, but at least we've given ourselves a little time."

"Let's not sit around here and give the poor woman a heart attack," said Lance. "We're only a few hours away from that rope of ours. Let's start walking while we figure out exactly how that amulet works."

We let ourselves out of her cottage and hiked northwest towards the rope.

After a few steps, I realized something was wrong. "Where's Gerald?"

We scanned the sky, and I whistled for him, but there was no sign of my beloved bird.

"Is he in Mrs. Halloway's house?"

"I don't think so. He didn't poop on my shoulder after the jump." I gasped. "Oh no! I think I left him back in Bletchleysbum!"

"Wait," said Eldrack, holding on to my wrist. "I think I heard something."

We listened for a second, and sure enough, we heard a bird calling out in the night. But it wasn't Gerald.

"Blast! How many ravens do they have looking for us?"

I caught a glimpse of the raven as it passed by the moon.

"We can't stay here," said Lance. "We're too close to the capital."

"Dash it all, Gerald!"

"He'll be fine, Nige."

"Yeah, but I won't. He saved my life!"

"That raven is flying right for the palace," said Lance. "That means the army will be on top of us within the hour."

We had to go, but I hated to leave Gerald even further behind.

"Should we make a break for the river?" asked Eldrack. "Maybe we can get there in time?"

"No. But I have an idea on how this thing works," I said. "Hold on to me."

I closed my eyes and zapped us into a small room. The room was lit by a single candle and featured a bed, a desk, and a rather startled-looking man who had been about to take a sip of tea.

"Hello, Lieutenant Thuffsburry," I saluted. "Cadet Nigel Pipps-Schrewsberry-Billingsbottom III reporting for duty, sir."

The poor man fainted.

"Is that who I think that is?" said Eldrack.

"It works!" I said.

"Why did you bring us here, you idiot?" said Lance.

We heard a knock on the lieutenant's door. "Are you all right, sir?"

"I've figured it out!" I said as I grabbed my friends. The door opened, and an intelligence officer poked his head into the room.

I had to hand it to him. The man was quick. He didn't pause to wonder how we, the kingdom's most-wanted, had suddenly appeared in his lieutenant's quarters. Nor did he faint, which seemed to be the popular thing to do.

No, instead he pounced, grabbing on to Lance just as I zapped us away.

As fast and quick-witted as the man was, however, he did seem startled by the fact that he was now lying on the ground, under a beautiful ruby maple tree, just inside the border of the Gorkish Kingdom.

But that didn't stop him from launching an attack at yours truly.

Knowing that the man was an intelligence officer, I had been under the impression that he was more of a paper-pusher than an actual soldier.

How wrong I was.

Once he regained his senses, he did a flip and landed a kick to the right side of my face.

I, rather sensibly, fell to the ground whilst uttering a pithy, "Ooof!" The man had walloped me so hard I was having trouble seeing straight.

Thankfully, Eldrack had the speed and agility to launch a counterattack

I'm not good at describing fighting scenes, but trust me, this was a doozy. Although the soldier didn't have Eldrack's strength, he outmatched her with a superior skill set, for it was soon evident that the man had spent years training at hand-to-hand combat. Eldrack, despite her warrior-like reflexes and tremendous strength, was just a teenage girl with no combat training of any sort. Not to mention the fact that she was still sporting a still-broken arm.

But what kept her in the fight was her anger, for she knew this officer. He had personally interrogated her and had inflicted an immense amount of pain on her. So she was fueled by fury and a desire for revenge.

Lance kept trying to intervene to help her, but the two combatants were moving around so quickly he was afraid to land a punch or kick for fear of hurting our friend.

I stood up and looked at the amulet, wondering how I could help, but I wasn't sure where to send us, or if I could even manage to get her away from this lunatic for long enough to make it work.

At this point, the officer realized we were only 200 yards to the east of Fort Phipps, for he turned and screamed, "Guards!"

Eldrack kicked him in the back.

He spun around and pulled out a long dagger. Why he had not pulled that out earlier, I wasn't sure, but I guessed it was because he hadn't had a second to do so with all the close grappling he had been involved in.

"I'm going to finish what I started," he growled. At least I guess that's how you'd describe it. Now that I think about it, I'm not entirely sure how one can growl the phrase "I'm going to finish what I started" without hurting one's throat in the process, but you get the drift.

Anyway, this chap performed some fancy flips and spins, showing off his prowess. He looked like he was just starting to get warmed up. I was suddenly afraid for Eldrack. This guy had thus far held his own against her without using a lethal weapon. There was no telling what he would do to her now that he had one.

"Eldrack!"

Lance tossed her his sword and, although she caught it just in time, she grabbed it by the blade instead of the grip.

She dodged the soldier's lunge and then swung Lance's sword down, smashing the bloke on the head with the hilt, and knocking him out.

"Score one for Theresa!" said Lance.

"Ow!" said Eldrack, looking at her bloody hand. The blade had cut a rather severe gash in her hand.

"Theresa?" I asked.

"The name of my new sword!"

"I don't know. Doesn't roll off the tongue like Wilma. Where's Smythe when you need him? He had a real knack for naming swords."

"You OK, love?" said Lance, holding Eldrack's wrist. "This looks bad."

All the noise of our battle had raised the alarm back at the fort, and I could see a small group of soldiers riding out on horseback in our direction.

"We need to go," I said, whipping out my sword and charging into the woods.

"Let's just use the amulet!" said Lance, as he and Eldrack caught up to me.

"Doesn't work that way. Come on."

We fled into the woods, with every step taking us deeper into gork territory.

Chapter Twenty-Four

"So how does it work?" Lance asked me. We were striding through the forest to keep ahead of the soldiers. Well, Lance was striding. I was huffing. In spite of all those pushups Smythe had had me do, I was still in pretty lousy shape, though to my credit, we had been walking for two hours.

"I think I can send us anywhere I've already been. Or anywhere I have seen, which is why I could send us to that maple tree. I saw it the day the soldiers brought us to Fort Phipps. But I can't send us places I haven't been, which is why I can't just send us to Mount Boo-Boo."

"How close is the nose?" asked Eldrack, who didn't look at all well.

"You need to lean on me, El," I said.

She did, wrapping her left arm around my shoulder. I supported her weight, and we plunged forward, through the trees.

"If I never see another blasted tree as long as I live, it will be too soon," I said. "Lance, see if you can bandage her hand with one of the towels Mom gave us."

He got to work on her hand, while I slashed away at the dense foliage. I have to say the swords we stole from those museum guards were positively brilliant. Their razor-sharp edges sliced through vines and dead branches with ease.

"How close is the nose?" Eldrack asked again.

"Hard to say," I said. "I don't have any perspective in that void. I only know it's closer."

"We should only use that thing if we need to," said Lance. "Let's not chance anything."

I tripped on a root, which caused Eldrack to hold my hand tightly. I quickly recovered but didn't let go of her hand.

"Hang on a second," I said, just noticing something for the first time. "You're not slimy!"

"Don't make me bite your face off," said Eldrack.

"Lance. Did you know she wasn't slimy? Feel her skin! It's like a snake's skin."

"Oooh! Very nice, indeed!"

And so it was! You know how snakes can look all slimy from far away but up close they're kind of leathery? This was much the same experience, only smoother.

"It's almost silky!" I said. "Tell me, do all gorks feel this nice?"

She stopped walking and lifted me by my armor, holding me in the air with only one hand.

"It is not okay to fondle women!" she said.

"Quite right!" I said, "Sorry."

"I'm going to put you down now. Are you going to behave?"

"Absolutely."

She did as promised, and we continued walking, though now she wasn't leaning on me anymore.

"I don't get it," said Lance, trying to relieve the tension. "That thing. I mean it's cool and all being able to instantly teleport to any place you've ever been. But it's hardly the greatest weapon of all time."

"Aww," I said petting the amulet. "Don't let him hurt your feelings. Who's a big bad weapon of mass destruction? You are! Yes, you are!"

Eldrack stopped walking to gape at me.

"Have you lost your mind?"

"Frankly, yes. I need to rest," I said. It was the middle of the night, and we had had quite an active several hours. Plus, I think using that amulet had drained me of energy. "Just a little shut-eye. Besides, I can't believe that patrol is going to come after us this far into gork territory."

"OK," said Eldrack.

"OK?" I said. "No comment about how pathetic we humans are?"

"Let's set up camp over there by that stream."

I couldn't believe it. "Are you . . . tired?"

She grabbed me by my armor again and pulled me close.

"You would be tired too if you had battled that scum-sucking torturer!"

"OK, El," I said, holding up my hands. "I was just having a go."

Her eyes softened. I noticed she had green speckles in her yellow eyes. They were kind of . . . well, they were kind of pretty.

"Sorry," she said before looking away.

"No, I'm sorry. I didn't think about how emotionally draining that must have been for you back there."

"Yeah, well, maybe think about other people for a change." She walked over to a tree and slid down it until she was seated. She closed her eyes.

Lance and I set our equipment down. I collapsed on to the ground, I was, as Lance would have put it, exhaustipated.

"I'll keep the first watch," said Lance.

I went through my pack and grabbed a blanket and rolled it up to use as a pillow. I saw Lance looking at something in his lap.

"What are you doing?"

"Reading," he said.

"What are you reading for?" I asked.

"Did you just ask me what I was reading *for*? Have you never read a book? You should try it sometime. Might learn a thing or two."

"I meant what book are you reading?"

"Elbo's book," he said, holding it up. "I grabbed it off the shelf in Mrs. Halloway's house. I thought maybe it would help us."

"Good luck with that," I said, placing my head on my makeshift pillow.

The next thing I knew Lance was shaking me.

"Nige! El! Wake up!" he whispered. "Someone's coming!"

You know how sometimes you wake up and you're raring to get out of bed and take on the world, like when you've perfectly timed your sleep cycle? This was not one of those times. I was fuzzy-headed and groggy. And even though I knew we might be in danger, I was struggling to wake up. I even stumbled into a tree while trying to gather my things.

"Good to know we can count on you in a pinch," said Eldrack.

"What did you hear?" I asked Lance.

"Someone was walking over there. But they stopped just shy of where I could see them."

"Let's go," she said.

"Ready mate?" Lance asked me.

"Always," I mumbled.

We started hiking east again while staying alert to the threat behind us.

"If we could just get clear of these blasted trees!" I said. "Maybe I'd be able to see a distant mountain peak and transport us there and save us miles and miles of walking."

No such luck. We walked for an entire day, slashing and hacking at trees, with no end in sight. I tried climbing up one tree to see if I could get above the treeline, but the trees were too flimsy for me to get high enough. Every once in a while we heard a noise behind us, which would cause us to stop and listen, but then the noise would stop, too. Nor could we get a good look at whoever or whatever was following us for they always stayed just out of sight. Eldrack offered to backtrack and fight our invisible friend, but we decided she needed to heal her hand first.

Eventually, we decided to settle down for the night.

"No offense, El," I said as dropped my backpack, "but yours is a crap country."

"I think it's beautiful," said Lance, always the suck-up. "Unspoiled by human or gork hands."

We busted out some of the food my mom made for us and enjoyed a rather pleasant evening of not walking or being chased by anyone.

"Anyway," said Lance, "back to my statement from yesterday. I don't see why there's all this fuss over that thing. It hardly even seems like a weapon."

"Well, I suppose you could instantly transport an entire regiment a thousand miles away," I said.

"But only if you've been there or seen that place before."

"Plus, that would require an entire army to hold hands, which I really can't see happening."

"Maybe we haven't figured out everything it does."

I held the amulet up for closer inspection. With all the fleeing and screaming and fighting we'd been doing, there hadn't been to analyze it properly. I asked Eldrack if she could understand the etchings, but she tossed it back to me. "That's Old Gorkish," she said. "I can't understand it."

I knew just what she meant. I had once seen Old Human written on an ancient parchment, and it might as well have been a foreign language.

"You should try to do something with it," said Lance. "Experiment."

"I have been."

"Well, try harder! What will happen if we get attacked again? Go back to your mom's?"

"I am trying!" I said, suddenly annoyed by how hostile he'd been towards me lately. I thought back to him insulting me about not having ever read a book.

"Don't point that thing at me!" he said.

"Oh yeah? Why don't you go read or something?"

And Lance promptly disappeared.

Chapter Twenty-Five

IT TOOK A second for Lance's disappearance to register, partially because I was swallowed up by the void once again and I was distracted by the ever-approaching nose, but also because I hadn't meant to use the dashed thing.

But when I emerged from the darkness, I stared at the spot where Lance has once sat, and I blinked.

I blinked again.

Lance did not reappear.

"What did you do?"

"I have no idea!"

"You must have done something!"

"Oh, dear gods!" I said, "What did I do?"

I turned the amulet over and over in my hand.

"I wish Lance would come back!"

He did not.

"Did you kill him?"

"I don't know what I did! He just disappeared."

We heard someone crunching their way through the woods.

"Oh that's just all we bloody well need right now, isn't it?"

"Shut up!" whispered Eldrack. "Follow me!"

She scurried through the woods and ducked behind a boulder. When I rounded the corner, I could see she had wedged into a crevice that was barely big enough for two. I hesitated. She sighed and pulled me in.

There we were, pressed up against each other. She was looking around the corner. I was looking at her. She was rather pretty now that I had gotten used to her being a gork. She had high, well-defined cheekbones. And her skin . . . well, I already told you about that.

Eldrack must have sensed that I was not on high alert. She glanced at me and then, realizing that I was paying attention to her and not to the fact that we were possibly about to die a horrible and tragic death, she did one of those double-takes that I thought only people in books did. She glared at me. And let me tell you, as someone who has been on the receiving end of many a glare, Eldrack was as good a glarer as anyone who has ever glared. Better than my mom, even, and that's saying something. She looked like she was about to hit me, and she probably would have, too, if we didn't hear approaching footsteps.

Eldrack turned to get ready to spring out at our stalker. She placed a hand on my face, ostensibly to help her get better leverage for her impending leap, but I think she was also sending me a not-so-subtle message. You have to admire someone who can get so much mileage out of a single action.

"Ah!" she yelled as she leapt out at our foe. I was going to leave that little detail out of the narrative, but it occurred to me that "Ah!" really is the best thing one can yell in mid-leap if one wants to avoid sounding foolish. "A-ha!" comes across as too effete. "Curses!" sounds like you're trying too hard. And "Boo!" . . . well, if you yell "Boo!" you're just asking to get beat up. Of course, you could try for a more surreal vibe and hope to gain an extra edge by thoroughly confusing your target. Months later, after all these shenanigans were over, I suggested that the next time Eldrack needed to leap out at someone, she should try yelling "Pancakes!" She told me she would take that under advisement.

Anyway, back to our story.

"Ah!" Eldrack yelled as she launched herself at our stalker and tackled him to the ground.

She raised her fist as if to smash his face in when she stopped.

"Ahhhh!" said Lance. "It's me! Don't kill me!"

This turn of events was, to say the least, rather startling.

"How did you get here?" asked Eldrack.

"Can you get off of me, please?"

She thought about it for a second and then did so.

"Oh, thank heavens, it's you!" I said. "I thought for sure I'd vaporized you or something."

"You know what you did? You sent me back in time. That guy who's been stalking you all day? That was me. I've been following us."

"Oh," I said. "Well. That certainly clears that up."

"It does?" said Eldrack.

"No. I have no idea what he's going on about."

"OK," said Lance, who had obviously been dying to have this conversation for a while now. "So a few minutes ago you pointed that thing at me—in spite of the fact that I specifically asked you not to."

"I am terribly sorry," I said.

"Yeah. Well, when you did, that thing sent me back in time to last night when we decided to rest. I didn't realize what had happened at first. I mean, one moment I was sitting right here with you and then suddenly it was dark. But I heard your voice. So, I made my way towards you when I heard me making fun of you for not reading. And suddenly I realized what had happened. But rather than burst in on the scene and try to explain things, I figured I would just follow you to this very moment. That thing," he said, pointing at the amulet and taking a deep breath, for that little monologue had tired him out, "is a time travel device."

"Wait a second! I was thinking about you reading when I pointed this thing at you! So, I guess I need to hold it like this—"

"Ahhh!" said Eldrack, diving out of the way. "Careful with that thing!"

"Sorry," I said, letting go of the amulet. "OK, then. Well, now we know that I can send people to other places and times! That seems like a pretty cool weapon, right?"

Our discussion was interrupted by a crash in the woods. Someone was coming. Quickly.

We froze.

"Is that one of us?"

We didn't have time to discuss, for a knight on horseback burst through the trees.

I don't know if you've ever seen a knight in full armor, but they truly are quite terrifying—especially when they are charging at you on a speeding horse, and even more so when they are swinging a war mace, quite clearly advertising the fact that they intend to use said mace to smash you on the noggin. That, my friends, is the stuff of nightmares. Only this was no nightmare. This was actually happening.

But then . . . well, I had my trusty amulet, now didn't I? Once I got over my shock, I grabbed it and pointed it at the rampaging knight and thought, *Wouldn't it be delightful if that knight were to smash headfirst into yonder tree?*

And wouldn't you know it, the knight promptly disappeared from the top of the horse and reappeared in front of a massive elm. And since he was still moving at whatever speed the horse had been traveling, he smashed into the tree, bounced off onto the ground, and didn't move.

I, on the other hand, moved quite rapidly. Not on my account, mind you, but thanks to Eldrack's quick thinking. For while I had made the knight disappear, I did not make the horse do so (I didn't want to hurt the poor animal). And so it kept right on charging at me. Eldrack lunged forward and knocked me out of the way, just in the proverbial nick of time. The horse, now fully aware that its rider was no longer on him, decided that he was rather tired of this whole charging about the countryside nonsense, and he promptly fled the scene.

"Thanks!" I said.

"Idiot!" said Eldrack, pushing herself off of me.

"You try using this thing! It's very disorienting to be thrust in and out of that void and expect to perform acrobatics at the same time!"

Lance crept over to the knight.

"Is he all right?" I asked. I stood up and brushed myself off.

"I think so. Hard to tell if he's breathing or not with all this armor."

"Ugh!" said the knight, clearing up that question.

"Who sent you?" I asked.

"Ugh!" he replied.

"Ah," I said.

"Well," said Eldrack. "What now?"

"You ask that question a lot you know that?" I said.

"Can we deal with Knighty McKnighterson over here?" said Lance.

"OK," said Eldrack, "We've got a time—"

"Ub-bub-bub!" I said, waving my hands to shush Eldrack. "Let's not give anything away in front of Moaning Melvin here."

I bent down to take a look at the bloke. He was not in good shape. His nose was bloody, and he had that dazed look of someone who had recently suffered a concussion.

"Listen, mate," I said, lifting his visor so he could get a better look at me. "I'm going to send you to get some medical attention. But if anyone asks," I raised the amulet so he could see it, "we have figured out how this thing works. And guess what? It's truly as powerful as the legends say it is. And, if you idiots don't stop chasing us, I'm going to use it to destroy the whole kingdom. Got me?"

"Ugh," he said.

"Well put."

I stood up and was about to send him to our school nurse's office, where he could get some decent care. But then I had a better thought.

"Actually, I hate to be a pest, my good man, but I need you to fall on some guards for me at Westgate."

"Ugh," he said.

"Thank you."

I focused on the amulet and—poof!—he vanished.

"This thing is seriously cool," I said after re-emerging from the void.

"'Fall on some guards'?"

"Now we know where that knight in shining armor who saved Eldrack came from," I said, clapping my hands together. "Well! Let's continue on our way, shall we?"

Questions! Oh boy, did my friends have questions for me. "But you weren't there when it happened!" said Eldrack, which, I realize, wasn't technically a question, but the idea was the same.

I strutted along, filled with confidence due to my new found abilities.

"I know," I said, "but I saw Westgate when we were scouting out the city. And, thanks to you, I knew exactly when the bloke would fall from the sky, so I just sort of put two and two together and got four."

I walked past Eldrack and winked at her. "You're welcome," I said.

"Is he strutting?" asked Eldrack.

"Indeed," said Lance.

"Should we be worried?"

"Clearly."

Chapter Twenty-Six

W E EVENTUALLY BROKE out of the woods and came to a clearing. I gasped. Miles off in the distance, past a vast field, beyond rolling hills, I saw mountains. These were the first mountains I had ever seen, and I'd had no idea that anything could be so enormous. Many of their peaks were higher than the clouds.

"I know those mountains!" said Eldrack.

"Are they on the way to Mount Boo-Boo?"

"Yes, but—"

I grabbed my partners' hands and whisked us off to the top of the furthest mountain I could see clearly.

"Nice, right? I just saved us months of walking!"

We were standing on a mountain peak. The wind howled, blowing snow all over us.

"Are these the Mountains of Death?"

"No, these are the Mountains of Doom. Totally different range."

It was freezing, and we could barely see anything, due to the clouds and the snow.

"Where do we go from here?" I asked, my teeth chattering away.

"I have no idea," she said. "I can't see anything!"

"Hmm," I said. And then I whisked us down to a lower spot I could see through the clouds. "How about now?"

"Comrade, seriously! You need to take it easy with that thing."

"Nonsense, my good man! Nonsense!" I turned to Eldrack. "Where to?"

We were below the clouds and could see practically the entire Gorkish Kingdom. She scanned the scenery for a bit and pointed at a distance plain.

"See that—"

Boom, we were there.

"Woah! Wow!" I said. "What a rush!"

I caught Lance and Eldrack glancing at each other.

"What?"

"You're enjoying that way too much."

"So would you! But, oh, wait! That's right. You can't use it. Only I can."

"How close is the nose?" asked Lance.

"Nose, nose, nose!" I said. "All you ever want to know about is that blasted nose!"

"Yeah, that's right," he said. "How close?"

"Never fear, my good man."

"Um, guys?" said Eldrack. "We've got company."

A small regiment of gork cavalrymen came sprinting up. On dire wolves, no less. That's one thing I'd always thought was awesome about gorks. I mean, riding a horse is cool and all, but come on! Who wouldn't rather ride on a dire wolf?

"Hallo, gents!" I said. "Good day to you, what?"

The gorks couldn't believe their eyes.

"Humans!" said the lead bloke.

"That's right, my good man. We're bloody humans! Except her. Eldrack, why don't you take a bow—"

"Silence!" said the lead gork, brandishing his sword.

"Oh no you don't," I said.

I zapped all twelve of them to the top of that frigid mountain we had left only moments ago.

"Serves them right," I said. "How rude."

I sat down, suddenly tired.

"Is anyone else hungry? I'm starving!"

Lance sat down next to me.

"I have an idea," he said. "Why don't you take that amulet off and give yourself a rest?"

"Why don't you go—"

"Stop!" said Eldrack. And thank goodness she stopped me, for I had been about to suggest that Lance go jump in a lake—Lake Beginshaw, to be exact, near our home.

"What?" I said defensively.

"You're literally drunk with power!"

"Zat so? Because I feel AWESOME!"

She eyed Lance.

"Don't go giving him googly eyes," I said, "He doesn't play for your team."

I stood up and walked over to her. "You know what, Eldrack? Remember that time when I said you weren't pretty? I was wrong. Way wrong! I think you're stunningly beautiful. And I don't care who knows it!"

Her jaw fell open, and she stared at me.

"And I love your name. I love it! I love how it rolls off my tongue. Elllldrack. OK, the drack part doesn't roll so well, but the Elllll part . . . hoo-boy is that fun to say! Elllll . . ."

"Hey, Nigel . . ."

"Yes, love?"

"Do you really think I'm pretty?"

"Boy do I. Your eyes . . . your nose . . . that is your nose, right? S'beautiful."

"I like you, too."

"Really?" I pumped my fist. "Yes! I've never had a girl like me before!"

"No!"

"No, it's true! They all like what's-his-face over there. Just cause he's handsome and has strong ears."

"Well, they don't know what they're missing."

"I know! That's what I keep telling them!"

She pulled me close and walked her fingers up my chest.

But then I backed away.

"Wait a minute! You only like me because I am the most powerful human in the history of forever!"

"No! I liked you from the start."

"No, you didn't. You called me all sorts of nasty cuss words."

"I was just covering up my true feelings. That's how I deal."

"Ohmygods, that's amazing! I cover up my true feelings with sarcasm."

"Can we have our first kiss all over again?"

"This is, and I mean it, the greatest day of my entire life."

"OK, close your eyes."

I did.

And then she bonked me on the head, knocking me out cold.

Look, I'm not proud of how I behaved. You try controlling the most powerful and evil magical weapon in the world and see what it does to you.

I came to the next morning. The sun was rising, the sky was pink and red and orange and we were surrounded by those towering mountains. It was the most beautiful sight I'd ever seen.

I bolted up and immediately regretted it.

"Oh, my head!"

"How you feeling, Nibes?"

I inhaled and slowly let out my breath, remembering everything that had happened.

"Oh. My. Gods," I said. I must have turned a bright red, for Lance started laughing. I looked at Eldrack, which was not easy to do, "I am so, so sorry for everything I said and did."

"You love me, you love me!" she sang. And then she laughed.

She had a great laugh. Hearty. Full. Giddy. It lit up her whole face.

"I . . . I . . ." I wanted to deny everything, but at the same time, I hadn't been lying when I'd rambled on like an idiot, and we all knew it.

She laughed some more.

"Don't worry about it, lover-boy. We're cool. But let's just keep this amulet away from you, OK?" She held up the amulet and slipped the necklace around her head.

"What if we need it?"

"We'll worry about that when the time comes," said Lance.

We ate breakfast and marched east, towards Mount Boo-Boo.

The next two days were uneventful, which was a welcome change of pace. We hiked across that vast and beautiful plain (which Eldrack told us was called the Plain of Sorrow) and then on through the Hills of Annoyance.

The whole time I kept scanning the skies, looking for ravens, but Lance told me I needed to chillax.

"Look, only the humans know we've got the amulet, and they're not about to go venturing this far into Gorkish territory."

"Well, those poor gork soldiers I sent to the top of that mountain must have figured it out."

"It'll be a while before they can reach anyone to alert," said Eldrack.

On the third day, however, we saw another gork cavalry patrol. At first, I thought Eldrack had been wrong, and they were already on our trail. I held out my hand for the amulet to zap them to the top of that mountain, but Eldrack backed me down with a glare. Instead, we simply stayed out of sight, and the gorks passed by without seeing us.

Frankly, it felt good to be away from the amulet. In his book, Elbo had talked about the ever-increasing weight of the Cufflinks and how they had filled him with more and more hatred and rage. That wasn't the case with the amulet. I just wanted to keep using it, and I didn't give a care in the world about that quickly-approaching nose. I mean, it's just a nose, right?

But, having been off the amulet for a few days, I now had a keener sense of the danger I had been bringing us towards, for that nose was getting very close indeed. I got the feeling I wouldn't be able to use the amulet too many more times before trouble would arrive.

What that trouble would be, I didn't know.

On the fourth day, we reached the Mountains of Death. Unlike the towering Mountains of Doom, which we had crossed by using the amulet, the Mountains of Death, were only 4,000 to 6,000 feet high, so we could hike over them on foot. I was a little nervous because back in the Age of Magic, these mountains were infamous for being home to some of the world's most fearsome creatures, including trolls, giant spiders, blob monsters, and dragons.

Lance assured me that all those creatures had all fled after the Really Big War, but Eldrack wasn't so sure.

"But they were only here for the magic," he said. "When that was gone, they split, too."

"But we're walking around with a magical amulet."

"Yeah, but it's not the same, is it? I mean, we have one item. They had loads of magical—"

"Ten," I said. "There were nine magical panties, plus the Cufflinks of Doom."

"OK, nerd," said Lance.

"See this?" she said, pointing at a beautiful blue flower. "This is dracksbane. I'm actually named after this flower. This plant only flowers when there's magic, and they haven't flowered for twenty-five years. Until now."

"Oh, come on," said Lance.

"I'm serious. Lover-boy over here . . ."

"Hey!" I said, "I thought we were never going to speak of that again!"

"It seems that *Lover-boy*," she said with a smile, "has awoken the presence of magic."

I picked a flower. "See how I bring beauty into the world, comrade?" I turned to Eldrack and bowed low, handing her the flower. "For you, my sweet."

She crushed it and let the petals fall.

"We need to be careful is what I'm saying," she said. "Who knows what beasts lie in wait for us up there."

"Well, I could just zap—"

"No!" they both said.

And so we started our hike into the ever-lovelier Mountains of Death.

Chapter Twenty-Seven

We hiked for two more days without seeing anything unusual, but Eldrack was growing ever more concerned. I thought it odd to see a girl getting upset by the presence of more flowers. We sat down for lunch on day three, and I watched a flower bloom in front of my eyes. It was miraculous.

Or, one might say, magical.

We finished our lunch, packed up, and resumed our trek.

"With any luck, we should be out of here by tomorrow evening," said Eldrack.

I heard a distant buzzing.

"What is that?"

"Dragons?" I said semi-hopefully.

Lance, who was the last in line, could better see what was coming.

"Hornets!" he said, sprinting ahead of us. "Run!"

I didn't stick around to confirm. I was terrified of bees, wasps, hornets, jacklers, snaplets, and all those other stingy creatures. I took off and tried my best to catch up to Lance.

The sound got louder and louder, and soon the entire sky was black. There must have been millions of hornets.

And they were all coming for us.

"Try to stay still—ah, blak, splah" said Eldrack, who had apparently gotten a hornet in her mouth.

I got stung.

I got stung again.

And again.

And . . . well, you get the idea. Dozens of stings. And there was no end in sight. They were crawling over every inch of my body. It was my worst nightmare come true.

"El!" I said, not wanting to open my mouth further.

She tossed me the amulet.

I wasn't sure this would work, but I slipped the necklace over my head and tried to keep my eyes open so I could see the horde, while getting stung again and again, and—

The hornets vanished. Well, most of them did. I gathered from this that I needed to actually see all of the objects I wanted to use the amulet on. The remaining thousand hornets regrouped and made a beeline (pardon the pun) for us, but then I zapped them away, too.

"Ow!" Lance said. He looked terrible. He had several stings on his face.

"What the cuss?" I said. I was angry. "I don't remember Elbo getting attacked by hornets!"

"Where thid you thend them?" said Eldrack.

"You OK?" I asked her.

"I got thung on my thung."

"Are you allergic?"

She shook her head and mumbled something. Probably to inform me that gorks aren't allergic to anything.

"Where did you send them?" said Lance, flicking away a hornet that had gotten stuck in his arm.

"Uh . . ." I said, suddenly realizing what I had done. You know, when a million hornets are attacking you, you don't necessarily have time to think things through.

"What did you do?"

I inhaled. "I sent them to Lieutenant Thuffsburry's quarters."

Lance and Eldrack looked at me for a second.

And then we all laughed hearty, full, giddy, evil laughs.

After we finished chuckling, though, Lance came over and held out his hand.

"OK, mate. Hand it over."

I hesitated a second, but I did as I was told.

"How close?"

"It's hard to say."

"How hard could it be?"

"Look, it's a void. There's nothing else there except me and that nose. I have no reference point."

"Can you see any nose hairs?"

"A few."

"That's too close. We need to be careful."

"We are!" I said. "But come on . . . what else were we gonna do? There were millions of hornets! They would have killed us!"

"Why were they coming after us? Are they attracted to magic, too?"

Eldrack, unable to speak very well due to the sting, shrugged her shoulders and started walking.

"Well said, my dear," I chimed.

She pushed me over.

We walked for a few hours until we came to a steep ridge. We had no choice but to climb. It was grueling work, requiring hand over hand climbing, but after about an hour we made it to the top.

I got there first and sprawled out on the ground in a desperate attempt to rest and catch my breath, but I felt something sticky on the back of my hand.

"Ayee!" I said, launching myself off the ground and trying to wipe off whatever had gotten on my hand.

"Yuck!" said Lance, looking down in the direction we were going to travel.

I slowly raised my eyes, afraid of what I would see.

"Oh, man," said Eldrack after she made it up to the top of the ridge. Her tongue had mostly healed from the hornet sting. "I forgot about the slugs."

Yep. Slugs. Giant slugs.

Now normally, when we say "giant," like with giant eagles, we're talking about things that are way bigger than a person. But in this case, these "giant" slugs were about a foot long and four inches thick. But still . . . yuck. And there were millions of them, stretching as far as we could see, from the north all the way to the south.

Apparently, Eldrack informed us, every three years the slugs in this part of the world go on a massive migration to their southern breeding grounds. And we were lucky enough to arrive right in the middle of it.

We were looking at a slimy river of slugs about a hundred yards wide. And we needed to cross it.

"Hand it over, my good man," I said.

"No way. We're doing this the old fashioned way."

"Are you serious? Look at that!"

"This is not a dire emergency."

"Come on, just a quick zap. I'll keep us slime-free!"

But it was no use. They were dead-set against me using the amulet.

So we trudged across.

At first, it was just kind of gross. Slippery. There was maybe an inch of slime. We had boots on, so it was more the thought of what we were doing and the way our feet skidded on the ground that was so gross.

But then I stepped on one.

I'm no fan of slugs, but I didn't want to hurt them. I had been shuffling my feet and trying to shoo them out of the way, but it was nearly impossible because they were everywhere and the ground was uneven, and, as I mentioned, slippery. About ten yards into my journey, my foot slid off a rock, and I stepped on one of the poor creatures.

The slugs in the immediate area stopped their southerly slither, and instead, they came after me.

"What the cuss!" I said. Dozens of slugs started crawling up my legs.

"Must be pheromones," Lance said. And then he said, "Oh no!" Because he too stepped on a slug.

"Get them off of me!" I said. And then I started to panic because more and more of them were climbing up me and it was getting harder and harder to get rid of them.

"Ugh!" said Eldrack.

"Can they hurt us?" I asked.

"Maybe?"

"Let's run for it!" Lance said.

For once, he was wrong about something.

You know what happens when you try to run on a river of slime?

You fall, that's what happens.

And once you fall, there's no getting back up again. Not with dozens of slugs climbing angrily over you and covering you with their slime.

"Lance!"

He didn't need me to elaborate. He threw the amulet.

But he threw it too far.

"Cuss!" I said.

I tried to scramble over to it, but it was hard to see with all the slugs climbing over me. My hands slipped out from under me, and my face wound up in the slime.

For a moment, I wasn't sure I'd get back up again. Slugs crawled up onto my hair, but I got lucky. My left hand found purchase on a rock that gave me just enough of a grip that I was able to push myself up. I pulled myself forward and saw the amulet. I managed to reach it and slip it over my head.

Had I been able to grab my friends, I would have transported us to the other side of the slime river, but I couldn't get to them.

That meant moving the slugs. I paused, unsure where to send them.

"What are you waiting for?" yelled Lance.

I briefly considered sending them all to our school bailey, or, better yet, right to Smythe's quarters (I had a brief chuckle at that thought), but I was afraid I'd be killing off the entire slug species. And as much as I wanted to see Smythe covered in slimy slugs, I couldn't bring myself to do that. It wasn't their fault we were dumb enough to wade in the middle of their migration. So, I merely moved the slugs about a hundred yards behind us, at the bottom of the ridge.

This time, as I plunged into the void, I tried to gauge just how far away that nose was. And I realized why it had been so hard to judge. The nose wasn't regular sized. It was enormous. Possibly even bigger than me. Knowing this, I was able to determine that it was probably close enough that I could hit it with a snowball.

I came bursting back to the real world.

Although the slugs were gone, the slime wasn't.

It took a good half hour of hard work to scramble across this river of slime.

I had slime everywhere: in my ears, up my nose, inside my clothes, and in other areas, too.

"I feel like I'm never going to be clean again," said Eldrack as we rested on the first bit of non-slimy ground we came to.

I was hungry, but I had no way of cleaning my hands well enough to eat.

"So far this adventure cussing cusses," I said. "What kind of crap creatures are these? What's next? Ants? Cockroaches? Fleas? Where are the trolls and dragons? Heck, I'd even take a giant spider, and I hate spiders."

"Should we keep going?" asked Lance after removing the amulet from my neck.

We did, though it was a challenging walk. We all kept slipping and falling on rocks. I was worried one of us would break a bone. There was no water in sight for us to bathe in.

"I'm dying of thirst," said Lance after a while. But we couldn't open our water pouches for fear of getting slime in them.

"Wait," I said. "I see a ridge up there." I was pointing to a spot about two klicks away. "I say we use the amulet to get us up there so we can scout for a river or lake or something."

We debated about it for a bit, but ultimately decided it was for the best.

I zapped us to the top, and for once we got lucky. Eldrack spied a lake about three klicks to the south. We decided not to use the amulet again, though it was mighty tempting, and we walked, ever so slowly and carefully, to the water.

We arrived just after sunset, and we spent a good hour bathing in the water, scrubbing ourselves to get clean, washing our clothes and all of our belongings, which had gotten covered in slime, and hoping against hope that there was nothing in the lake that would eat us.

Luckily, nothing would try to eat us until the next day.

Chapter Twenty-Eight

I HAD THE FINAL watch of the night, so I was already awake by the time Lance and Eldrack woke up. We ate the last full meal my mom had packed us (which miraculously didn't have any slime on it). Food-wise, all we had left now was a loaf of bread.

We packed up our things. Unfortunately, our map and Lance's copy of Elbo's book had been destroyed by slime, but everything else came through just fine. Things were still wet from last night's cleaning session, but we needed to keep moving.

Off we went.

"So, I know I keep asking you this," said Lance, "but really, how many more uses of that thing do you think we have?"

"Five? Six? Seven? Hard to tell."

"OK. And Eldrack, how far do you think we still need to travel?"

"Hundreds of miles."

"Hundreds."

"Hundreds. We still have to cross the Sea of Destruction, the Forest of Terror, and the Pit of Damnation. And that's just to get to the Mean

Mountains. We still have to climb up a few twelve-thousand-foot peaks to reach Mount Boo-Boo."

"And we have maybe half a dozen uses of that thing to do it?"

"Not to mention that we have to do all of this again. On the way back. Without that thing."

"Oh my gods, whose stupid idea was this?" I said.

It was hard not to despair.

"It's one thing to look on a map," I said. "It's another thing to actually walk through all these awful places."

What were we thinking?

Had we done this right and sat down in a cozy room with some hot tea, examined maps, figured out our supplies, and plotted our course, we would have tossed out this idea as an idiot's quest.

"Elbo did it," said Lance.

"Yeah, well he had a lot of help. Remember that one part where they got a lift from some giant eagles? Where are these bleeding eagles? Why don't we just zap ourselves over to them and ask for a ride?"

"I've always dreamed of flying on a giant eagle," said Eldrack.

"They're gone."

"But maybe they've come back!" I said.

"Yeah, Elbo had help," said Eldrack, "but he also had to face trolls and ghouls and all sorts of creatures that we haven't had to deal with. Heck, we barely made it past a few slugs! Ashokenah help us if we actually faced something dangerous."

"Well, to be fair, those hornets . . . excuse you, mate!" I said, wafting my hand over my nose.

"Huh?" said Lance.

"Look, I don't care that you let one rip, but at least say 'excuse me' or something."

"Let one rip?" he said. And then he smelled it. "Oy! Nasty! Nigel, what did you eat this morning?"

"Me?" I said.

"He who smelt it, mate. That's all I'm saying."

"Ack! You humans are disgusting!" said Eldrack. "Seriously!"

"That's brimstone," said a deep and melodious voice from above.

I looked up and was immediately sorry I had done so, for, flying above me was—you guessed it—a dragon.

It was amazing that something so huge could have snuck up on us, but there it was. He was a beautiful, majestic beast, and even though his overall color was that of a bright yellow, his scales gave him a shimmery glow. He floated above us, maybe fifty feet away, slowly flapping his enormous wings, without making a sound. I could have watched him all day.

"Dragons smell like farts?" I said. "How come, in all the books no one has ever mentioned that? That seems like a critical detail. If I ever write a book, that's the first thing I'm mentioning."

"I smell something, too," said the dragon, alighting on a boulder. "Something I've not smelled in ages."

"Soap," I said, holding up the bar we had used last night. "You should try it."

Eldrack looked at me.

The dragon took a deep breath and exhaled, "No. Something more ancient and wonderful. Magic!" He pointed a claw at Lance. "You've got something. Something very powerful."

Lance whipped the necklace off his head and tossed me the amulet.

"Now he's got it," he said.

"So he has," said the dragon. "And now I want it."

And with that, he opened his mouth and shot two fireballs at me.

A flurry of thoughts assaulted my brain, which was profoundly disorienting, as my mind is usually deliciously void of any thoughts whatsoever.

But, I guess when a dragon blasts fire in your direction, your brain tends to go to work.

The first thought was a mixture of surprise and outrage. I mean, blimey! The stinker didn't even give me a chance to hand the amulet over! Again, this is where I feel the old books have let us down. In Elbo's book, for example, the dragon demands the Cufflinks of Doom, and there's a bit of negotiating, and Elbo acts all brave before running away, resulting in a rather smashing chase scene. Our dragon, on the other hand, was clearly from the Shoot-First-Dig-Through-the-Ashes-Later school of thought, which was super annoying.

The second thought I had was how much more frightening fireballs are when they're coming straight at you, as opposed to flying away towards some distant building. I guess this goes without saying, but my brain felt the need to say it to me anyway.

My final thought, which, if my brain had been worth a damn would have been my first thought, was that now would be a smashing time to use the amulet. I did so, and the fireballs vanished.

The dragon's eyes widened. "You've got the Amulet of Ashokenah!" He licked his lips. "Oh, goody. I've always dreamed of having that."

He shot another couple of fireballs at me, but this time I was better prepared, and I used the amulet to send them right back into his face.

"Ha! Take that!" I said.

"Awufffuff," the dragon said, sputtering and howling with pain and disdain. "That was low, human!"

I tried to use the amulet to send the dragon to the Great Hall in our school. In hindsight, I realize this would have been rather cruel—after all, there were plenty of cadets, instructors, and others who didn't deserve to have an angry dragon suddenly appear in their midst—but the hall was the only place that came to mind that might contain this enormous creature—even if just for a bit. At any rate, it didn't work.

"Ha!" he said. "You can't use magic on a magical creature, you fool!"

He flew into the air and circled, looking for a way to get us. Suddenly he snapped his head forward, trying to bite me. I was prepared for this. I grabbed my friends and zapped the three of us over to a distant cliff, so the dragon chomped down on his own teeth.

"How close is the nose?" asked Lance.

"Let's worry about that later."

We could see the dragon, who was several hundred yards away looking around for us.

"Maybe he won't be able to . . ." but that was as far as Eldrack got. For the dragon took a deep breath and snapped his head right in our direction. He launched himself into the air and, with only a few flaps of his mighty wings, flew to us.

As if that wasn't scary enough, we heard another sound behind us. My heart sank. A red dragon had landed on a rocky outcropping to our left.

"Oy! What you got there, Reg?" she asked our yellow dragon. She had a high, shrill voice. Reminded me of Mrs. Avery, our librarian.

"He's got the Amulet of Ashokenah!" said Reginald the Dragon.

"He's got wot?" said his female friend.

"Argh, didn't you pay attention in school?"

Two more dragons joined the party.

"Did you say Amulet of Ashokenah, Reggie?" said a pale blue dragon.

"I thought that was a myth!" said a dark green dragon.

Eldrack whispered in my ear, "You should probably take this moment to send us somewhere far away from here." That seemed like good advice because we were now surrounded by a dozen dragons.

"We'll find you no matter where you go," said Reginald.

"Blimey! You've got good ears!" I said.

"What are we waiting for?" said a grey dragon, arriving on the scene. "Remember that other git? See, the reason he got away from us was we spent too much time socializing and not enough time attacking. I say we all fire at once. Who's with me?" And he and all the other dragons got ready to shoot.

"Wait! No!" said Reg.

But it was too late. Everyone except Reginald fired at us. I zapped us back over to the other cliff just before the fireballs hit. It had the desired effect. They dragons all shot each other. They rolled around on the ground in pain for a few seconds. Then we saw Reginald point at us.

"After them!" he screamed loud enough for us to hear.

"Forget this!" I said. And I cast my eyes on a distant peak, which I later learned was called Mount Doozy. It was over 14,000 feet high. I say "was" because I aimed the amulet at it and zapped the entire mountain right on top of the dragons, smooshing all of them.

It took a few seconds for us to register what I had done. Parts of the mountain fractured and broke apart. Boulders crashed down the sides, knocking over trees and flinging massive amounts of dust into the air.

My friends stood and stared, their mouths wide open.

"Egads!" said Lance, who looked at me with a touch of horror in his eyes. "That thing really can move mountains."

"You'd better let me hang on to that," said Eldrack holding out her hand.

But, having just used the amulet three times in quick succession, I was starting to feel power-drunk again.

"I'm good," I said, swirling the amulet around on my finger.

I winked at Eldrack and strolled eastward, continuing our journey.

They caught up with me a few minutes later.

"Nigel the Dragon Slayer!" I said, spreading my hands out in front of me as though I was reading the words on a giant tapestry.

My friends didn't say anything for a second.

"Has a nice ring to it, doesn't it?" I prodded.

"More like 'Dragon Squisher,'" Lance said.

"Oh come on, you have to admit that was pretty sweet! I mean, who else has ever killed a dozen dragons at once?"

"Look, mate, don't take this the wrong way, but you're starting to act funny again."

"If by funny you mean awesome? Then yes, I am acting funny again."

"What are you gonna do when Lord Smoron shows up?" asked Eldrack.

"Punch him in his large, stupid nose," I said.

We walked in silence.

I was angry. I mean, here I had saved everyone with some pretty quick and rather creative thinking. And here they were trying to take my amulet away from me.

"What was I supposed to do? Let the dragons kill us?" I said. "And another thing—"

Once again, our conversation was interrupted; only this time, it wasn't a voice that did the interrupting; it was a sound. A sickening crinkle, followed by a series of ticky-tack noises that are hard to describe but which immediately suggested that we were about to be set upon by a giant insect of some sort.

I was wrong, but only slightly.

Eldrack gasped.

I spun around to see a giant spider rushing straight at us. It was an even more horrifying sight that I might have imagined, for this thing was as big as a house. The top of its body was a good four feet taller than a grown man. And it was fast. It took a second for me to comprehend the fact that something so enormous could also be so agile. There was no way we could outrun this thing.

There was only one thing for me to do. But as I fumbled for the amulet, Eldrack put her hand on my shoulder. "You can't keep using that thing!"

"Are you kidding me?"

I aimed at the spider, and it vanished. I plunged into the void. The nose was so close now I could almost touch it, maybe six feet away, tops. When I re-emerged from the blackness, I saw the spider fall off the cliff to our left. A second later, we heard a splat.

Lance raced over to the edge and quickly turned his head away. "You don't want to look over here."

"How close?" Eldrack asked me.

"You let me worry about the nose."

"No more using that thing!"

"Hello!" I said. "Giant spider!"

"We could have taken it."

"Could have taken it? The three of us? Fight that house on legs?"

"I don't know about a house. It was more like the size of a large shed," said Lance.

"Oh. Just a shed, was it?" I said. "Forgive me. I should have let us fight a Giant spider the size of a large shed . . ."

"More like a mid-sized shed," said Eldrack. "And yes. We could have taken it."

"A bunch of lunatics," I said, and I stormed off into the scrub. "I'm surrounded by loonies."

I walked about twenty steps or so when I came upon a clearing. And in that clearing were about forty round, spikey objects, the size of boulders.

"Eggs," said Eldrack. "She was protecting her eggs." She turned angrily to me. "You killed a mother rushing back to protect her eggs."

"So I'm supposed to feel bad about this?" I said. "Not a moment ago you were saying how you would have killed her by fighting her to death. At least I made it quick."

"Guys," said Lance. "Let's keep moving before any of these eggs hatches because that would be bad."

We needed to get to the other side of the egg field, but it wasn't like the eggs were placed in rows. They were scattered haphazardly, almost like a maze.

"I could zap us—"

"No!" she said.

"OK, don't have a spider, love."

We started walking through the egg maze.

Well, you can guess what happened.

First, one egg started hatching.

Then another. And another.

One by one, spiders—the size of jail carts—started crawling out of their eggs and heading towards us.

"Argh!" Lance said. "I hate spiders!"

"Nigel, no!" Eldrack said, seeing me grab for the amulet.

"Run!" said Lance.

I had been planning on sending us away, but Lance made that impossible by running, so I couldn't get a grip on him. That left me with only one option.

ZAP!

I sent all the eggs to the slug river.

Now there were just a dozen spiders to deal with.

ZAP!

Now they, too, were in the slime.

"Stop!" said Eldrack.

"OK!" I said. "They're all gone!"

"Guys!" said Lance. He was running towards us.

"Uh-oh," I said.

A dozen more spiders came pouring over the ridge behind him.

They were just about to catch up with him, and he was too far away for me to reach, so I had to—

236 · SCOTT MCCORMICK

ZAP!

Make them all disappear.

The nose was almost on top of me now, but more spiders were pouring over the ridge.

Lance dove to us.

I had no choice. I had to use it again. And because I couldn't see all the spiders, I knew I wouldn't be able to zap them all, so my only option was to teleport us. And since I couldn't see any safe place up ahead to send us, I had to send us back somewhere we had already been.

I thought of the field where I had confessed my feelings for Eldrack. I was pretty sure I hadn't sent any creatures there, but I wasn't positive. (It was getting hard to keep track.)

The spiders were almost on top of us . . .

BAM!

An explosion sent us flying.

When I could see again, the three of us were lying on the ground in the Plains of Sorrow. Crouching next to us was a figure, dressed in shining black armor with a black cape.

"Behold, mortals!" he said, standing up. "For—ahhhhh! My eyes!" The man screamed and fell over. He attempted to cover his eyes with his hands, but he seemed unable to move his arms.

"Arghhh!" he said, writhing on the ground like a headless snake.

The three of us looked at each other, unsure of what to do.

"Little help?" said Lord Smoron.

Part Four

Chapter Twenty-Nine

WE STOOD UP and looked upon the pathetic little figure wiggling around in the grass. I say little, for he was shorter than me, and I'm about average height for a fourteen-year-old.

"This is the evilest villain in history?" Lance said.

"Once again," I said, "I feel the history books have failed us. Remember the slugs? Those were scary."

"Are you just gonna stand there?" yelled Lord Smoron, flopping about like a half-dead hake.

"We could laugh," I said.

"What's wrong with you?" Eldrack asked him. She seemed disgusted by the sight.

"You try living in a void for two thousand years and see how you do! My eyes need time to adjust to the daylight!"

"Well, why can't you stand up?" asked Lance.

Smoron stopped squirming. He took a deep breath. "I haven't used my muscles in two millennia. I guess they've atrophied."

"So," I crouched down. "Let me get this straight. For two thousand years, you've been trying to emerge from the void to continue your quest for world domination, yes?"

"Maybe."

"How's that going?"

"Laugh it up, tough guy. But soon I'm gonna regain my eyesight and strength, and then we'll see who's laughing."

I stood up and dusted off my hands.

"What are you thinking, comrade?" Lance asked.

I grabbed the amulet.

"No!" said Eldrack.

"Why not?" I asked. "Smoron's already here!"

"Oh. Right. OK, go ahead, I guess."

I aimed the amulet at him. Smoron started laughing.

"Let's see how you laugh once you're locked up in Lieutenant Thuffsburry's jail."

Nothing happened.

Smoron laughed some more. "You can't use that on magical creatures," he said.

I remembered having that same issue with the dragons, "Keep an eye on him. I'll be right back."

"Where are you—"

I zapped myself back to the bank of the Moor River. Thankfully, I didn't plunge into the void this time. My trip was utterly instantaneous and much more pleasant. I guessed that since Smoron was now in the real world, my journeys into the void were a thing of the past.

I looked around for the rope. It was right where I'd left it, still tied to two trees on opposite sides of the river. I walked up to it and whipped out my sword. I was about to cut the rope when laughter startled me. I turned around and there, rolling on the muddy ground, was Lord Smoron.

"What are you doing here?"

He laughed some more. It was really more of a cackle by this point.

I rolled my eyes and sliced the rope. I let go of it and watched the current catch it and drag it downriver.

Smoron was still cackling away, so I just ignored him and zapped myself across to the other side of the river. Unfortunately, Smoron came along for that ride, too, though by this point he was completely hysterical, writhing away next to me in some dead leaves.

"How is it possible that you keep traveling with me? I'm not touching you!"

He laughed some more. It seemed I wasn't going to get an answer out of him.

I grabbed the rope and sliced this end away from the tree. I sheathed my sword and started coiling.

"I can't believe you're the one who's laughing," I said. "Do you know how ridiculous you look?"

This sent him into a spasm of laughter. In fact, he was laughing so hard he started coughing, "Ow! Ow! Oh man! It hurts!" But that didn't stop him from laughing.

By this point I was getting rather annoyed with all of this, so I zapped myself into a shallow part of the river, where the water was only up to my thighs. But it was deep enough that Smoron couldn't lift his head to the surface. I couldn't see him struggling for air because the water was so muddy, but I could see bubbles popping up, and the water was agitated from his struggles.

I relished the silence.

Then, after thirty seconds or so, I started to feel guilty. I mean, I knew he was the worst bad guy of all time and everything, but I couldn't bring myself to drown him, especially since he hadn't done anything to me or my friends.

I sighed a long sigh, and then zapped us back to the spot where I'd left Eldrack and Lance.

"Right!" Smoron said after sputtering up a gallon of water. "I'll do you for that!"

"What the heck is going on?" said Eldrack. "We thought you were in trouble."

I tossed the rope to Lance. "You're good with knots. Will you tie him up so we don't have to worry about him?" Then I explained what had happened while we were gone.

"So, what, are you linked to the amulet?" Eldrack asked Smoron.

"Of course I am! I made the bloody thing!"

"No, you didn't!" said Eldrack. "Ashokenah the Creator did!"

That sent Smoron into another fit of laughter. Having had rather enough of his laughter to fill a lifetime, I sauntered over to him and kicked him in the groin.

He spent the next few minutes cursing at me and telling me about all the terrible things he was going to do with me, but he eventually calmed down.

"You made this amulet?" said Eldrack, trying to steer him back on course.

"Funny story," Smoron said. "I'm Ashokenah."

"Liar!"

"Do you have anything to eat?" he asked. "I'm famished."

"No! And even if we did, we wouldn't give it to you!" said Eldrack.

"That'll teach him," I said.

"Ashokenah gave the amulet to the gorks a thousand years before you were ever born."

"I'm really old," said Lord Smoron. "The first piece of magic I perfected was to make myself immortal. But I got bored, so I made that thing. Figured I'd try to conquer the world."

"How'd you ever lose it? I mean, this thing can literally move mountains."

"I didn't lose it," he said with a sniff. "It was stolen from me."

"By whom?" said Lance. Of all my friends, only Lance would use the word *whom*.

"I'm not telling you losers anything else."

"Losers?" said Eldrack. "You're the one who's all tied up."

He didn't have a response to that. And I took the lull in conversation to give the man the once-over. I don't know about you, but when I imagine the most-evil bloke in history, I tend to think of a tall chap with lots of muscles and chiseled features and an angry, powerful expression. Maybe even a mustache. This chap? He looked like a banker who had dressed up as a knight for a costume party.

"You're staring at my nose, aren't you?" Smoron said after a few moments.

"Huh? What? No, I wasn't."

This was true, after all, his nose wasn't all that big.

"See why I tried to conquer and destroy the world?" he said, "It was bad enough that my last name was Smoron, but to also have this for a schnozz? The kids never stopped making fun of me."

"You tried to destroy humanity because some kids made fun of your nose?"

"OK, in hindsight I can see that it was a bit of an overreaction. But once I started conquering the world? I couldn't stop myself! It was exciting! Everyone was doing what I told them to do! Girls paid attention to me! I could—get this—I could get candy any time I wanted it!"

We nodded and glanced at each other, unsure of what to make of this fellow with a nose complex.

"Speaking of food . . . please, can I have some? I'm famished. Haven't eaten in two thousand years. And I can smell something delicious in Lance's backpack."

"Good to see your giant nose is still working," I said.

"I'm going to relish destroying you and your mother."

"How did you know my name?" asked Lance.

"And about my mother?"

"I've been watching you guys ever since Nigel, or should I say, *Nibel*, woke up the Amulet."

"How are you still," Lance began, "you know . . ."

"Alive? Ha! I told you. I made that amulet. I attached part of my soul to it, so I'd never die."

"You're not Ashokenah!" said Eldrack. "Besides, Ashokenah lived a thousand years before you did."

"You don't have to believe me. That's cool, as you kids might say. Do kids say that? 'Cool?' Back in my day, kids said 'cool.' Anyway, the fact of the matter is I made that Amulet. In fact, I even created the gorks. How's that for awesome?"

Eldrack huffed at that last revelation.

"You made this insanely powerful weapon?" asked Lance. "How?"

"Oh, it's too complicated to explain unless you know a lot of quantum physics, which I'm assuming you don't know . . ."

"And you created gorks?"

"Advanced Biochemistry. Crazy stuff."

"Who stole this weapon from you?"

"I see. You think I'm going to make the mistake that every bad guy makes by explaining everything to you so you can exploit it later? Ha! I'm not falling for that. You're getting no information out of me whatsoever!"

"I'll bet his mother took it away from him," Eldrack said.

"Shut up!" said Smoron. "She did not!"

"Aw . . . wittle Smoron got into twouble wif his mummy?"

He lay there quietly, but I could tell he was fuming. Clearly, we'd touched a nerve.

"I get it," I said. "You fell asleep one night, thinking everything was fine, but your mom slipped into your room, stole the amulet, and hid it from you, thus ending your plan for world domination."

He still wasn't speaking.

In fact, he wasn't flailing about, either, and that unsettled me.

"What are you doing?"

He didn't answer. It was almost like he was in a trance or meditating like the Shiffu Monks of the far east.

The amulet started to flutter on my chest. And then it lifted off of me and floated in the air, pointing right at Smoron, like he was a magnet.

Smoron started to do one of those evil, rumbling laughs the bad guys do in books.

"What's happening?" I asked. I pushed the amulet down, but it flew right back up again.

"It's trying to get back to its owner," said Lance.

Smoron started laughing again.

But then Eldrack kicked him in the groin. She obviously hit him harder than I did, for he didn't curse like he had last time, he just moaned in agony.

"Wow. That is really satisfying," she said.

The amulet landed back on my chest.

Chapter Thirty

"OK," SAID LANCE. "So I think our course is pretty clear. He's obviously gaining strength if he's able to use his magic again. And we can't keep kicking him in the pants every ten minutes."

"Awww. But it's so fun!" said Eldrack. She placed another kick to emphasize the word fun.

Lance turned to me. "Eventually he's gonna get that amulet and then it's game over for humanity."

"I say we just kill him right here and now," said Eldrack. "Give me your sword. I'll do it."

I hesitated. "I don't know, El."

"Oh, come on, kid," said Smoron. "Be a man! Let's see what you got!"

"I'll do it," said Lance, whipping out his sword.

"Oh no! Not Theresa!" said Smoron in fake horror.

"I still hate that name, comrade," I murmured to Lance.

"Why aren't you more scared?" Lance said to Smoron.

"I'm indestructible."

"You look it," I said. "You got bested by a bunch of fourteen-year-olds, mate. You're all tied up and covered in mud and dead leaves. You can't even move!"

He flicked his left hand at me—for although his arms were tied tightly against his body, he could still move his hands—and the amulet flew off my chest, trying to get to him. I grabbed it just as the chain broke around my neck. One second later and the amulet would have been in his possession. The pull was strong enough that I had to lean back or risk falling over.

Lance sprung into action. He lunged forward and slammed his blade down on Smoron's chest. Although the sword managed to slice through Smoron's armor, it did nothing to his skin.

"Oof!" Smoron said.

The pressure on the amulet released, causing me to fall backwards. I quickly stood up and got into sword-fighting position. I didn't want to be surprised again.

"You can't kill me, kid. There was a time when I could have been killed, but they blew their chance."

"Who?"

"Dash it all! You got me talking again!"

"Let me hold it." Eldrack held her hand out. She was quite a bit stronger than me.

"Smart girl," said Smoron. "He's the dangerous one!"

"Shut your yap, Nosey," I said. OK, that wasn't the greatest insult of all time, but I was annoyed.

"Ever since I showed up back here in reality, a lowly invalid, unable to stand or see, all you've done is beat me and stab me and tie me up and say mean things about me. What did I ever do to you?"

I laughed. Actually, now that I think back on it, it was more of a snort. I mention this only because one doesn't get to snort very often. It felt good.

"You started the Really Big War!" I said.

"Well, you started a war, and no one is giving you grief!" he replied.

"What are you talking about?"

He looked at me with a curious expression. And then he laughed. "You mean, you don't know?"

"Know what?"

He squirmed around on the ground for a bit, scanning the horizon.

"What are you doing?" Eldrack asked.

"See that hilltop over there?" Smoron said, "Pop us over there, will you?"

"What kind of trick—"

"Oh for the love of beets, just do it already."

I looked at the hill. There didn't seem to be any kind of trap, so I grabbed my friends and zapped us over.

"Now what?"

"Look."

He nodded towards a field maybe three hundred yards away. We could see thousands of humans and gorks engaged in a fierce battle. People slicing at each other. Arrows finding their marks in gork and human bodies. There were cries of pain and agony. People were getting slaughtered on both sides. Blood ran in the grass.

It was horrific.

"This is the fourth such battle that has happened since the war started, or, I should say since you started the war."

"I did no such thing!"

"No?"

I couldn't watch the battle anymore, so I zapped us to the spot in the woods where I had accidentally made Lance disappear.

"You're saying I started that? How exactly did I start the war?"

"Remember those dragons you so ruthlessly squished?"

"Crushed, you mean? What about 'em?"

"That first fellow, Reginald? The yellow dragon with the bad B.O. What do you think happened to those first two fireballs he shot at you?"

"I don't know. I sent them—" I gasped. "Oh, no!"

"Oh, yes!"

I fell backwards.

"It wasn't my fault!"

"What are you talking about?" said Eldrack.

I jumped up and grabbed on to my friends and zapped us back . . .

. . . just in time to see those very same fireballs fly through the air towards Fell's Palace.

We stood on that rocky hill I had noticed that morning when we cadets had hiked to the parade grounds.

I held up the amulet and tried to make the fireballs disappear, but the amulet didn't have any effect on them. The dragonfire slammed into the palace, collapsing the two towers, which crumbled on to the rest of the building, destroying it entirely. Debris and smoke engulfed everyone on the field. I scanned the ground, looking for the past versions of Lance and myself, but I couldn't see anyone in that ash cloud.

"You destroyed the palace?" said Lance.

"I . . . I didn't mean to," I said vacantly. "I just . . . when the dragon shot at me, the last thought I had before the fireballs hit me was that I thought they looked familiar. And I guess I inadvertently thought of this moment."

"It's awful," said Eldrack.

I sat down, staring at the chaos below.

Smoron, seeing that I was distracted, used this moment to try to summon the amulet. It almost worked, too. The force of Smoron's spell yanked me up and towards him. Thankfully, Lance jumped in the way, but there we were, Smoron, Lance, and me, all pressed up against each other, in some kind of squiggly, scream-y sandwich. It wasn't until Eldrack popped Smoron on the head that he let go, causing Lance and I to topple over.

I stood up and cursed at the villain. I even kicked him in the face, which felt great for a brief second. But then he laughed at me. He was right to laugh.

Disgusted with myself, I turned to face the damage I'd wrought. People were screaming and crying and running in circles. I could hear a child yelling for his mother.

I couldn't take it anymore. I transported us back to the Plain of Sorrow.

"Thousands of people have died," said Smoron. "Thousands more will die. The Gorkish Kingdom? That's going to fall. And the humans will eventually wipe the gorks out of existence. All because of you."

"How do you know that?" I said.

"Come on, kid. I'm Lord Smoron," he winked. "I know things."

I couldn't think straight. I needed to get away from him and this stupid amulet that had caused so much grief.

I handed it to Eldrack, and I went for a walk.

It's not every day you discover you are responsible for the destruction of a palace, the start of a war, and the obliteration of an entire race. It was such an overwhelming revelation I was having a hard time wrapping my head around it. How could one mistake have caused so much pain and suffering? I wanted to cry. I wanted to scream. I wanted to gnash my teeth, whatever that is. I felt awful. And yet at the same time, I felt totally dead inside. It was all too much to bear.

Lance caught up to me.

"Look, mate . . . I don't know how you feel, but I know this: You're a decent bloke. Sure you've destroyed pretty much everything you've ever come into contact with, but you're also the kindest person I know. Heck, you couldn't even bring yourself to kill Lord Smoron when you thought you had the chance. You actually felt compassion for him. I'm sorry you started this war, but I also know you never meant to. You're still my best friend."

I looked at him. He wore a kind smile.

"And you know what else I know?" He did that squinty thing on the word "else," which almost made me smile.

"What's that?"

"I know you can fix it."

Chapter Thirty-One

THAT PEP TALK had been just what I needed to hear. We stormed back to Eldrack and Smoron, who were having a discussion.

"But you want to destroy the world," I heard her say.

"No, I want to rule the world," Smoron said with a shrug. "Look, what do you have now? An old fool of a human king and his idiot son? The angry and volatile Gorkish King Skidmark? I'll be a much better ruler. I've had thousands of years to figure this out. For example, first thing I do after assuming control? Universal healthcare. Boom! Second thing? A livable minimum wage for everyone. You're welcome. Third thing? And I'm just spit-balling here, but I love this one: Casual Fridays! BAM! It's on!"

"You're back!" said Eldrack, looking relieved to see me.

"I'm back all right." I held out my hand for the amulet. "And I've got a plan."

She gave it to me, and I grabbed her hand.

Smoron guffawed. (I hated to admit it, but the chap had a cracking guffaw.) "I can see you're looking for a way out—"

I zapped us to a dark hilltop in the middle of the woods. There was snow on the ground.

"—of this," Smoron said.

"Hey! I know where we are!" said Lance. "In fact, there we are!"

He pointed to a group of kids frolicking about in the snow and making their way to this very spot. And sure enough, we could see Lance and me in the crowd.

"You don't want to run into your old . . ." Smoron cut himself off in mid-sentence.

"Huh? We don't want to run into our old selves? Why not?"

"Wow, I really have to stop talking. What's wrong with me?"

I didn't know whether to believe anything he said, but I suspected he had actually let something slip.

The kids were getting closer to the hill, and I didn't want them to see us, so . . .

ZAP!

I moved us down the hill, to the other side of the path where the merchant's cart would be coming in a few minutes.

"What would happen if I came into contact with my old self?" I said.

"Beats me," said Smoron. "Why don't you go find out?"

"You wish."

The clip-clopping of hooves distracted me. I looked down the road, and sure enough, there was the merchant's cart.

"You can't use the amulet to change your past," Smoron said.

"Why?"

"Paradoxes. See if you make this event never happen, then you don't get sent to that awful military academy and blah blah blah, you don't end up with the amulet, which in turn would make this event never happen, and around and around we go."

He looked at us.

We looked at him.

"Never mind. Go for it if it makes you feel better."

Why should I trust him, I thought. He's the most diabolical villain of all time. But I figured I had to give it a try. I had to see if I could divert that horse before I threw that blasted snowball.

The horse and cart came riding up. I held up the amulet to see if I could zap the cart into the village unharmed.

Nothing happened.

"See?" jeered Smoron. I wanted to smack him, but I was still focused on changing the future.

Who needed the stupid amulet?

"Guys!" I said, "We need to stop that horse!"

We ran out into the road. Smoron got dragged along on the ground as I sprinted forward.

On the hill I could see the other Lance, whom I'll call Past Lance, throw a snowball.

We still had time to change the future, for it wasn't until the fourth or fifth snowball that I hit that poor horse.

The three of us stood in the middle of the road and yelled at the driver to stop. He continued as though he couldn't see or hear us.

"What's wrong with that guy?" I asked Lance. "Lance?" I couldn't see him, even though he had been right next to me only a second ago. I waved my hand in front of my face. I couldn't even see my own body.

The horse was right in front of me, totally unaware that I was standing there.

BAM! The horse got hit in the face with my snowball. He whinnied and reared back and took off running right through us, into the square.

"I told you," said Smoron. "The amulet won't let you change any history that prevents you from getting the amulet."

I sank onto the ground. Then I cursed because I had forgotten that the ground was muddy and wet from the snow.

"Ugh!" I said. I grabbed my friends' hands and zapped us back to the place where Smoron had first joined us.

"I can't stop the Palace from falling," I said. I was sitting in on the ground, trying to soothe my soul with the beautiful scenery around me. Mostly I was staring at a fleerflower and feeling powerless.

"I guess not," said Eldrack.

"So I can't stop the war."

"Nope."

"Give up, yet, kid?" said Smoron.

I stared at him.

"No!" I said it the way a little kid might if you were to ask him if he would like to give up candy for the rest of the year.

But then I collected myself. "You know what? I might not be able to stop what's already happened, but I sure as heck-fire can stop you from taking over."

"Atta boy, matey!" said Lance.

"Let's end this. Grab on to me!" I turned my back to Smoron. I was going to need total concentration for what I was about to do. I didn't want to have to worry about Smoron trying to summon the amulet, so I figured if I had my back to him, at least my body would be in the way should he attempt anything.

Lance and Eldrack clutched at my arms.

I zapped us to the farthest spot I could see towards the east. We landed on a small rocky hilltop. We were standing at the eastern end of the Mountains of Death. From here, I could see a hundred miles further east to what looked like a body of water.

"What—" Smoron began, but I zapped us all the way to the edge of the Sea of Destruction. It was enormous. I had no idea a body of water could be so big. That lake near my house, Lake Beginshaw, was maybe half a mile wide at its widest point. This sea in front of me was so vast I couldn't see across to the other side, which meant I couldn't zap us to dry land.

But that didn't stop me.

"—are—" Smoron continued.

BAM! I zapped us a mile out into the middle of the sea.

"—you—"

BAM! Before we could sink into the water, I zapped us out another mile.

"—doing—"

BAM! Zapped again.

"—ahhh—"

BAM!

"—ahhh—"

BAM!

"—AHHH!!!—"

BAM!

I'll tell you why Smoron was yelling.

As I was zapping us across the sea, I'd had an idea. I picked a spot, a cloud, miles up in the sky. And I transported us there. We started to fall, of course, but then I chose another cloud. And another. And another. We were traveling dozens of miles with each jump. Why hadn't I thought of this sooner?

"—HHHHHHHHHHH!!!!! You're crazy!!!!"

We stopped, perched atop the highest tree in the middle of a vast forest.

"Is this the Forest of Terror?" I asked Eldrack, who was desperately trying to cling to both me and a flimsy branch.

"I think—"

BAM! We were back in the sky again, still over the forest.

BAM! at another spot, but now there was no forest below us, just a giant hole in the ground.

"Is that the Pit of Damnation?" I shouted at Eldrack.

Up to this point we kept being surprised at how misleading Gorkish place names were: the Plains of Sorrow were beautiful, the Mountains of Death were simply tall and snowy, the Sea of Destruction was nothing more than a large body of water, and the Mountains of Doom were fairly innocuous (except for the hornets, slugs, and dragons, of course). But this hole was so big it was scary. When I say there was a giant hole in the ground, I'm not doing it justice. The hole was ten miles across and so deep that we couldn't see the bottom. The sight of it was unnerving in a new and terrible way.

And we were plummeting towards it at a terrifying pace.

"Ahhhh!" she said, which I took as a yes, confirming my theory that nothing good could possibly be named Pit.

Smoron must have sensed my unease, for he chose this moment to launch a counter-attack and try once again to summon the amulet. The force jolted me back against him. The amulet pressed into my chest, trying to bore through me. But I was not about to be deterred.

BAM!

I zapped us to another distant spot, way high in the air, to disorient Smoron.

"Lance!" yelled Eldrack.

We were falling again, but I managed to look back.

I saw my friend free-falling into the Pit of Damnation. Smoron's action must have lurched me out of Lance's grip.

"Cuss!"

BAM!

We were at Lance's side. Eldrack grabbed him.

BAM! Back in the air. As we fell, I spied a distant mountain.

BAM!

We were standing on a snowy windblown mountain.

"OK, I gotta say, that was AWESOME!" said Smoron. "I floated around in that void for two thousand years and not ONCE did it occur to me to use the amulet to freakin' FLY IN THE AIR!?! YOU'RE AN ANIMAL! I LOVE IT!"

He whooped it up for a second, but then he caught his breath.

"You know, and I mean this, I'm honestly going to be kind of sad when I destroy you. I never feel bad about destroying anybody. But you're awesome. I will raise a glass in your honor. After, you know, I destroy you."

"Are we where I think we are?" I asked Eldrack, ignoring him.

"There it is!" she said.

She was pointing at the red, glowing tunnel on the face of the next mountain over. Actually, it wasn't a mountain. It was a volcano. And not just any volcano. We were looking at Mount Boo-Boo.

BAM!

Chapter Thirty-Two

I ZAPPED US TO the entrance of the famed Tunnel of Victory on Mount Boo-Boo. This was easily the most-famous yet least-visited place in the world. It had been a harrowing journey for us, and we had had a magical amulet to help us. I couldn't imagine how hard it must have been for Elbo.

"I can't believe we're finally here!" Eldrack said.

"Lance! We made it!"

"Mmm," he said. He looked up and saw my confusion. "Sorry, comrade. In my head, I'm still plummeting to my death into that pit."

Eldrack put her hand on my shoulder. "You feeling OK? Not drunk with power or anything?"

"Not at all."

"Yeah," said Smoron. "That was a little spell I put on the amulet to make people want to use it more so I could get out of the void. Clever, right?"

"So," said Lance, looking like he had recovered, "who's ready to destroy that thing?"

"No!" said Smoron.

"You're about to lose, mate," I said to Smoron. And then I stormed towards the entrance to the volcano. As I walked, Smoron slid behind me on the rocky ground, being pulled by an invisible force of attraction.

"Wait, Nigel!" said Eldrack rushing up to me. "This won't work."

"She's right," said Smoron in a panic. "Don't do it!"

I was confused. After all, this had been the big plan ever since I had tackled her into the river—take the amulet to this very spot and throw it in the fire to destroy it. Why all of a sudden was it not going to work? And furthermore, if it wasn't going to work, why was Smoron so afraid that I would go through with it?

"Think about it," she said. "The minute you let go of that thing, he'll just summon it right to him."

Ah.

"OK, let's think. You have to hold the amulet to make it work, right?" I said. "What if we tie his hands so he can't hold it. And then we toss both of them down into the lava."

That plan sounded good to me.

"That won't work either," said Lance. "He's indestructible, remember? The ropes will burn before the amulet does. Then he can just zoom away and conquer the world, and we'll be stuck here."

"If he doesn't kill us first."

He started laughing again. "Got you in a tight spot, don't I?"

I nodded at Eldrack. She kicked Smoron in the face.

I still wanted to see the famous spot where Elbo had destroyed the Cufflinks of Doom, so I marched into the cave, dragging Smoron along with me.

Boy was it hot, which kind of figures, given that it was an active volcano, but I was not prepared for the temperature. I could feel waves of heat flowing over me, and I started to sweat. Once inside, I looked for the ledge Elbo mentioned in his book, and sure enough, there it was, leading into the middle of the mountain. I walked to the edge and looked down. I could see a roiling and broiling lava lake a thousand feet below me.

"What if I just jumped?" I said, the thought hitting me from nowhere.

"What? You can't do that, mate!"

"He's going to destroy the world! I don't know how to stop him. And besides! Look at all the pain and suffering I've caused. At least this way I can try to do something right for a change."

"OK, first of all, you're crazy," said Eldrack. "Second of all, you don't even know if that will work."

"Only one way to find out!" said Smoron.

"There's got to be another way, mate," said Lance.

Smoron took advantage of the fact that we weren't on high alert, and he flicked his hand again, summoning the amulet. I managed to hang on to it, but, because I wasn't ready for him, I fell forward and started sliding towards Smoron. Then he did something dastardly: He stopped pulling.

The suddenness of this caused me to roll off the ledge.

"Noo!" screamed Eldrack.

I plummeted, maybe twenty feet, but before I could zap myself to safety, he resumed his attack, pulling the amulet towards him as hard as he could, which caused my body to whip downwards, towards the lava. The force of it nearly ripped the amulet right out of my hand. I honestly don't know how I managed to hang on.

But my troubles weren't over, for now I was flying up at him without the ground to slow me down. It was only because I managed to regain my senses that I was able to zap myself up to the cave entrance.

Smoron appeared at my side and once again tried to pull the amulet towards him. He pulled so hard he yanked himself upright, and we flew towards each other. My instinct was to raise my right knee to brace myself for impact, and it was a lucky thing I did, too, for that was the only thing keeping me away from him.

Lance dashed forward and slammed his sword on Smoron's head.

Smoron cursed, and his spell-force let go of me, which caused both of us to fall. I jumped up and started yelling at him.

"What's wrong with you?"

He tried again. This time, he was using two hands. Once again, I fell forward, but Eldrack was ready. She grabbed me by the waist and pulled back. It hurt like a . . . well, it hurt a lot. I felt like I was being torn in two.

Lance smashed away again and again and again at Smoron's face, but it didn't seem to have any effect at all. He was determined.

And I don't know. My mind works in weird ways. But something about fighting Smoron and the fact that he was indestructible made me think of something he had said. I had a new plan.

Eldrack was already holding on to me.

"Lance!" I yelled, reaching for him. He stopped smashing Smoron and grabbed my hand.

BAM!

We all collapsed on the ground.

"What happened?" said Smoron. He stopped trying to summon the amulet, and instead looked around in an attempt to figure out what I was up to.

"Did we just travel?" said Lance. "Because it felt like we just traveled."

The reason for everyone's confusion was that we were in the same spot, but what I knew and they didn't was that we had traveled twenty-five years into the past to VS (Victory over Smoron) Day. I didn't say anything because I didn't want to alert Smoron to my plans.

I scrambled up and away from him, putting Eldrack in between him and me, lest he try anything again.

"Where are they?" I said, looking at the cave entrance.

"Where are who?" whispered Eldrack.

I remained silent. I handed her the amulet so Smoron wouldn't follow me, and I ran outside the cave.

I looked to the West, and sure enough, the sun was setting.

This was the moment I had read about.

I peered over the edges of the mountain, looking for climbers, but no one was there.

"What are you up to?" asked Lance, trotting up to me. I glanced back to make sure Eldrack and Smoron were still in the cave.

"They should be here. This is the famous moment!"

"Who?"

I looked at him and decided I'd hold my tongue a little longer. I jogged back inside to make sure Smoron wasn't giving Eldrack any grief.

"Well?" she said.

Just then something flew past my head, causing me to duck. I reflexively turned towards the cave entrance, unsure if more projectiles were coming to bombard me, but the sky looked clear.

"What was that?" said Eldrack. She was looking over the ledge, down towards the lava lake below us.

She had seen it too.

Suddenly there was a burst of light from down below.

We heard a distant explosion. Lance and I bolted outside and, way off to the north, we could see a tower crumbling.

"What is that?" Lance said.

It was the Tower of Numendrack, the headquarters of Smoron and his army during the Really Big War. Elbo had destroyed it when he threw the Cufflinks of Doom into the fires of Mount Boo-Boo.

But where was Elbo?

"What's going on, mate?"

I had to think, which as you know is not one of my strengths, but the answer on how to destroy Smoron was near . . . I just had to see it.

Then I saw it.

"Where is Riverfell?" I asked Lance, referencing the famed city of elves, where we had initially planned on going in our quest to find the mythical/magical Relic of the First Age.

"Riv . . . how the heck should I know? West. Way west of here. But why?"

I ran back into the cave.

". . . and you could be my queen," Smoron mumbled to Eldrack.

"Are you hitting on her?" I said. "She's fourteen! I mean, come on! There's gotta be some law against that kind of thing."

"Oh, shut up," said Smoron.

"I don't know," Eldrack said. "He's kind of charming."

I stood there, gaping at her, even though I knew she was joking.

She laughed. "What's the plan, Lover-boy?"

"The amulet, please."

She handed it to me. I closed my hand over hers, so we were both holding onto it. Lance grabbed my arm.

BAM!

Chapter Thirty-Three

"NIGEL!" SCREAMED MY mother. We had startled her, causing her to drop a bowl, which promptly smashed on the ground, further fraying the poor woman's nerves. I had zapped us into her house back in the present day. It was getting rather hard to keep track of time, but we arrived at my mom's house maybe two hours after I had brought Smoron back to the real world. The light was streaming in through the window, birds were chirping outside, and my mom was furious at me. I felt right at home.

"Sorry, Mom."

"You can't keep popping into my house whenever you feel like it! And why is this person tied up? What have you done now?"

"Oh, sorry. Mom, meet Lord Smoron."

"Ma'am," he said.

But she wasn't paying him any mind. She pointed her long, bony finger at me. "You know what I'm going to do? I'm going to rearrange the furniture!"

This was a rather puzzling threat until I realized what it meant.

"You wouldn't!"

"I will!"

"Huh?" said Eldrack.

"Wow, that's evil!" said Smoron. "See, if she moves the furniture, your boyfriend here won't know where to make you reappear. For all he knows, he'll pop you right into the middle of that table! Ouch! Man, I thought I was evil. But you, ma'am . . . simply diabolical! And against your own son, too!"

"Who is this idiot?" said my mom, her juices flowing.

"I'm Lord Smoron."

"You can't be Lord Smoron," she said. "Smoron's dead."

"I was, sort of," Smoron said, "But your son brought me back."

"NIGEL!"

"My bad!" I had handed the amulet to Eldrack and was now rummaging through my dad's old books.

"'My bad'?" she said. "You can't bring back the lord of all evil and simply say 'my bad' and hope it all goes away!"

"Look, Mom, I just need to borrow a book."

"You most certainly may not!" she said. "Get out of here at once."

"Sorry, ma'am," said Lance, "but it really is important."

"Important how?"

"I have no idea because Nigel can't say in front of you-know-who," he thumbed at Smoron. "But he seems very excited about it."

I found what I was looking for and held it aloft. "Aha!"

"The atlas? What do you want with that?" she asked me.

"Not now, Mom," I said, flipping through the pages.

"Why, the nerve!"

I found the map I was looking for. "Blimey! It's on the bleedin' other side of the world!" I said.

"You know what you're doing?" Lance asked me.

"Hardly."

"Then let's go," said Lance.

"Is that bread I smell?" asked Smoron. "May I have a slice? I literally haven't eaten in two thousand years."

"I dunno . . ."

"I promise you will be the last human I destroy."

"Well, in that case—"

BAM! I zapped us back to the hill where I'd thrown the snowball, only now it was daylight, and the snow had long since melted.

"Hey!" said Smoron.

BAM!

BAM!

BAM!

I started flying us through the air again, this time going west.

We all clung desperately to each other, trying to keep Smoron behind me, in case he tried anything.

He tried something, all right.

"You"

"jerk!" screamed Smoron as we zapped our way through the air.

"You"

"left"

"before"

"I"

"could"

"get"

"a"

"slice"

"of"

"BREAD!"

Man, I had no idea someone could be so put out by not getting a piece of bread, but boy was he peeved. Right as he said the word bread, he used everything he had to summon the amulet to him. This was his most power-ful effort yet. Had I not positioned myself with my back to him, he easily would have been able to yank the thing right out of my hand. In fact, I totally lost my grip on it, and it flew into my chest and tried to bore through my leather armor.

When he pulled this stunt we were thousands of feet up in the air, and, because he distracted me from my attempt to pilot us, I was unable to figure out how to deal with this dire situation. I had two people clinging to me, and Smoron pressed up against my back. Plus, we were tumbling in a free fall, spinning end over end. I couldn't see the ground well enough to find a place for us to land. What's more, I needed to place my hand on the amulet, but with two people clinging to my arms, that was challenging to say the least.

I guess Smoron's plan was to let us crash; being indestructible, he'd survive. We'd be squashed like three teenage-sized grapes, but he'd be just fine.

I understood where he was coming from. After two thousand years, he had finally made it out of the void, only to be hogtied by some kids who were geared up to destroy him. Couple that with his hanger issues, and I get that he was ready to do whatever it took to triumph. But still, as I tumbled through the air trying to pull my right arm up to grab the amulet against all that centrifugal force, I couldn't help but marvel at the sheer cold-bloodedness of his act.

I finally managed to reach my thumb up and touch the amulet. And in that second, I zapped us to a spot on the ground I had spied a second earlier.

BAM!

I must have miscalculated that last teleportation because we landed hard, causing us to tumble and roll a few yards. I heard a cracking sound in my chest and felt a sharp pain in my side, but worst of all, I lost control of the amulet, and it rolled away from me.

As you have learned from reading this book, I don't always make smart decisions, but this moment was the rare exception. Rather than try to find the amulet, I rightly guessed that Smoron would simply summon the thing to him. So the minute I got my bearings I leapt on to him, which caused me a tremendous amount of pain, given that I had just cracked a rib.

I managed to get to Smoron just as the amulet did, and both of our hands closed on it.

I don't really know what happened next. The two of us were trying to control the amulet, and we were each simultaneously trying to send us to different times and places. At one point, I saw a herd of olyphants charging at us. Then I think he tried to zap us into a forest fire. He even transported us into the hornet-infested quarters of Lieutenant Thuffsburry. He was trying to kill me anyway he could. He was even biting me, which was just downright rude. For a guy who was somehow still tied up and who had severely atrophied muscles, he was putting up a desperate and powerful fight.

Meanwhile, I kept trying to send us back to Eldrack and Lance. With my cracked rib, I would need their help to pry the amulet away from Smoron. They later told me what it looked like from their end. One minute we had crashed into the earth; the next Smoron and I vanished. Then we reappeared, covered in dust (from the olyphants, I think), then we were gone, only to appear again, our clothes smoldering, disappearing and reappearing again, this time with hornets buzzing around us. Eldrack jumped on board, and she elbowed Smoron in the face. He wasn't giving up, however, as he then zapped us into that river where Eldrack had nearly drowned.

It was incredibly disorienting, suddenly being underwater. Once I realized where we were, I was afraid Eldrack might panic and let go; but to her credit, she held on. We were underwater, so it impossible to punch Smoron, but then I zapped us back to where Lance was, and he seized the moment and kicked Smoron in the head, which was just what we needed to make him let go of the amulet and put an end to this insanity.

I pried the amulet away from him and rolled away, gasping for air, and quietly cursing at the intense pain in my side.

"You OK, comrade?"

I couldn't respond, so exhausted was I from that fight. Instead, I simply raised my hand and gave him a thumbs-up.

"How much farther do we have to go?" Eldrack asked. "I don't know that we can go through that again."

Just before Smoron had pulled that stunt, I thought I had spied a tall, green mountain with what looked like a giant, orange willow tree near its peak. I tried to sit up, but my rib was causing me too much pain. Eldrack gently pulled me up and held on to me while I scanned the horizon. There it was, the famed Elder Tree, which was thought to be over four thousand years old and which was the symbol of the Elvish Kingdom.

I took a deep breath. "Let's do this." I grabbed on to my friends and zapped us to that peak, being more careful with my aim this time.

Chapter Thirty-Four

WE STOOD UNDER that dazzling tree, looking over a lush cliff. A beautiful waterfall was flowing next to us. Below us lay a glorious city. I could have sat there all day, but I was on a mission. I peered down at the city, but couldn't find what I was looking for, so I decided to get a closer look.

BAM!

We were now standing in the middle of the city square.

"Where are we?" said Eldrack. I detected no small amount of wonder in her voice, and for good reason, for this was the most beautiful place I'd ever seen, and even that comment vastly undersells the splendor of the city. Granted, I hadn't seen many cities, but if you had asked me to draw up a picture of the most beautiful place I could imagine, that drawing would have paled in comparison to Riverfell, city of elves.

There were gorgeous, tall, effervescent waterfalls everywhere you turned. Mist rose and swirled ever so gently into the air. The waterfalls made a faint whooshing sound that would have been the perfect background noise for a pleasing night's slumber.

"This way," I said. I wasn't entirely sure I was going in the right direction, though ahead of us was a majestic building that looked like it could be King Selron's palace. I figured we could get some answers there.

We passed lush, green tree after lush, green tree, dragging Lord Smoron along behind us as we walked. Plants and ferns hung everywhere one would want to hang a plant or fern. One cottage had a gorgeous garden with moss so thick it seemed to be begging for me to lie down and take a nap.

The buildings were ancient but well kept. Columns, arches, and looming spires ascended high into the misty blue sky.

"Nice architecture," said Smoron. "I can't wait to destroy it."

It was heavenly.

An elf approached us. She was, as I had hoped, the most stunningly beautiful person I had ever seen. Long, flowing brown hair, high cheekbones, and eyes you could swim in. She floated more than walked.

"Welcome to Riverfell," she said. Her voice washed over me like a gentle breeze.

"Hi!" I said, trying to stay focused. "Where's the Gazebo of Althowen?"

"Is that a gork?" she said, looking disapprovingly at Eldrack.

"A gork who's gonna kick your butt unless you point us in the right direction," Eldrack said.

"I'll take it from here," said another elf who drifted into view from behind a column. He was tall and thin, but muscular. He, too, had long flowing hair, but his face had chiseled manly features. He was wearing a low-cut blouse that showed off his muscular chest.

"Wow," murmured Lance. I raised an eyebrow at him. I thought he didn't like elves.

"I am—" began the elf.

"Well if it isn't King Sugar Bums!" said Smoron.

Selron, King of the Elves and former owner of one of the famed magical panties, arched an eyebrow. You could tell he was not used to being interrupted. But then a look of fear and confusion washed over his face. "Smoron? How . . . Atheleweth!"

A hundred elves appeared on to the scene, all pointing arrows straight at us. Where they had come from was a mystery, but elves were like that.

"Long story, my friend, long, long story," laughed Smoron.

"Thealaweth!" A volley of arrows smashed into Smoron's face.

A couple of things about this that impressed me: 1) I liked that Selron didn't waste any time with idle chitchat or questions. He just acted. And 2) Every single arrow found its mark.

"Woah!" I said. After all, it's one thing to know that elves are excellent marksmen, but it's quite another to have dozens of arrows zipping past your face. "Time out!"

"Ow!" said Smoron.

The elves readied another set of arrows and were looking like they were going to fire again.

"Hey!" Lance said, waving his arms. "Can everyone chillax for a second and listen to my friend?"

"Chillax?" said Selron. "I like that! Can I use that expression?"

"Sure?" said Lance.

"Listen," I broke in, "I'm Nigel—"

"The Amulet of Ashokenah!" said Selron, pointing at the object in my right hand—elves were known for having keen eyesight. "You must be the Dragon Squisher!"

"Come on, man! *Dragon Slayer*! Boy, you drop one mountain—"

"Why have you brought this villain and that vile weapon here?"

"Or how about Dragon Crusher?" I continued, ignoring the king. "Can't we meet halfway here? Dragon Crusher acknowledges that I didn't exactly slay any dragons, but it still sounds manly. I mean, come on, what girl wouldn't want to date the Dragon Crusher?"

Both Eldrack and that beautiful Elvish woman raised their hands.

Selron merely stared at me and raised his eyebrow. I decided to answer his question.

"I would love to explain everything, your majesty, but there isn't time. Please show me to the Gazebo of Althowen so that I can defeat this big-nosed lunatic once and for all."

Selron peered at me, as though he was trying to read my mind right through my eyeballs. "Very well, but Lord Smoron will have to stay with us."

"Would if I could, bruv," said Smoron, "but where that amulet goes, so do I. We're joined at the hip."

Selron sighed and gestured for us to follow him.

We walked down a beautiful path, framed by tall, vine-covered columns.

My only complaint about Riverfell was the harpists. The harp was definitely the musical instrument of choice, and there were harpists around every other corner. That might not have been such a terrible thing, but what got me was how each harpist looked like they were getting way too much enjoyment out of their own music. They had these angelic, almost pained, expressions on their faces as they strummed their harps. It was kind of embarrassing. I wanted to tell them to take it down a notch. After only a few minutes' walk, I was ready to smash every harp in the place.

We rounded a corner, and there in front of us was the famed Gazebo of Althowen. It was an ancient structure, thirty feet in diameter, with tall white columns supporting an elegant dome. Around its perimeter were white marble benches, and in the center was a white podium.

"Well?" said Selron.

I took a deep breath, grabbed my friends' hands, and took the plunge.

BAM!

The four of us appeared in the same spot, twenty-five years earlier.

There, seated on the benches in the gazebo, were some of the most famous people in history: The Group of Nine. In the middle seat was Brondork the Beige. To his right were Elbo, his friend Spam, and their two irritating halfling comrades. To Brondork's left was the handsome elvish warrior Lotsoleg, Gimlet the dwarf warrior, Gregorigorn, who would one day become Olerood, king of Amerigorn, and finally, the past version of Selron. I wondered if he was wearing his magical panties.

On the podium, in the center of that gazebo, were the Cufflinks of Doom. Here we were, at the very meeting where the Group had decided how to destroy the Cufflinks and rid the world of Smoron. A shiver went down my spine.

Our sudden appearance at this little get-together proved to be quite a shock to the Group, especially since this was supposedly an ultra-secret meeting. Lotsoleg immediately drew his bow. His reflexes were astonishing.

I zapped his bow and arrow into a distant waterfall, which surprised the heck out of the poor elf.

"A gork!" said Gimlet, who immediately charged at us. I zapped him over in front of a column, which he ran into and knocked himself out.

I half expected Smoron to summon the Cufflinks, but I guess he figured he'd have to hard time putting them on with his arms all tied up, so he just lay there, watching things play out.

There was a lot of confusion and shouting and scurrying about, and before we knew what was happening, the four of us had all sorts of weapons and wands pointing at us.

"That Amulet of Ashokenah!" said Brondork.

I held up my hands in front of me, trying to bring the tension down a bit. "Hallo there, famous heroes of yesteryear!"

"Who are you?" asked Brondork.

"Me?" I said, "Nigel, the Dragon Crusher. And this? This is Lord Smoron."

Well! You can imagine the commotion that caused!

While everyone was distracted, I zapped us over to the podium, grabbed the Cufflinks, and then I sent us over to the town square.

There was much confusion back at the Gazebo, which was maybe a hundred yards from us.

"The Cufflinks!" someone said.

"They're gone!" said another.

"Over there!" said Lotsoleg, pointing at us.

They were all rushing at us. I didn't have much time.

"Hold him!" I said to Eldrack, motioning towards Smoron.

I tried to put on the Cufflinks. It wasn't easy.

"No, look," said Lance, getting annoyed with my feeble efforts, "you fold this bit and slip it into the hole there. Ugh! Let me do it!"

"You had to make them Cufflinks?" I said to Smoron, "Seriously? The most annoying jewelry in the world? Why not a ring?"

"Too showy," he said.

"There!" said Lance.

The air changed. The world turned a little slower. Elves who, only seconds ago, had been rushing at me, their faces distorted with furious thoughts of vengeance, suddenly smiled, took deep breaths, and—most importantly— lowered their weapons.

"You look brilliant, mate!" said Lance.

"Hey, handsome," said Eldrack. She was so charmed by me she had totally forgotten her duty to hold Smoron.

"Hold him!" I told her, pointing at Smoron.

An elf glided towards me. She was that same beautiful woman I had seen in the future. She gazed deeply into my eyes, bowed, and said, "How may I serve you?"

"Oh. My. Gods," I said. "These things are AWESOME!"

"Right?" said Smoron.

"I'll say this: you're an evil bloke, but dang, you've got some mad skills."

As all of this was happening, I could also see, in the back of my mind, a vision that could only be described as a rapidly approaching nose.

Suddenly there was a big flash.

"Ah HA!" came a booming voice. "You have—Argh! My eyes!"

And just like that, the past version of Lord Smoron collapsed in a heap in front of me.

"OK," said Future Smoron, looking at his past self. "I can see why that's funny." And then he said, "Uh-oh."

Future Smoron realized, just a few seconds too late, what my plan was.

I shoved him into his past self.

I didn't know what would happen, but I remembered a comment Smoron had made back when I was trying to prevent that horse from getting hit by my snowball. He had said something about not running into the past version of yourself. I was hoping that that wasn't just another one of his lines, and I was (perhaps recklessly) putting the fate of the world on that hope.

On the plus side, my plan worked. On the slightly-less-than-awesome side, I was really hoping for a big explosion. But what we got instead was an implosion, which is the exact opposite. So, rather than a loud boom, the moment Future Smoron touched Past Smoron, Future Smoron simply collapsed in on himself and disappeared with a muffled *floop*.

I'm not gonna lie: It was a total letdown. I guess I shouldn't have been all that surprised since my adventures had disabused me of so many of the notions I'd gleaned from our historical epics. But still, there was one rock-solid concept on which every single saga had agreed, and so I had taken it as an indisputable fact of nature: Bad guys are supposed to go out with a bang.

"Seriously?" I said. "All that work for a floop?"

"What just happened?" said Past Smoron, who still couldn't see a thing.

His comment snapped me out of my disappointment. I still had a job to do.

I sniffed and struck a heroic pose, trying to regain some of the lost drama. "You just lost, mate," I said. And then I ripped the Cufflinks from my sleeves.

OK, to be quite honest, that last part didn't happen. I tried, but even if I had been in better physical shape, it would have been nearly impossible to do. In my mind, I was going to pull off a powerfully dramatic moment that might one day be immortalized in a famous painting . . . but what happened instead was I said "You just lost, mate," and then I spent the next couple of minutes tugging at my shirt sleeves, fumbling with the clasps of the Cufflinks, and cursing in embarrassment and pain (for I was still suffering from a cracked rib) until I finally gave up and asked Lance for help. All the while, Past Smoron was squirming on the ground and chatting away: "Who lost? What's going on? Where am I? Who flooped?" But eventually, thanks to Lance, we got them off.

I cleared my throat. "OK, as I was saying . . ." once again I struck that heroic pose and held my amulet aloft. "You just lost, mate!"

BAM!

I sent the Cufflinks into the fires of Mount Boo-Boo.

Smoron exploded right in front of me.

It was deafening.

It was blinding.

It was disgusting, for we were all covered in blood, flesh, and tiny pieces of bone. (We were, as Lance so eloquently put it, "absolutely smattered with Smoron.")

But it was most definitely not a letdown. The history books were finally right about something.

It took a moment for all the folks in Riverfell, including the Group of Nine, to understand what had just happened.

"My panties!" cried King Selron.

Chapter Thirty-Five

"So that's it?" said the man who would one day become King Olerood.

We were all seated at a large banquet in our honor, eating the most delicious food I'd ever tasted.

"Yep," I said.

"Wow," said Lotsoleg. "You just saved us a lot of time and trouble. It would have taken us months to travel to Mount Boo-Boo."

"Dang it!" said Gimlet the dwarf. "Now I don't get to kill anything."

"Don't let it get you down, old sport," said Lance, patting him on the back. "You still look amazing in that warrior getup of yours."

"You think so? It's not too much?"

"I think you look rather dashing. Just the way I'd always imagined a dwarf would look. How old are you, by the way?"

"Fifteen. Why?"

Lance smiled his brilliant smile and held out his hand. "Name's Hightower. Lance Hightower."

"I have a question that's been bothering me for years," Eldrack whispered to me, "In the original timeline, why didn't the Group of Nine just fly to Mount Boo-Boo on a giant eagle and be done with it?"

That was a good question. Why indeed?

"Speaking of Mount Boo-Boo," said Elbo the Great with a sigh. "I mean, I know we should be happy, seeing as you rid the world of Lord Smoron and everything, but now none of us will be famous heroes. I was looking forward to writing an epic tale about our brave adventures. I thought it might be nice for halflings to have some heroes of their own. We're not exactly a beloved race."

Huh. That gave me pause. Without Elbo's book, we never would have been able to complete our quest. It had been our guide—albeit a flawed one—on our journey to Mount Boo-Boo. This brought me to a further troubling question: by destroying the Cufflinks myself, how had I not created a paradox?

Then it hit me.

I leaned in close to make sure I had his attention. "You're right, Elbo. The world needs a halfling hero and an epic tale of adventure, and I think you're just the chap to pull it off. You need to write a book about how you lot destroyed the Cufflinks of Doom. Use your imagination. We won't tell anyone it's not the truth."

"Speaking of the truth," Brondork the Wizard said gravely, "I believe we have come to a moment of truth. The Amulet of Ashokenah is too powerful of a weapon to trust in the hands of any single person, especially a teenager. Furthermore, we don't know for certain that Smoron is truly gone for good." He walked over and looked down his beard at me. "Give the amulet to us. We'll be sure to keep it safe."

"Sure thing, mate," I said, looking up into the sky. Something had caught my eye. "Just as soon as I'm done with it!"

I grabbed my friends and zapped us a thousand feet into the air.

"Hallo there!" I said to the giant eagle on whose back we had just landed, "Mind giving us a lift?"

"I can't believe it! I'm flying on an eagle!" said Eldrack with a glorious laugh.

"OK, I have a ton of questions," said Lance. "First, how come destroying the Cufflinks didn't change your future? Second, how come Future Selron didn't recognize you? Third . . ."

"Hey, mate?"

"Yeah?"

"We're flying on the back of a giant eagle. Chillax and enjoy the ride."

"Good point, comrade."

And off we flew.

Epilogue

"AND THERE BEFORE us, stood a mighty dragon," read Elbo.

Eldrack, Lance, and I were relaxing in Elbo's lovely underground cottage home. He had invited us to be the first to hear his newly completed book, *Remember That Time When I Saved the World?* The title had been my suggestion, and he was, to his credit, rather embarrassed about it, seeing as he had done no such thing.

A fire was crackling away, and I was sitting in a comfy chair, sipping on a delicious cup of tea with my feet propped up on a cushy ottoman. Eldrack lay on the floor next to me, with her hands behind her head, eyes closed, smiling at Elbo's words. Lance was pacing around the room, paying strict attention to Elbo's grammar and word choice. After all, he knew Elbo's book better than Elbo did.

As I lay there, I was only half paying attention to Elbo. Mostly I was thinking about our recent adventures.

It had been six months since we had flown away from the Group of Nine on the back of that eagle, and we had been busy. As happy as I was that we had defeated Smoron, we still had a lot of unfinished business to attend to.

So, after giving Eldrack some time to enjoy her eagle ride, I zapped us back to the future to begin our work. After a bit of research, we were able to track down the time and place of the first battle of the war I'd started. I zapped the three of us to that battlefield just in time to see the human and gork armies charging at each other.

"Here goes," I said.

I aimed the amulet at both armies and raised them two feet off the ground.

WHAM!

Four thousand soldiers and horses and dire wolves and heavy weaponry all came crashing down, shaking the ground with the impact. We could hear the groans of thousands of people and animals. I'm sure I had broken plenty of bones, but as far as I could tell, no one had been killed.

Then I zapped each army to pre-selected places in their own kingdoms in order to keep them permanently out of the war.

Rinse and repeat.

Smoron had told us there had been four battles of this war, so we zoomed to the next two battles scenes and did the same thing, hoping to minimize injuries and avoid any deaths.

We were determined to stop this war before it got out of hand.

There was not much we could do about the fourth battle, which was the one we had witnessed with Smoron. I tried to use the amulet to prevent it from happening, but it wouldn't let me. I guess preventing that battle would have changed my history, so instead, we hid in a copse and waited for our past selves to arrive on the scene and leave. Once gone, I lifted the armies in the air and put a stop to the battle. Maybe I was able to save a few hundred lives.

After that, it was time to put an end the whole war.

It took some doing and several dozen uses of the amulet, but we managed to capture King Olerood and King Skidmark. I wanted to lecture them in a quiet spot, so I asked Old Mrs. Halloway for some help. She had thankfully forgiven me for destroying her barn and agreed to host the discussion in her lovely cottage. She even served us tea and cookie cakes. I explained to the two kings that it was my fault the war had started and that if they insisted on continuing this stupid conflict, I would sick millions of giant slugs on them. I won't bore you with the details, but they eventually gave in and agreed to peace. The kings still hated and distrusted each other, so there was no guarantee that the peace would last, but at least I had ended the war I'd started.

With the war at an end, we took Eldrack home. She hadn't seen her parents in almost three years. We arrived outside of a quaint little cottage, startling two middle-aged gorks, who had been attending to a vegetable garden. After getting over their shock at our sudden appearance, Eldrack's parents rushed up to her and showered her with affection. They had thought she was dead.

I almost couldn't believe what I was seeing. All my life I'd been brainwashed into thinking that gorks were these evil, war-like hunter-gatherers who did nothing but sharpen swords and gnash teeth. It had never occurred to me that they might have houses and gardens, let alone parents who loved their children.

"I didn't know gorks cried," I said after introductions had been made.

"Shut yer hole," Eldrack said, wiping away her tears.

Her parents invited us to stay for dinner.

"Thank you," I said, shaking Eldrack's father's hand, trying my best not to wince under the strain of his powerful grip, "but there are still a few things I need to sort out."

I turned to Lance. "Want me to take you home, Glancey old boy? Let me help you sort this thing out with your folks. After all, you're a hero now! Surely they can find it in their hearts to welcome you home."

He smiled sadly and placed a hand on my shoulder.

"Can't do it, comrade. It's not that simple."

"We just stopped a war. What could be more complicated than that?"

"Family."

I opened my mouth to say something snappy, but instead, I simply reached out and hugged him. There were so many thoughts coursing through my head, and so much I wanted to say to him to express the depths of my friendship, but all I could muster was a simple hug.

"Oh my gods, when did you become such a sap?" he said, surprised by my action, but he soon returned my embrace. When we let go, he wiped a tear from his eye.

I bid my friends goodbye and told them I'd catch up with them later.

I zapped myself in front of a door, startling a young woman who had been passing by.

"Sorry," I said.

I'd gotten so used to startling people over the past few months I had fallen into the habit of automatically apologizing every time I apparated anywhere. Sometimes I braced myself to catch people, as rather a lot of them had taken to passing out, but I sensed this person wasn't about to fall over, so I simply apologized and turned to knock on the door.

"Nigel?" the woman said before I could knock.

"Hmm?" I turned. It took me a second to recognize her. I don't know why, for she looked the same as the last time I saw her, only different somehow. "Oh . . . hi."

". . . Melissa," she said.

"Right, yes. Sorry about startling you. One of the hazards of using this thing." I raised the amulet.

"I'll bet." Her eyes lit up, and she glided towards me.

"Listen. I hate to be rude," I said, "but I've got something rather important I need to do."

"Oh, of course."

"Good seeing you."

"Look me up some time."

I nodded. I took a deep breath, ran my hand through my hair, and knocked on the door. I heard a voice call out, "Just a minute."

Something landed on my shoulder.

"Gerald!"

My beautiful tufted titmouse friend pecked lightly at my ear, and then pooped on my shoulder.

"I missed you too, old chum." I stroked his head.

The door opened, revealing my mother. She seemed puzzled to see me.

"May I come in?" I said, totally unsure what her reaction would be.

She smiled, opened her arms, and gave me a giant, warm hug.

"You smell like bird poop, dear."

I was finally home.

"And there before us, stood a mighty dragon," read Elbo. He tapped on his paper, which snapped me out of my reverie.

"This is the only part of the book I don't love," Elbo said. "I want to immerse the reader in the moment, but I feel like I don't know enough about dragons to really do that. Thanks to you, I have a good idea of what they looked like and how they talked, but I still feel like I'm missing some part of their character that would truly make them come alive for the reader. Maybe you can tell me . . . what do dragons smell like?"

Lance laughed out loud at that. "Here's your chance, comrade! Time to set the record straight!"

I opened my mouth. And then I closed it.

I realized to my great disappointment that I couldn't tell him. After all, if he were to write that dragons smelled like farts, we would have known what to smell for when we had been on our journey to destroy the amulet. And if we had smelled the dragons coming, I might have zapped us away at first stench, which might have prevented our encounter with Reginald and, ultimately, the destruction of Fell's Palace.

"Well?" said Elbo, for he could tell I had much to say on the subject.

"Brimstone," I said finally. "Dragons smell like brimstone."

Lance looked at me like I was bonkers.

"Brimstone?" said Eldrack. "But . . ." I shot her a look.

"I love it," said Elbo, writing. "By the way, what is brimstone?"

"Exactly," I said, leaning back and putting my arms behind my head. "Please keep reading, Elbo. I can't wait to hear how the story ends."

THE END

About the author

When he's not flustering emus or stymying mambas, Scott McCormick enjoys annoying his children until they tell their mother. Scott lives on the western edge of the easternmost part of southern North Carolina, right smack in the middle of it all.

You can contact Scott at:
storybookediting@gmail.com
www.scottmccormickonline.com
Twitter: @ScottsYABooks
Instagram: authorscottmccormick
Facebook: www.facebook.com/AuthorScottMcCormick/